The Asuras of Antariksh

Veena S Rao

Vitasta
LET KNOWLEDGE SPREAD

Published by
Renu Kaul Verma
Vitasta Publishing Pvt Ltd
2/15, Ansari Road, Daryaganj
New Delhi – 110 002
info@vitastapublishing.com

ISBN 978-93-86473-60-8

First Edition 2019
MRP ₹395

This is a work of fiction. All characters in this book are fictitious. However, some people may find images of themselves or of people known to them in the characters of this book. All such resemblance is coincidental.

Cover and layout by Somesh Kumar Mishra
Back cover illustration by Sathish B
Printed by Vikas Computer and Printers

When Justitia's hands and scales are held
By distant, unseen strings,
Then pen gets mightier than the sword
To free her scales again.

She lifts her head and scans the world,
She grips her sword, she snaps the cords,
She flings the sword and grasps the pen,
And sternly smiles in hope again.

Asuras are a class of supernatural beings in the Vedic period, who in Indian mythology tend to be malevolent and constantly at war with the *Devas* (gods).

Antariksh is the Sanskrit word for outer space.

The back cover picture is an adaptation of the *Samudra Manthan*, the churning of the ocean, a legend from Hindu mythology. Both *Devas* and *Asuras* churn the ocean in search of *amrita*, the nectar of immortality. Amidst much intrigue and action, the pot of nectar is found, and the *Asuras* and *Devas* fight for it. The *Devas* are finally able to secure the *amrita* through divine assistance.

They hurled a sack of deadly, bitter lemons
I turned them into lovely lemonade

This book is dedicated to
Naresh Kaushik and Chirag Madan
gentlemen with high ethics and no avarice

Mumbai, August 2, 2002

IT WAS A hot and steamy day in August. The kind of day that happens when the monsoon dribbles along for a while, and then suddenly becomes alive again, with its martial thunder that makes windows shake, its fiery streaks of lightning that split the sky and reach the earth, and violent torrents of never-ending rain.

It was 3 o' clock in the afternoon. Dr Maharishi Nath, MN, as he was called by his close friends, was sitting in his office, his chair facing the sea. He had a sense of tired contentment. He had achieved his lifelong ambition, and just a week ago had been appointed chairman of the Indian Space Agency, popularly called the ISA.

He had just returned from Delhi after paying his respect and tributes to all those who had helped him to get this position. He had called on the minister, and on all the other Delhi bigwigs whom he would now be rubbing shoulders with, as an equal, or superior.

Well, now the initial euphoria was beginning to recede. The congratulations and felicitations from the scientific fraternity, from his own organisation, from fellow scientists across the world were gradually thinning out, and he was now back on the ground.

First, he had to take stock of what he must deliver to shine more than his predecessors. ISA was a strange sort of a place. It had started on the strength of brilliant and innovative pioneers, who went through enough trial and error and failures, but were able to make India enter the exclusive club of space nations. But gradually, like in most government organisations, brilliance was replaced by the typical Indian hierarchy, which at a certain point becomes the mother of mediocrity, sired by godfathers. How many mediocre bosses he had to put up with, to reach the top. Well, by God's grace, and perhaps some luck, he finally had reached there. He knew he was the best rocket scientist in the country, innovative with scarce resources. Yes, he had seen some failures, but that was part of science. He always rose again, and there were always enough godfathers to protect him.

Managing ISA would not be difficult. He knew everyone who headed the various divisions of the organisation and their capabilities. He was fairly popular and knew how things worked—what was to be told to the bosses and what not; what was to be told to the subordinates and the public, and what should remain concealed; how to handle the bureaucrats with their cocky, supercilious manner—either ensnare them to your side, or banish them. Such unnecessary creatures they were, outsiders interfering with their lofty, charmed world of science, snooping around as if they knew everything. But this was government, and they had to be endured.

But Maharishi had really never had a problem with any of the bureaucrats so far. He knew how to handle them. They all had a price, and it was a matter of time that their price would be discovered. Most of them were his friends anyway, though he still had to test their loyalty to him and not to his predecessor. As for the new ones whom he did not know so well, it was just a matter of time and he would discover their price. All quite routine. And now that he was the lord and master of his empire, he could do things his way.

Presently, he was a little concerned about his meeting with Dr Satyadev, his predecessor, which was to take place in the next half hour. Satyadev was a smart scientist. He had worked with NASA for several years and done some research on sensors. He then skillfully used all his networks to pronounce himself as the leading satellite man of India, and the influence of a particularly powerful mentor to get himself appointed as head of India's satellite programme, after which he went on to head the ISA.

Satyadev had been chairman ISA for a good six years and Maharishi could almost predict his demands, which would certainly be couched in innocuous language—that his general patronage be respected, that his favourites remain untouched. Well, that could be adjusted through a balancing act. Then he would ask that his favourite projects and grants continue—that was reasonable; that his mistress' position remain undisturbed—could be managed, a little this way or that.

MN was ruminating on these expected demands and mentally preparing his answers. It would be easy, he thought, and the meeting would be smooth.

His eyes traversed the walls of his office, the office that he had entered the past two decades in different positions as a subordinate, sitting at the meeting table, 'sir'ing and flattering everybody. Well, this was his office now, and he was the boss.

He kept looking at the pictures on the wall, of the rockets and launch vehicles that he had created, which had brought great honour to ISA and India. Small, baby steps they may appear now, but they were important at that time, and he was part of them. He loved them.

How beautiful they looked. Tall priapic symbols, with payloads latched on, adding to their size, their phallic splendour. In his dreams, he would make love with them in space. They made a woman's charm appear so insignificant. What were they anyway… charming, churlish creatures… wells of interminable demands ….

Maharishi Nath kept gazing lovingly at the pictures, and found himself getting aroused. The rocket was the sexiest thing in the world. He believed it was the perfect therapy for men slipping into the nightmare of erectile dysfunction disorder. He never needed Viagra. It was his rockets that helped him each time he was to meet his mistress or his other paramours, or even sometimes, his wife.

He was in this stage of meditation when his predecessor Satyadev was ushered in by his former personal secretary, Ms Shukra Devi, still lodged in his office.

He rose, shook his legs, adjusted his trousers to look decent, and the two men shook hands and embraced each other.

"Well, well, congratulations, Maharishi. I can only say it feels wonderful, wonderful, to come back here again, especially to this office. It feels so good."

"Most welcome, sir, anytime."

Saytadev looked a little uneasy and Maharishi tried to cover up his own unease by trying to look as expressionless and friendly as he could. One of the best weapons in this world of science and intrigue.

"Now, Maharishi, I've not got too much time. Have to catch a flight to Delhi at six. And there is something important I need to brief you about. Something that no one else can."

Maharishi smiled inside his mouth, continuing his expressionless and friendly expression. "Go ahead, sir." His mind had moved away from the priapic rockets and the sexy satellites that mated with them before they ascended his beloved space.

"Now, you know, our Gagan Vayu, GAVA, is not doing too well. It's meant to be a business, commercial corporation, but we, and our damned government procedures never allow it to do any commercial work. But anyway, I used all my power and influence to ensure that it remains free from all those useless government regulations, and enjoys complete autonomy to take decisions as it chooses in its best interest. Just don't make any rules, so there'll be none to follow. Simple. And quote national security and secrecy to anyone who asks anything. What do you say? Remember that for the future."

Maharishi gave a pleasant laugh. "That's brilliant, sir. I will remember that." But knowing Satyadev, he knew that the real mission of the visit would trickle in gradually. And it didn't take long.

Satyadev continued in a somewhat monologic tone, "Well, talking about GAVA, we have been in long discussion with a company called Oriont Telecom in the US for the last few years. It's headed by a fine American gentleman, Dr Georges. Think he's of German descent. An extremely decent gentleman. And he has a brilliant number two, from our own parts, one Dr Karmaswamy."

Maharishi was listening and watching Satyadev's face intently. He had heard these names before and also a little gossip about some deals being discussed by them and ISA. But he didn't know the details, as he was not part of the negotiations. Satyadev started looking a little distracted, somewhat unusual.

He continued in his monologic tone, "You would know that there is a huge mobile telephony market emerging in the world. All kind of new technologies are coming into the market, about hand-held devices, audio and video on the palm, hybrid technologies with space and terrestrial segments. So, if we want to be forward looking, and want to do something for our organisation and country, we must be proactive and aggressive, and steal a march on the other players who are vying for our market. And who do all the great telephony companies come to for getting their spectrum? To us, and to our satellites. Why should GAVA not get the profits, and also the country?"

"Yes sir, quite right." He wondered what Satyadev was really trying to say.

"So, they, that is Oriont, will be coming over sometime in the next month or two. You must carry on the negotiations with them for setting up an Indian entity for the hybrid telephony market. I will ask Vidyasagar to brief you about it."

"Okay, sir", Maharishi continued with his expressionless, friendly expression.

"By the way, do you know anything about Oriont Telecom and what's been going on with them and GAVA?"

"Not really, sir. I was told here and there, that there were some meetings you had held with them when you had visited the US last year. But I know nothing about the details."

"I'll also ask Gurupriya to brief you. She may be from the IAS, but she's a fine officer. Completely loyal to us, and very committed. You know her quite well, I think. She's a good friend of yours too, isn't she?"

"Well, we've had no problems whenever we've had to deal with each other professionally. She seems competent enough."

"And yes, be careful of the other bureaucrats. There's the deputy administration and finance officer, Sushil Ramu, who's been with us for a while. Watch him. He's good, but I always thought he was a little slippery. I'm not quite sure how trustworthy he is. A man with too little conviction. But I think you can win him over quite easily. Just send him abroad for a trip or two, and put him in this committee for the GAVA negotiations with Oriont. He'll be yours."

"Yes, I've dealt with him now and then. He seems easy enough to manage."

"But, the new one who's just come in as the chief administration officer, Manal Kumar, he's the one you have to be careful about. He appears far too independent and aloof. And far too intelligent. And I believe he's a bachelor, so even more unpredictable. Test him well before you entrust anything to him. And watch him carefully."

"I see. Well, I don't know him at all, but will try and find out. Perhaps through some intelligent use of Gurupriya. One thing I have noticed about these IAS chaps—they do seem to respect their seniors, even if it's just for show." They both laughed.

"This is a tough deal. It has to pass several stages—through the bureaucracy, the ministry, the cabinet. So, keep everyone on your side. Either by passively involving them, or keeping them in secrecy."

"Yes sir, thank you for your advice."

"And before I leave, keep Shukra Devi in your office. She's a good PA, very reliable, and very useful in many ways, many many ways." Satyadev smiled and stared into Maharishi's eyes.

"That should not a problem, sir." Maharishi smiled in return.

"And remember, the Oriont deal has the blessings of everyone in government. Everyone. So, don't let it fail." Satyadev drilled the words into Maharishi's eyes.

Maharishi understood, and felt a little irritated. Inheriting a mistress was not such a bad idea. But inheriting a half-done deal, with somewhat secret, shady undertones was a little disconcerting and uncomfortable. Anyway, he had never trusted the wily Satyadev.

New York, April 2002

NEW YORK WAS turning a little more pleasant. The suite in the Waldorf Astoria was splendid, with luxurious leather sofas and walnut furniture of antique style. Tables on one side laden with fruit and artistically presented snacks and nuts, tables on another side laden with the most exotic wines and beer, tea, coffee, and fruit juices.

There were only five people in the sitting room. Dr Satyadev, Chairman ISA, the Indian Space Agency, Dr Martin Georges, Chairman, Oriont Telecom USA, New York, Dr Karmaswamy, Vice President, Oriont Telecom USA, Dr Vidyasagar, Managing Director, Gagan Vayu, GAVA, and Ms Gurupriya, Financial Advisor, ISA.

The steward, a tall young man with an East European accent walked in and addressed Dr Georges, "I'm Johann, sir. Just came in to check if all is okay. Would you require anything else? Please press this buzzer if you would like anything."

"Thank you, Johann, we'll probably ask for lunch after about an hour."

"May I pour the wine, sir?"

"Yes, please do. Wine for everybody?" Dr Georges fanned his glance around his guests, both his arms extended in good cheer.

"Sure, thanks. Wine is fine. Perhaps champagne later. When we celebrate our agreement." Dr Satyadev smiled, and extended his right arm in goodwill.

Johann placed the wine bottles and the glasses on a tray—mostly French wines and some superior California wines.

"Any preference, Dr Satyadev?"

"Ah, I like the Napa Valley wine the best. White. It beats all French wines."

"Okay, let's all have the Napa Valley white," Dr Georges gestured to Johann.

Johann did his job and left. The door clicked shut.

"Well, cheers, Dr Satyadev. To our collaboration. And to everybody's good health and success." Dr Georges raised a toast.

The gentlemen and lady clinked their glasses.

He continued, "I must tell you, Dr Satyadev, I really appreciate your dynamism and initiative for bringing both our organisations together. It's a win-win for both of us."

Dr Satyadev took a sip of his wine. "Wonderful wine. And a wonderful future for all of us. Our agreement is in place. Oriont Telecom will set up an Indian entity which Karma will head. I have some excellent former employees of ISA who will join him to set up Oriont India. I've already sounded them, and they are very excited about this new venture."

"That's a commitment?" Dr Georges asked.

"Yes. It's a commitment. We then set up a joint venture of Oriont India with GAVA. We will from ISA then construct a communication satellite, and allot the transponders to it for the mobile telephony market in India, which is growing exponentially each day. The profit for both GAVA and Oriont India will be enormous."

"But Dr Satyadev, you just have another few months as chairman ISA. Can all this be accomplished by then?"

Satyadev was irritated. He hated any reference to his retirement.

"Georges, yes, I am to retire by July end, but I have every reason to believe that I shall continue for at least another six months, if not another year. My political bosses have assured me this."

"But you have an election coming on in another two months. What happens if the government changes?"

"Don't worry, Georges, support for the scientific community cuts across party lines. It should happen even if the opposition party comes to power. I have very influential friends there too. And even if I have to retire, my influence over ISA will not cease. ISA has fine traditions regarding its past chairmen."

Georges changed track to focus more on the agreement.

"Okay, great to hear that. So, let's get back to our agreement. One, Oriont Telecom will establish an Indian entity with your support. Two, there will be discussions with GAVA for setting up a joint venture for entering the telephony market. Three, we will bring in the technology and you will provide the satellite and the spectrum, and four, we will jointly do the marketing. Am I right?"

"Yes, that's agreed. As soon as I get back to India, I will invite you to make a presentation to ISA and GAVA, and the bureaucrats. So that would make it completely transparent."

"Brilliant, let us know when. We'll be there. But are you sure the political cover from all sides is assured? That's the way your system works, isn't it?"

"One hundred percent."

"Wonderful. So now we'll order lunch."

But before ordering lunch, Georges took Satyadev aside. "There's a small token of my gratitude that I owe you. You bailed us out when we were in a rather tricky situation in that Malaysian affair. Let me know how I can deliver it…."

"Not now," Satyadev replied, "we'll talk about it later."

Mumbai May 5, 2002

DR SATYADEV WAS true to his word. He invited Dr Georges and Oriont Telecom USA to make a presentation to ISA and GAVA about the proposed joint venture, ten days hence. Before that, he called for an exclusive meeting with the scientists and his senior bureaucrats, and explained to them the JV proposal and the forthcoming visit of the Oriont Telecom top brass, all as part of a new and dynamic GAVA strategic partnership initiative.

He got together a band of his loyal scientists who were no longer in ISA—some retired, some forced to retire because of impending disgrace—and informed them that they were required to form a company for the future telephony market. There was hardly any discussion, as they were all his staunch followers. Of course, they all agreed wholeheartedly.

The meeting and the presentations were a spectacular success. Apart from the scientists who had no option but to attend, the presence of Ms Gurupriya, the seniormost bureaucrat and financial advisor was strongly seen and felt. The deputy administration and finance officer

Sushil Ramu was present, but the chief administration officer Manal Kumar was in Delhi. He was attending a meeting called by the health ministry about how to take telemedicine into the villages of Arunachal Pradesh where primary health care was just not reaching the villages, and it was extremely difficult to secure the services of doctors and nurses. Satyadev was not too happy about this.

Dr Georges did not come, but sent Dr Karmaswamy, whom he thought would be a better representative. An Indian who could speak the local language, bond easily and be one of them.

Finally, it was agreed that Oriont Telecom USA would set up an Indian entity, Oriont India, and a separate committee within ISA would be set up to work out the nitty gritty of its collaboration with GAVA, before it was presented for approval to the GAVA Board, and then to the minister and the cabinet.

Oriont USA was quick to set up its new Indian entity, Oriont India. Satyadev's loyalists immediately pitched in, bringing in token sums of share capital totalling a mere rupees two lakhs. The company was registered and then got cracking, setting up a posh office in Colaba, in a nice, peaceful interior street. Within two months, they were able to get permission from the finance ministry to receive funds from abroad, and immediately after that came their first grant of USD 1 million, to start the preparatory research and startup activities for the ISA collaboration.

The national election was to take place in June. Satyadev was confident that the ruling party would be returned to power, and he was certain that he would remain in this position for at least another six months, if not a year. Everyone in government had high regard for him. After all, during his tenure, he had sent up four communication satellites, providing the nation with unprecedented television access; three polar satellites that helped India's security forces get much more information than ever before. Politicians across the board showed great respect to him, though of course, many of them knew that apart from being an expert on satellites, he was also a great expert on magnifying his achievements manifold at the right political fora, and downplaying his non-achievements correspondingly. And since his political bosses were not scientists, he could talk his way through quite successfully. Satyadev had no doubt that regardless of the outcome of the elections, he would be around for enough time to see the Oriont deal through.

He appointed Dr Haridas, who was head of the Satellite Research Centre at Hyderabad, as chairman of the committee to study and work out the details of the GAVA Oriont collaboration. Dr Haridas was a hard-working scientist, reasonably mediocre, and had a penchant for ordering and accumulating a huge inventory of unnecessary material, which would under no circumstances be required in the foreseeable future.

He would cleverly fit the value of purchases, which were really wasteful expenditure of public money, within the limits that were prescribed within his discretionary purchasing powers. There was a nasty audit report indicting him on that, but ISA generally had great disdain for these useless, mundane audit reports, which they merely transferred to the bureaucrats, and then sent them vague and obfuscatory replies. But, stealthy whispers in his office corridors were always accompanied with a wink—purchases were always a productive occupation bringing great gain to both the purchaser and purchasee.

Satyadev should normally have ordered a discreet internal enquiry into the rather serious audit observations. However, he sat tight on the report, but would keep referring to it obliquely whenever he had to speak to Haridas about something that he wanted him to do. Haridas understood this, and though he loved satellite research greatly, he loved his swelling assets even more. Luckily for him, he had developed enough contacts in Singapore during the course of his research, that he had no problem in secreting them discreetly.

Satyadev knew that. After all, the scientific club was a small cozy one, where everyone knew who had made what deals, who had profited how much, and where it was salted.

So, Haridas was appointed as chairman of the committee to draw up the road map for the GAVA

Oriont joint venture. With the nasty audit report hanging over his head, Satyadev was confident that there would be no hurdles in getting the required report for the collaboration.

Satyadev also made sure that in addition to the key scientists of the organisation, the key bureaucrats, particularly the deputy finance and administration officer, Sushil Ramu was also included. That would compromise them sufficiently, so that they could not make a noise about it later.

All the more this was important because the bureaucrats would not understand a thing about the science and would only be scouring the rules and regulations. A perfect situation, because there were no rules and regulations in ISA for such collaborations that happened in GAVA. And the science, whether real or bluff, would fly over their heads.

But then the unexpected happened. The national election results delivered a terrific shock. The ruling National People's Party which was completely confident of forming the government again was voted out, and a tenuous coalition of assorted parties headed by the Indian Democratic Party formed the new government. Very few people had expected this, and almost each one of the television channels and their renowned anchors had to bite the dust for their useless poll predictions.

Satydev was a little concerned. He would have to

start negotiations for his continuation with the new government with whoever the new minister for scientific development and his secretary would be. Anyway, the scientific community was a small well-knit club, and he had his supporters everywhere. But then, he also knew that scientists were famous for turning towards whichever direction the wind was blowing. Besides, he also had his deals to save. Transitions in deals were always tricky, but the big business houses behind the deals had by now mastered the art of ensuring their smooth transition. And if that did not work, there were always his American friends, who were important and had influence over the US law makers and government. After all, the Oriont deal was as important to the US as it was to GAVA and himself. He waited in anticipation for the appointment of the new minister and his principal secretary, both of whom were critically important for his continuation.

The new prime minister, Shamlal Kanwar, who belonged to the royal family of Kaashi, had repeatedly spoken about accelerating India's scientific and technological development in his very aggressive election campaign. He appointed his close friend and political colleague, Dr Pratap Singh, as minister for scientific development, mainly on account of his academic excellence. Pratap Singh, originally from Gaya in Bihar, was a brilliant young aeronautical engineer. He came from a family of freedom fighters, was a graduate from

IIT Kanpur, had researched and taught in MIT, and returned to India only after he was invited by Shamlal Kanwar to help him in his political work, particularly for India's scientific advancement. He had worked with Shamlal for about three years and was head of his scientific think tank. Pratap Singh could think out of the box, and had given Shamlal Kanwar many ideas and shortcuts for reaching parity with China in the realm of both advanced and basic technologies. He was delighted that they had all been included in the election manifesto committee of the Indian Democratic Party. He was also rather amazed and did not quite resist the quantum of resources that came his way in his new role. Indian politics was indeed a gold mine, he realised.

Pratap Singh was elated at his appointment. Clearly, he had taken the right decision to return to India. This was indeed such a great opportunity, and challenge. He was full of plans for making India a leader in the scientific world. What he needed foremost was a sound principal secretary, to keep the fine balance between science and his new political role.

The new principal secretary for scientific development, of course, would be important as far as Satyadev's future was concerned. But he was not unduly concerned about him. He was bound to be part of the existing scientific fraternity over whom he could flaunt his scientific superiority, and then handle him with a few carrots and sticks.

But Satyadev was in for another shock. The minister did not appoint any of the scientific academy chairs or think tank leaders who ubiquitously abounded Delhi, and were always visible at all high places. These, he knew quite well and could muster their support. The minister, in a surprise move, decided to appoint one Dr Yudhistarachari, Vice Chancellor of the old and famous Gangotri University in Kaashi, a good and sound Brahmin from Uttar Pradesh, as his principal secretary. Yudha, as he was called, was a mathematics genius, especially when it came to money and its safe storage, its profitable handling and multiplication. In this context, he had the most congenial relations with every leading politician of UP, all of whom were full of praise for him and his impeccable integrity and efficiency as guardian of their money, and for raking in the most profitable returns for them. No one minded the percentage he kept for himself, as he never cheated on the principal amounts. Yudha also had a huge amount of scientific research papers to his credit, his favourite subject being the Game Theory propounded by John Nash.

Not surprising then, that Pratap Singh took the advice of all his well-wishers who had supported him so staunchly in his election. He had no hesitation whatsoever in appointing Dr Yudhistarachari, strongly recommended by all his supporters, as his principal secretary. After all, he was also highly respected in the academic world, particularly in the field of mathematics, something that was not very fashionable anymore. And besides, he belonged to the prime minister's own constituency.

Satyadev wasted no time. He immediately asked for an appointment with the new minister and his principal secretary for the customary courtesy call. He got it immediately for the next day. He had already given his finishing touches to the standard ISA presentation, and with his team, the satellite chief, the GAVA chief, and the financial advisor, the IAS lady, whose main value rested on efficient navigation of Delhi's bureaucratic alleys, he departed for Delhi.

To begin with, the meeting with the minister and his principal secretary was extremely cordial and went off smoothly. The routine presentation, explaining the origin of the ISA, its growth and development, successes and failures, future plans, etc. etc.

The Minister smiled at the end of it, but his principal secretary started looking sullen. Satyadev noticed that. Yudha was thinking of how he had ascended from being Vice Chancellor of just another university to a position of scientific and political power, where he could now pass judgement over all these arrogant ISA scientists who went around with a huge chip on their shoulders when dealing with other science mortals, treating them as second-class scientists. Well, he decided, he would start by shooting off a few home truths which they were certainly not accustomed to hearing.

"This is all very well, Dr Satyadev. I have gone through some of your old annual reports and your plan documents. Why is it that you take ever so long to complete your projects? Look at some of them. The Weather Sat series—they were approved by the cabinet six years ago, and you still have not been able to send up even the first one. Look at your Navasat 5 for the Navy. Approved seven years ago, but still not ready. And as for your great promises for societal purposes, how many villages have you reached with your tele-education, leave alone your telemedicine? You built a whole satellite for that, and now you don't know what to do with it. You know, you gentlemen are really lucky that common people don't understand your operations and how much public money all of you waste. Or else your offices would be in a state of gherao most of the time. You have no contact with the common people, so you can go on in your unaccountable ways. And just because you shoot off a rocket in the air now and then, even if it belongs to the primitive space age, you make yourself into some sort of heroes. Just go through your own annual reports and budget documents of the last five years, and see how much you have achieved, and how much you have not."

Satyadev was seething in anger, but contained it. Just another upstart. A nondescript vice chancellor from somewhere having the nerve to pass judgment over the haloed ISA, which had brought so much achievement and honour for the country, despite its few failures. Well, he had no alternative but to stomach it.

He decided to reply and addressed the Minister. "Sir, I do agree there have been delays in several projects. But I must explain that there are valid reasons for that. Often, it is very difficult to get the critical components for our rockets and satellites. You know that sanctions have been imposed and we cannot import a whole list of components which are most essential for us. We try our best to indigenise and substitute, but that provides no immediate solutions. Scientific research takes time. However, we do try our best. Delays, yes there are, I admit. This is a matter that concerns me very seriously too."

"Well, Dr Satyadev, I will soon be doing a detailed review of your department and of GAVA too. Please be in touch with me personally, and tell me all your problems. I'll do my best to help you out."

"Thank you, sir. I will, most certainly. Please let me know if your need any information about anything concerning our organisation."

"Yes, I will. Surely."

Satyadev took his leave and returned to his camp office in the fashionable Lodi Estate. His team started dissecting the meeting. On the whole, it had been good.

The minister had been cordial and friendly. And who the hell cared about what his principal secretary was saying. He was only displaying his ill breeding and inferiority complex, and would soon fall in line.

But Satyadev was disturbed. The vibes were not good. The principal secretary seemed hostile, and he somehow felt that his continuation would be under threat.

Just a few minutes later, he received a call from the minister asking him to see him as soon as possible.

He immediately returned to his car and directed the driver to South Block.

The minister received him, affable and smiling, and said, "Dr Satyadev, I am aware of the hard work that ISA has put in to make your organisation a success and an envy of the world, especially all our neighbours."

"Thank you, sir. But I agree, we have yet to put in even more effort to overcome our deficiencies. After all, this is an effort that should never stop."

"Yes, that's the right attitude. I just wanted to tell you not to be offended by what my principal secretary said. He is a brash man, but means well, and is very highly respected in the academic world."

"Not at all, sir. We must take criticism in a constructive spirit. There is no doubt that we must improve in many ways."

"Now, what I wanted to ask you is what is the latest position about the Oriont collaboration?"

Satyadev was stunned. He felt his blood rush up to his face, and immediately concentrated all his energy on keeping his face and eyes expressionless. The minister was watching him intently. Who had told the minister about it? Some fifth columnist from his organisation? A disgruntled scientist? A perfidious bureaucrat? Or Orient itself?

Satyadev gathered his wits quickly. He realised he must speak the truth, and gave the minister a brief summary of the background and the commercial importance of the proposed collaboration, ending with the recent Oriont USA visit and presentation, and the constitution of the committee that had to work out the details of the joint venture.

The minister intervened. "No, no, Dr Satyadev. Don't make it a collaboration or joint venture. Collaborations always get into trouble. Too many watchdogs who can criticise and find fault with anything they like. Make it a lease. Can't you lease the satellite to Oriont, the transponders? ISA has done it before. I think you should work on those lines. It's better for both parties. And less messy."

Satyadev was astonished, but continued keeping his face and eyes expressionless. What on earth was going on? How the hell did the minister know everything about the whole deal, and about past ISA deals?

"Sir, this would be a very important decision. We can

certainly consider it in this manner."

"Then, consider it." The minister's words had a ring of finality. The message was clear, and Satyadev understood it.

Satyadev returned to his guest house, and immediately called Vidyasagar to his room. He informed him of his conversation with the minister and his instructions. "Well, the Oriont lot seem to have wasted no time in welcoming the minister as their new partner in the deal."

Satyadev was not too happy that they had done so without informing him. Or perhaps, the minister had been informed from some other source. Anyway, soon, he would come to know, as the Oriont representatives would be present at Haridas' meeting. But he kept experiencing a sense of disquiet.

THE ISA TEAM returned to Mumbai the same night. The next day, Satyadev summoned Dr Haridas to his office. Haridas looked a little nervous. He hoped it would not be yet another session about the audit report and his excessive purchases.

"Sit down, Haridas," Satyadev commanded.

"What is the progress on the committee meeting about the Oriont collaboration?"

Haridas turned pale with fear. He had still not called

for the committee meeting, as he had been preoccupied with a little disaster that had struck his family. His niece, his elder brother's daughter, had eloped with someone from Delhi and was nowhere to be found. The two were working together in IBM, and though she had told her parents that they wanted to marry, her parents had refused permission. So, she decided to elope, but in all fairness, she gave notice of it to her parents. As she was above eighteen years of age, no police complaint could be lodged, only a missing person complaint. Since Dr Haridas worked in a government organisation, his brother thought he might be helpful in tracing her without making any police complaint at all. Haridas used the influence of Gurupriya to contact the boy's family in Delhi and find out about the well-being of his niece. That is what had kept him busy during the last week.

"Sir, I must confess, I have not yet called for a committee meeting. I thought I would do it this week after studying all the papers thoroughly. And, besides, I was in the middle of a terrible family problem."

Satyadev showed no interest in his family problem.

"Haridas, I'm disappointed. Call the meeting immediately, and place the subject with two options. One of collaboration and joint venture, and the other for constructing a communication satellite and leasing the transponders to them at a reasonable cost to ISA. Perhaps the second option would be preferable."

Haridas digested the words. The boss wanted the second option and expected him to steer it in the committee.

"Yes, sir. I have already prepared the papers. I will now prepare the second option. Please give me a week."

"Okay, hold the meeting next week definitely, and keep me briefed."

"Yes sir, I will show you the papers in the next two days."

"Good. Hope your spending over unnecessary items has reduced."

The Damocles sword reappeared on Haridas' head.

Dr Haridas called the committee meeting for the following Monday. He worked day and night for three days and prepared the papers for the committee, citing both options of collaboration and of leasing out transponders. He refused to give any SWOT analysis of either option. Why should he? Let it come from the committee which had heads of the major ISA divisions—a bureaucrat who was the deputy administrative officer, and two retired scientists from the Space Research Institute who were well respected in the scientific world. No doubt, the boss would have instructed them what to do. It would be interesting to see how they would marshal their arguments.

After completing his papers, Haridas had a long briefing session with Satyadev. Both viewed each other with polite suspicion.

They went through the technical papers—the design of the satellite, the power of the beams, the uplinks and downlinks, the speed of data downloads, configuration of receivers, the ground segment plan, the audio video compression systems, the unfurlable antenna, etc. etc., all coming from the X band, the most powerful spectrum that is reserved for security purposes.

This would be a momentous initiative for ISA, at a time when a host of new technologies were emerging in the telephony market, combination of the ground segment with the space segment, devices with internet and email held in one's hand.

But Satyadev did secretly have some worries. ISA did not have the latest technology. Oriont too did not have the technology, even though they were funding the Lincoln Labs, the leading research organisation in telecommunications, and were confident of having the technology within a year. When Satyadev had mentioned this to the previous principal secretary, he had just laughed.

"We all know that Dr Satyadev. But we are completely confident that Oriont will produce the technology—they will beg, borrow, buy or steal. Oriont has our complete confidence. And remember, the minister is aware of all the facts."

"Yes, I know that." The former minister had great trust in Satyadev. And besides, the negotiations had gone well so far, and the minister was pleased with the progress. The *nazranas* (gifts) had been good and the future collaboration spelt good tidings for all partners. The profits would be phenomenal once the transponders started beaming.

Satyadev decided that it was now time for him to brief the new minister Pratap Singh about the progress of the Oriont deal and also to push for his own extension. He would be retiring within the next two months, and why the hell was he sweating it out so much for something that would not be in his hands after that.

He got an appointment for the next day, and was off to Delhi that night. Fortunately, the principal secretary was out on a conference in Bangkok.

He gave a good brief to the minister about the progress of Oriont India—that the new company had already been registered and had started some preparatory technical work; that the Haridas committee had been constituted, and its first meeting was scheduled for the coming Monday; and that the committee would build up a case for constructing a satellite and leasing its transponders to Oriont India.

The minister listened patiently.

"Yes, I'm aware of the developments. Now, you must follow up everything and complete the formalities quickly. How soon can the contract be signed?"

"In another three months, at the earliest," replied Satyadev.

"That's too long. Can't it be done within two months?"

"A little difficult, sir. There would have to be detailed technical discussions among the scientists, legal experts, financial advisors. Then the bureaucrats will have to be brought on board and kept satisfied. Then, it would have to go to the GAVA Board for approval. It's only after that that the contract can be signed. So, nothing less than three months, as I see it. Besides, it would be better, sir, if all the procedures are followed properly, without shortcuts. Wiser. Anyhow, sir, we will try our best to complete it within two or two and a half months. I will personally monitor it."

Satyadev continued, "Sir, I must also inform you that I am to retire by the end of July. So maybe it would be better if I stayed on for another year, just to make sure that the satellite starts getting constructed."

The Minister nodded, but said nothing. Satyadev was disappointed. Several MPs and ministers had spoken to Pratap Singh about his extension. Satyadev knew that.

But what he did not know was that Maharishi Nath, the next most senior scientist and head of the Rocket Research Centre in Thane, had also gathered his loyal MPs and ministers, mostly from Uttar Pradesh, the state to which both he and the minister belonged, to plead for his appointment as ISA chairman. Besides, he had the support of an extremely influential scientist turned politician, Kabir Sufi. The minister, in all fairness, had listened to each one of them. Fresh blood and brains were always required in any organisation was their argument, particularly in a scientific establishment.

THE HARIDAS COMMITTEE met as scheduled during the last week of June, and most members attended. The deputy finance officer, Sushil Ramu, wanted to avoid the meeting after he read the short background note that accompanied the meeting notice. He somehow could smell that something was not quite okay. He also found out that he would be the only bureaucrat at the meeting, something that made him a little uncomfortable. And not being a scientist, there was no way he could contribute to such a meeting which would be regarding finalising the design of the satellite and antenna and the payload, about all of which he had no competence to express any views. And if it was a question of finances, that would arise only later, after the technical decisions had been taken.

He requested approval for a tour to the ISA tracking station near the forests of Bidar, which was receiving threats from Naxalites entrenched nearby, and since he was also in charge of security, he believed a visit from him was necessary to boost the morale of the security platoon stationed there. His tour programme was turned down immediately by Satyadev.

"Mr Sushil Ramu, I cannot approve your tour programme. There's this very important meeting of the Haridas committee coming up where an important decision has to be taken. The minister has been calling me every day asking about its progress, and you say you want to go on tour. I cannot permit this. Complete the meeting and then go."

Sushil Ramu had no option but to attend. As he had anticipated, he had nothing to contribute. The papers contained drawings, mathematical calculations and several other physics formulas, and there was no way he could comprehend any of them, or judge their merits or demerits.

Then there were several sets of financial calculations drawn up by GAVA—cost of collaboration, investment for construction of satellite, setting up ground stations, marketing strategies. He wondered how on earth would GAVA handle all this?

There was nothing much beyond layman's logic that Sushil Ramu could understand. Certainly, none of the technical details. That damned satellite could well be a washing machine for all he cared. But he felt a most unpleasant sense of entrapment into a deal which he felt was somewhat sneaky, something he did not feel too good about. Anyhow, he'd try and make sure that he did not get involved in it any further, even if he had to feign illness to miss the next meeting.

The meeting ended with some agreement about the design of the satellite. It was decided that they would meet again the next Monday to work out financial projections, and take a decision whether it was technically and financially more prudent to have a commercial collaboration or whether they should simply build the satellite and lease out the transponders to Oriont. That way, a certain revenue to ISA would be ensured with none of the hassles of commercial operations.

This was tricky, thought Sushil Ramu. He had to start working on how to avoid the next meeting. Let his boss Gurupriya attend it, if someone from finance was required. She was greatly trusted by the senior scientists, and was their great favourite.

He decided he would apply for leave after a few days days. He hadn't quite decided whether he would feign a viral fever, or whether he would use the excuse of his mother's ill health to scoot from the scene to his home town in Palghat. He chose the latter, because leave would be more assured.

Haridas held his second and final committee meeting the next Monday. The two options of collaboration and lease were discussed and the financial projections of both options placed forward. Gurupriya was present as Sushil Ramu had sent her a letter on Friday saying his mother's health had turned serious, and as her only son, he had to leave for Palghat immediately.

Gurupriya cursed him, and saw no alternative but to attend. She couldn't let her organisation down. She had been part of the negotiations from the start, and she owed it to ISA to see the agreement through. After all, her son, studying law in Stanford, had benefited greatly from the generosity of Oriont. She owed it to Oriont too.

The Haridas committee came to a safe conclusion. After studying the financial projections prepared by GAVA, the scientists were unanimous in their decision that it would be technically and administratively more prudent to opt for the leasing of the satellite transponders to Oriont, rather than going in for a commercial venture, fraught with risk, which would require a lot of additional manpower and marketing expertise, which they were not too confident of. Marketing by government was always a tricky business, unless buy back agreements were in place. Besides, entering the sphere of commercial marketing would require a million approvals from several layers in the governmental system, always an unsavoury exercise. The scientists had been tutored well, and knew which way the wind was blowing.

Haridas quickly drafted the proceedings of the meeting, and went to see the chairman.

"Well, sir, I've delivered what I had promised. Here is the decision of the Haridas committee. They have all agreed that it would be more prudent and financially less risky if ISA makes the satellite and GAVA leases out the transponders to Oriont. Oriont should pay an upfront capacity reservation fee of USD 15 million, and a fixed reasonable annual lease fee of USD 8 million. This would be better than going in for a JV commercial agreement, where we would be stepping into uncharted territory, and wouldn't be very sure of what the financial results would be."

"Okay, good. Let me go through it," Satyadev said.

"And besides, sir, this is not the first time. Even earlier we have done the same thing for TerrAkask, and the arrangement worked well."

"Good work, Haridas. Now send it over to GAVA and tell Vidyasagar to immediately draft the agreement with Oriont. I will call for a meeting on this tomorrow."

"Yes sir." Haridas did as he was told. He was aware that Vidyasagar had already completed two long sittings with the Oriont herd and had almost finalised the draft agreement. Anyway, he was relieved that his job was over. Now Vidyasagar and his boss Satyadev could sort out the rest.

Satyadev phoned the minister to inform him of the progress, but was informed by his PS that he was in a meeting with his constituents from Allahabad, and couldn't be disturbed.

The GAVA Board meeting was called in record time on July 20. There was enough quorum, though the non-official members, both heads of leading industrial empires in the telecommunication world, Deccan Technologies India and TerrAkash Industries were absent. There were the usual agenda items about financial accounts and the last year's balance sheet, financial results of the first quarter, plans and projections for the future, new foreign agreements about launching payloads for nearby countries like Malaysia and Singapore. And lastly, almost like a footnote, an agenda note on the GAVA Oriont Agreement was circulated for approval.

Chairman GAVA, none other than Dr Satyadev, explained the agreement in a few sentences, and used another ten sentences in announcing the recommendations of the Haridas committee report.

He continued, "Gentlemen and lady," he said, looking for a while at Ms Gurupriya, who was also present as the financial advisor, "We in GAVA have been following up on the telephony market as it has been exploding in India. There is an insatiable demand for it. Many market surveys have also been appearing in the papers about it. The world is now waiting for a multimedia telephony system, with audio visual capabilities. This requires a new technology, and we are lucky that we have found the perfect partners to enable this. They are Oriont India, headed by Dr Karmaswamy, who is one of our own persons having achieved great distinction in the USA as head of Oriont Telecom, USA. They have the technology and we have the spectrum. Together, we can become leaders in the field and bring our country great economic benefit. And as you all know, we have enough spare spectrum allotted to us in the X band which remains unused year after year. I am of the view that 50 mhtz of this spectrum, as recommended by the Haridas committee, can easily be allotted to Oriont for a period of 15 years, which is the entire life of the satellite, at the rate indicated in the note. Once the board approves and the agreement is signed, we can seek cabinet approval and start constructing GeoS 10. And if all goes well, we can follow it up with GeoS 11. We will give Oriont that option. This way, we can satisfy the multimedia telephony demand of our country through our own indigenous satellites, instead of depending upon foreign companies. The cost on the consumer would also be much less. You can see the projections and the costing in the agenda note."

Satyadev looked around the room. Everyone was listening. No one was flipping pages to see what the agreement contained. Most of them had seen the contents at the Haridas committee meeting. And no one cared whether they were the same or different. There wasn't a murmur.

Satyadev continued. "So, we can see that the board has approved this. Thank you, gentleman. Now we can proceed with signing of the contract."

"And lady, my apologies, as usual," Satyadev turned towards the financial advisor, Gurupriya, who smiled coyly. The meeting ended with a vote of thanks to the chair, and everyone proceeded for lunch.

Satyadev was exhausted by the end of it, but was jubilant. He had proved his worth to the minister and successfully achieved the objective in record time. He thought he should inform the minister, but then decided that he should first fix the date for signing the contract.

He sent for Vidyasagar, and said he would like to have a meeting with the Oriont team and him the next day, to work on the nitty gritty of signing the contract and the procedures that were required.

"So now, what next Vidyasagar? Good work."

"With your blessings, sir," Vidyasagar replied, not deviating even an inch from the prescribed texts of sycophancy.

"So, let us meet in my office tomorrow at 10 am with Karmaswamy and his team to go into the next phase of signing the agreement."

"Yes, sir. But before that, the science council, chaired by you must clear it. We can get the approval through circulation, as sometimes it becomes difficult to get all the members together."

"Yes, we could do that. But I would like to see the board meeting proceedings in the next two days, so that we can send off the proposal to the science council members."

"Yes, sir. But sir, can we have the meeting after 12.30 in the afternoon or even after lunch?"

"Why Vidyasagar?"

"Because, sir, from 11 to 12.30 is *rahukalam* (inauspicious time). Let's avoid it. No good and auspicious work should be done during that time."

Satyadev laughed, "Okay, okay, if you say so. But let's have all the papers ready by then."

"Yes, sir."

"And remember one more thing, the proceedings must not be sent to any bureaucrat, not even to Gurupriya."

"Yes, sir."

Satyadev immediately telephoned the minister. He was lucky to reach him at his constituency near Allahabad.

"Yes, Satyadev, hope all his going well," the Minister started.

"Yes sir, things are going well, with your blessings. Sorry to disturb you, sir, but I just wanted to inform you that the GAVA board has approved the Oriont contract for construction of GeoS 10, to be followed by GeoS 11, when the time is right. I just thought I should keep you informed."

"Good, so when do you expect to sign the contract?"

"Within the next two to three weeks, sir. There'll be a lot of legal vetting and financial scrutiny required. Then approval from the science council. Procedures."

"Yes, follow them all. Let the paper work be perfect."

"Yes, sir, of course."

"And one more thing, Satyadev."

"Yes sir."

"In future, don't phone me up about this subject. You can always keep my PS informed, if there's any problem. And if there's something more important, you can always come and meet me."

The minister sounded friendly, but cold and clipped, obviously wanting nothing more to do with the deal, now that it was done.

"Bastard," was the first word that came to Satyadev's mind.

The contract was signed in the last week of July as promised, after following all the mandatory procedures. As instructed, Satyadev did not telephone the Minister to inform him. He merely instructed Vidyasagar to inform the Minister's PS of the contract, and also send him a signed copy of it as an email attachment. This was for the record. After all, Satyadev and his team also had to protect themselves.

The last week of July had started, and there was still no word from the Government about whether Satyadev would continue after retirement. ISA headquarters went into an eerie huddle. At the best of times, its natural environment was grim, and the suspense about their future chairman only added to its grimness. Satyadev and Maharishi were nowhere to be seen. It was said that they were both doing inspections of the various ISA centres that existed all over the country. But everyone in ISA knew that each of the centres they visited was near some important MP's constituency or near Delhi.

And then one fine day, Maharishi was spotted in ISA holding a meeting with the Satellite Research Centre chief. But Satyadev was still nowhere to be seen. The same evening, news flashed from Delhi that Maharishi Nath had been appointed the new chairman, ISA.

There was a sense of relief in ISA. The shadow boxing of their bosses was over, and everyone now was clear about where and how to dissent. The old and new boss would get busy with farewells and welcomes.

Satyadev cultivated a perpetual smile on his face to hide his acute bitterness. He had navigated the whole Oriont deal, thinking he would be rewarded for it. Instead, he had been given the royal boot. Maharishi, in his elation cultivated a rather profound and philosophic smile, and sought everybody's cooperation and goodwill for living up to the great responsibility that had come upon him.

Officially, and on the face of it, handing over charge was an uncomplicated affair. The usual sendoff and welcome, speeches, flowers and dinners. But there were several other matters behind the scenes that had to be dealt with in the transition—unknown commitments to business partners which had to be honoured; protection of favourites; smooth transition of incomplete secret dealings not known to the rest of the organisation, and how their commitments were to be handled. These were the ones for which instructions normally came from above, and they had to be dealt with very deftly, maturely and discreetly.

THE FIRST THING that Vidyasagar wanted to do after Maharishi Nath took charge as ISA chairman was to give him a good and honest brief about the GAVA Oriont contract. But he thought it would be more prudent to consult Satyadev about when he should do so. He did consult him and was told that Satyadev himself would brief Maharishi shortly.

Maharishi had heard some stray details about the Oriont deal from some of his loyal scientists. He knew Karmaswamy and some of the former ISA and GAVA employees who were now part of Oriont India. Well, well, he sighed, the Oriont deal was also part of his inheritance along with the other baggage and trappings of his position.

He went to Delhi to call on the minister and pay his respect. The minister spoke politely but did not discuss anything official, least of all the Oriont deal. He told Maharishi that he would during the next month be coming to Mumbai to do a detailed review of both the ISA and GAVA.

Maharishi was certain that both Satyadev and Karmaswamy would have kept the minister informed of the latest on the Oriont contract. One of Maharishi's old staff who was now in Oriont had told him privately that Karmaswamy had already met the minister, and presented him with a beautiful slip of paper with some unintelligible gibberish written on it, but with a prominent ten figure number of the Bernard Lichtenstein Bank, with the name of one Maria Dolan.

It was now back to business for Maharishi. His predecessor had delivered the contract and briefed him about it. Well, so far so good. The transition was over, and now the deluge of phone calls from the minister's office had started. Not to him, but to all his subordinates—Vidyasagar in GAVA, Gurupriya in the secretariat. What was happening with the Oriont contract? When would the cabinet note be ready? And then, Karmaswamy wanted an urgent appointment, for which he replied—any time.

Maharishi realised that he had now to seriously get down to procedures, and take his Oriont inheritance to the cabinet. From what he could figure out, Satyadev, Haridas and his committee, which included almost the entire ISA top brass, the minister's office, some key bureaucrats, and GAVA, were already part of the deal making process. So that was a safety factor there. And he was, after all, just an inheritor of the deal.

Maharishi gave an appointment to Karmaswamy and the Oriont team for the next day. Vidyasagar was also present and the meeting went off smoothly. It was *bonhomie* all the way, wonderful conversation about the future, of how GAVA and Oriont would conquer the telephony market of the world with their bold and audacious enterprise.

"But what about the technology?" Maharishi asked with a somewhat bemused expression. "You still don't have it, do you?"

"No, sir, not yet. But just give us a few more months. Our scientists are working hard at it with Lincoln Labs. And we've almost concluded a collaboration with Leon Mercurius, the Canadian company which is already experimenting with it. Just give us a few more months and we shall have it."

"Make it a commitment. Because, if you don't get it soon, it can turn out to be a terrible fiasco. And GAVA will be put to a terrible amount of embarrassment. And of course, me as well."

"Not to worry, sir. We give you our word. By the time you get your cabinet approval, we will have the technology. We give you our word."

"You'd better. By the way, Karma, let us discuss everything at dinner this evening. I have a long string of meetings for the whole day. We'll meet at the Taj. Just us—Vidyasagar and you and your deputy, Vasudev. We can discuss everything in detail then."

"This is very gracious of you. Let us have the honour. Would you also like us to invite some of your other officers from the secretariat? Ms Gurupriya? She has been most helpful and supportive."

"No, no bureaucrats. Let's just keep this to ourselves, to begin with. I'm still not too familiar with them here. They're generally known to be rather tricky creatures, though I do think that's a bit of an exaggeration. Many of them are a nice lot, but yes, their tentacles spread everywhere. If they want to help you or harm you or sabotage you, even without any reward for themselves, they can do it. All they have to do is ring up some batchmate or cadre mate, or a friend of a batchmate, never mind which ministry or which state, and tell him, fix this guy or help this guy or keep this in cold storage, and they succeed. I've seen this several times over the last few years. Once or twice, in my previous assignments, I had asked my administrative officers to get something stalled or pushed in the Ministry of Defence or Telecom, and they always succeeded. Their networks are really stupendous. You've got to admit that. Wish we had them too." He looked at Vidyasagar, who couldn't help smiling.

Karmaswamy was taken aback. Obviously, Maharishi was still not too friendly with any of his secretariat officers.

The dinner at the Taj was a dull, drab affair. All four men drank themselves senseless, and enjoyed the marvellous food—jumbo sized prawns, juicy lobster and crab, and delicious, innovative vegetarian delicacies. In their relaxed haze, they also had a fairly serious discussion about future plans, goal posts, time lines, finances.

Before leaving, Karmaswamy whispered into Maharishi's ears, "Sir, there's a sealed cover waiting for you in your office."

"What is it?"

"Just a token of affection and gratitude from Mr Georges. He asked to deliver it to you personally. Nothing much, just a little slip of paper. That is all."

Maharishi saw it the next day. It was a little slip of paper with a strange name, and a number of the Bernard Liechtenstein Bank.

THE NEXT DAY, Maharishi summoned his senior most bureaucrat, Ms Gurupriya, the financial advisor. He didn't know her too well, but had dealt with her at several purchase committee meetings, parliamentary committee meetings, and planning commission meetings. He remembered the joke that went around about her among the scientists—that her mood for the day was to be judged by the amount of cleavage she 'accidentally' showed, and by the number of times she orchestrated her sari pallu to slip downwards. Also called was Vidyasagar, the MD,

GAVA, who was now the real key player in this whole affair. Vidyasagar brought along the secretariat assistant who was to start the cabinet process in the secretariat. He was a fine young man called Salim Khan, always a friend of the scientists.

Maharishi started the meeting. "Now Vidyasagar, by when are you planning to send the draft cabinet note for construction of GeoS 10 to Salim. It must be processed fast. The minister's office has been asking for daily progress reports. The details are all there in the agreement. It should not take much time."

Vidyasagar did not need to be told. He had started preparing the draft cabinet note well before the agreement had been signed, and he had already started refining it in accordance with the contract, to fit the format and requirements of the cabinet secretariat.

"Ms Gurupriya, just help him out, in case he needs some assistance," Maharishi said. He looked towards her and found her all covered up, which meant that she too was a little nervous. Anyhow, she was a partner now, having signed the Haridas committee proceedings, and had no room at all to retract. Things seemed to be moving well.

"Sure, sir. Dr Vidyasagar, just let me know when you need any assistance from my end. I'll be more than happy to assist."

"Thank you, madam. Let me get the first draft done, and then I will request you for your advice."

"By when will I have the cabinet note?" Maharishi asked Vidyasagar quite firmly.

"My draft should be ready within two or three days. But after that, it has to pass through the entire secretariat, then sent to the planning ministry and finance ministry. That would take at least a couple of months. That's a fairly realistic assessment. Would you agree, madam?" he asked Gurupriya.

"Yes, sir. I think that's realistic enough. Of course, we'll have to keep pushing it in both the planning and finance ministries. Sometimes, they can be quite difficult, but we'll keep up the pressure on them."

"Good," said Maharishi, "let me know if there's anything you need from my end. But work fast. You know the number of telephone calls we all receive everyday about this."

"Thank you, sir," Gurupriya said rising, her sari pallu showing some signs of slipping. Maharishi kept his smile to himself.

The meeting was over. Both Gurupriya and Salim Khan left.

Vidyasagar stayed on. He asked Maharishi, "Sir, should we inform the cabinet about our contract with Oriont, that we have already leased the transponders of GeoS 10 to them?" He was thinking of the college fees that Oriont had just paid for his daughter in Washington University.

"Hmm. That's a point. Let me think about it. I don't think there are any rules that we should. And I don't think we've done it earlier for several other cases, for example, when we built the satellite for TerrAkask or for the Singaporians."

"But, sir," Vidyasagar continued, "we have to clearly state the justification for building this satellite in the cabinet note. So, what do we say? Why are we building it? There must be some justification."

"Well, we can say that GAVA is entering into the state-of-the-art telephony market that is on the boom, right on our threshold."

'Even so, sir, we have to state the financial benefits. We cannot do this unless we refer to the Oriont contract."

"Let me just think about it. Perhaps we should," Maharshi said, with his mind quite distracted.

"You get on with the rest of it. About this particular aspect, I will inform you within the next few days. In any case, you also require a few days to get the cabinet note ready, place it into the administrative channel of the secretariat and then to the chief administration officer." He remembered the little slip of paper with the strange name and number of the Liechtenstein Bank. He felt good and satisfied, but he realised that from now on, he had to be very careful and play it very safe.

He decided to make a visit to Delhi to meet the minister, and brief him of the progress of the Oriont cabinet note, and also about several other projects on telemedicine and tele-education which appeared to be progressing well in the tribal areas of India, and some other launches that were scheduled in the near future.

He called up the minister's office and made an appointment for the next day. It would be an interesting meeting. One of his loyal cronies in the newly created Oriont India had made oblique references to the fact that the minister was happy with Oriont.

"What do you mean, happy?" he asked him.

"Well, happy, sir. Oriont US is in the business of keeping all its partners happy. You know how it is."

Maharishi put a stop to this conversation, and remembered the enticing piece of paper left in his room by Oriont.

Well, he thought, a curious kind of a *leela* (play) was in motion. Just as he was being informed about the 'happiness' of the minister, there was every possibility that the minister too was being informed of the 'happiness' of chairman ISA. So, it was 'one all' as of now, he thought, though he did wonder what economic formulae were used to quantify their respective quota of 'happiness.'

Maharishi left for Delhi early the next morning, as he was to meet the Minister in the afternoon at 3 pm.

He drove into South Block, after a light lunch and short nap. He was dot on time, and the Minister was in his office to receive him.

"Good afternoon, sir," he said, and waited for the PS to leave the room.

"Well, sir, everything has gone well so far with the Oriont contract. We are in the process of taking the construction of the satellite GeoS 10 to the cabinet. I just wanted a few clarifications from you, before we finalise the cabinet note, and your guidance in the matter."

"Yes, what is it?'

"Well, sir, I've already had discussions about the cabinet note with GAVA, and also with the chief financial advisor, Ms Gurupriya, an IAS officer of the Union Territory cadre. She is the only one who knows about the Oriont contract right from the beginning, and she has also attended the second Haridas committee meeting and the GAVA Board meeting which approved the contract. Her deputy, Sushil Ramu, attended the first meeting, but not the second, as his mother was very ill. So, Ms Gurupriya had to attend from the secretariat. Now, it is these people and their secretariat through whom the cabinet note will be processed. And they wanted to know whether it is wise to mention the Oriont contract in the cabinet note, and that the transponders of GeoS 10 are intended for them."

"What is your opinion, Dr Maharishi?" the Minister asked.

"Well, sir, for us it does not matter, one way or another. We can always justify the case for Oriont India, as a single vendor, and no one in the organisation will counter our claim. We will see to that. But the chief financial advisor has been part of the negotiations from the beginning, and has attended both the Haridas committee meeting and the GAVA board meeting. She's the only one who really knows about the whole contract from beginning to end. And the deputy finance officer has attended one meeting of the Haridas committee. So clearly, he knows about it too."

"So, what do you suggest?" the Minister persisted.

Maharishi was beginning to feel a little trapped. This was no way of treating a scientist who had behaved so loyally.

"Sir, there are no rules and regulations that cover this aspect. Previously, in some cases we have informed the cabinet, in some cases not. I just thought I should consult you, before I send up this note for your approval, for submission to the cabinet."

Both men were thinking of the Liechtenstein Bank slips. The minister decided he would put an end to Maharishi's one club bid.

"You know, Maharishi, now that I think of it, perhaps it would be wiser if you avoid names. That would unnecessarily arouse curiosity among the media, and all our political enemies. There could be so many accusations. And who is Oriont India? Just a few of your old employees who left either in disgrace or in disgust, many of them Satyadev's favourites. And we all know that

Satyadev is really the architect of this contract, whether it was the previous regime or this one. It would just cause a lot of unnecessary speculation and accusation politically, and negative reporting in the press."

He turned silent for a while. "So, you can just write that you have one serious interested party, with high merit for qualification. And your word will be final. No one will question it. No one has any authority to do so."

"I understand, sir. We will have no problem with our financial advisor, Gurupriya. She is completely loyal to our organisation. As for the deputy administration officer, we will ensure that he does not speak. We know his price. Apart from these two, no one else in the secretariat knows about the contract."

"Quite a concentration camp you run, I see," the minister laughed.

"Not really, sir. Everything is on a need to know basis. And you'd agree, that's the best way to run a high security organisation."

The minister laughed again. He knew Maharishi was no fool. Maharishi had done enough research to know that the naming of Oriont would compromise the former chairman, whose relatives now thronged Oriont USA. Maharishi also knew of the investments being made in foreign shores on behalf of the minister and his principal secretary in this new company that would capture the multi-media telephony market in India.

The message was clear, and Maharishi knew what he had to do. The minister, like him, was also an inheritor of the deal from the previous regime, and seemed comfortable with it. Really, thought Maharishi, what a lot goes on in this capital city of ours… and what are we scientists… just little pawns in the game…. But he again remembered the Liechtenstein Bank slip, and turned to the more practical realities of his life.

Maharishi took a little more time explaining the progress of some of the forthcoming launches, relating to marine fishing and climate change. The minister listened patiently, and after being informed that there were no serious problems about anything, Maharishi took his leave.

"Thank you, sir, for all your support. The cabinet note will reach you shortly. In just the way that we have discussed."

"Good, Maharishi. And before you leave, I just thought you should know. There are a lot of complaints about some Shukra Devi, who was PS to your predecessor. Apparently, she is running some sort of a real estate business right from your office. Just thought I should tell you."

"Yes sir. I've been hearing about that too. I'll see what I can do about her."

"Best of luck. If the people of India only know what goes on among all of you. Frankly, even I was pretty shocked at all the things I heard."

"Like what, sir?"

"Ah, nothing much. All your intrigues, your favourite men and women, your extravagant cultivation of the press—no doubt, they love all the goodies that you give them—your complete subjugation of the SCs and STs, your arrogance with the scientific world. And it's your good luck that the common people cannot understand a thing of what you're really achieving, and what you are not achieving."

"Sir, I hear you. And I assure you—I give you my word that I will do my best to correct all I can to your satisfaction."

"Thank you. Good night, Maharishi."

Maharishi rose and trooped out of the door, dispirited and a little unhappy.

His only achievement was that the Minister had given him a clear indication of what he wanted regarding GeoS 10 and the Oriont cabinet note.

Maharishi had a pen in his pocket which had a nice rounded pen cap, and in it was a smart recording device in it. It had been presented to him by Dr Karmswamy. Some instinct for self-preservation had made him record the conversation. And some strange instinct had made the Minister also record the conversation.

ON THE NEXT day at his ISA office, Maharishi summoned Vidyasagar and Gurupriya, and gave them clear instructions, "The cabinet note must not contain the name of Oriont India. Just make it general and write that there is serious interest being shown by a leading international company in this field, with high credentials."

Gurupriya insisted, "Sir, but what is wrong if we state it? Would it not be better to do so, for all concerned." Her cleavage was covered.

"Well, I've had discussions in Delhi, and that's the way they want it, to avoid any premature speculation and sabotage."

Gurupriya was thinking of her own child being educated in the US, through the bounty of Oriont.

"I understand, sir," she said, still soundly covered.

"So, Vidyasagar, get on with the cabinet note soon, just as I have told you."

Turning to Gurupriya, he added, "Please ask your deputy finance officer, Sushil Ramu, who is also doubling up for the deputy administration officer, to keep this in mind when the cabinet papers pass through him. He is due for his next promotion. Remind him that he must perform well in the interest of the ISA. And in the interest of his own promotion."

"Yes, sir," Gurupriya was a little startled. That the

soft-spoken Maharishi Nath could sound so ruthless.

Gurupriya knew, but Maharishi probably had still had not been informed by his in-house spies or the Oriont guys, that Sushil Ramu had also received the little slip from the Liechtenstein Bank. So had Gurupriya.

The stage was set. Vidyasagar worked hard on the draft cabinet note with all the respectable facts of the background and the proposal. The cabinet note was meant for getting approval for construction of a communication satellite, not for leasing out its transponders, so he kept it purely technical and financial, as was recommended by the Haridas committee. A lot of scientific gibberish, which would fly over the heads of all the secretariat hands, and the financial estimates and rates of return that justified leasing out transponders. As instructed, Vidyasagar completely avoided any reference to the agreement with Oriont India for leasing out the transponders for the life of the satellite, adding only that GAVA was already approached by a very qualified company for collaborating in the multimedia telephony technology, and was in discussion with them.

The note went up with extraordinary speed through the lower staff of the secretariat—through the deputy administration officer, who had been instructed to remain mum, and on to the chief administration officer, Shri Manal Kumar, the new and unknown commodity, always distant, always aloof, with no desire to endear himself to anyone around, least of all the scientist community.

Manal Kumar went through the cabinet note meticulously. He had no idea that the transponders of the proposed satellite GeoS 10 had already been leased out to Oriont India. As a bureaucrat in the ISA secretariat, he had no authority to question any of the facts stated by the MD, GAVA, who was a responsible officer of the organisation. Besides, the draft had the approval of chairman GAVA, who was none other than the chairman ISA, before it came to the secretariat. So too, the technical details had been scrutinised to finality by the communication and satellite chiefs, for which they were responsible and accountable, and were not his responsibility. Manal Kumar's job was to ensure that the note was in accordance with the cabinet secretariat guidelines, that it had internal consistency and logic, and that the financial projections were correct, as per the budgetary provision and guidelines. He attended to these aspects, sending the note back several times to his subordinates for corrections and amendments.

Maharishi was monitoring the progress of the cabinet note on a day-to-day basis, the secretariat underlings keeping him informed of every detail. He knew it had sailed smoothly until it had reached Manal Kumar, who had by now sent it back at least three times, suggesting several changes to make it more specific and avoid the vague language that Maharishi wanted it to have. He had also questioned some financial parameters. All that was fine, but it was getting unduly delayed. But perhaps, it was all for the best. Manal Kumar was doing his best to ensure that the cabinet note would be perfect, and would not be returned from the cabinet secretariat with some useless bureaucratic query.

He had also gathered by now from his underground contacts in Delhi that the cabinet secretary, Mr Chandrakanth Arin, was 'friendly' about this whole issue, and also that his deputy finance officer had also received a little slip from the Liechtenstein Bank.

Maharishi did not think it was necessary to interfere with the secretariat on speeding up the matter, though he would casually review it during his routine official meetings with them. And no one in the organisation, including the formidable Ms Gurupriya with her flexible sari pallu, could discover whether Manal Kumar had a price, and if so, what it was. This was a little unsettling, as it disturbed the harmony and synergy that had long existed with the regular bunch of bureaucrats who had inhabited the ISA. Manal Kumar was just a little too aloof and nonchalant, extremely intelligent and analytical, and did his work with perfection, something he had not seen too much of among the other bureaucrats. And it was good that Sushil Ramu, the deputy administration officer had stuck to his word and not stated anything about the Oriont contract even though he had been privy to it as member of the Haridas committee. So far, so good. His impending promotion and the little slip from the Liechtenstein Bank had taken care of him.

No, he would not interfere, thought Maharishi. It was best to leave Manal Kumar alone, with or without a price. After all, it was his professional responsibility to move the cabinet note forward, and there was no way he could stop it, despite the questions he was asking.

Finally, it was done, after all of Manal Kumar's questions were answered and the facts had an internal consistency for a proper cabinet note for construction of GeoS 10. Sushil Ramu still remained mum about his knowledge of the Oriont deal, and the cabinet note was sent to Maharishi Nath, who signed it with a smile. And then it went to Gurupriya, the financial advisor, who merely flicked her signature, and sent it for approval of the finance minister, not mentioning a word about the Oriont GAVA saga that she had witnessed from beginning to end. The finance minister took about a month to approve it, asking several questions, and after several visits from Karmaswamy.

The cabinet note then went to the minister for scientific development, who chuckled when he saw how meticulously it was written. He saw the finance minister's approval, and signed it without much ado. And bingo, it was in the cabinet secretariat the next day, for placing it before the cabinet secretary, Mr Chandrakant Arin.

Chandrakant Arin had been a good old friend of Satyadev, Georges and Karmaswamy, and had been involved with the entire history of the Oriont deal both in the previous and present Government. The cabinet note was of special interest to him, and he read it carefully. He did not like what he saw. He immediately summoned both Maharishi and Vidyasagar to Delhi.

Maharishi and Vidyasagar decided to stay at Hotel Taj Akbar, which had a very private, well equipped office suite. Chandrakant Arin drove into the hotel that evening after office hours, and settled into the luxurious sofa in the office suite. Maharishi was busy pouring him a drink, a good single malt whisky that he liked.

Chandrakant Arin went straight to the point. "Now listen, Maharishi, I've gone through your cabinet note. It's perfect. But you've got to change one thing. Don't say that you've been approached by just one party. That's going to cause problems. Say, you've been approached by a few or more than one."

"I don't understand. Why?" asked Maharishi.

"You see, we've been going through some rough times in other contracts which are single vendor. They have to be justified very strongly, and obviously, that is not what you would want to do. I know you have your own financial rules, but this is important. There have been too many single vendor contracts which have caused a political uproar, with demands for a vigilance enquiry and so forth. We certainly would not want something like that to happen here. So just change that line, and say that you have been approached by a few or some serious interested vendors and are negotiating with them. That should not be difficult."

"But, for that we will have to send it back to the secretariat, and that could ring alarm bells."

Chandrakant Arin continued coolly, "Not really, just make the change here. After all, you are the signatory of the cabinet note. Just change the sentence, and send it back to me, and we will then circulate it."

"But, sir, what about the finance minister's approval. How could we possibly change that?" Maharishi persisted.

"Don't worry about that. These are small matters. We will handle them," replied Chandrakant Arin, with an air of deep reflection and concentration.

Maharishi stared speechlessly at Chandrakant Arin in awe. Vidyasagar, who had a soft copy of the note, was quick to make the change of sentence in English. His Delhi liaison officer made the change in Hindi, and the new set of notes were put together by the liaison officer, signed by Maharishi, and given to the cabinet secretariat the next day. The originals had already been returned to Maharishi. But the liaison officer committed one little mistake. Out of sheer force of habit, he did not retain the date of the original note, but changed it to the date of the clandestine revision. Neither Maharishi nor Vidyasagar noticed this as Maharishi signed the new cabinet note. It hardly mattered at that time.

The cabinet note sailed through the cabinet without a hitch. Maharishi was present at the cabinet meeting, and was asked to enter the cabinet room to answer a few questions put forth by some of the ministers, an experience that put him on a new high. The questions mainly dealt with the kind of multimedia telephony communication that the satellite would be capable of delivering. As soon as he answered the questions, the minister for scientific development added that it was important that we set up our own indigenous companies to provide multimedia telephony services for countering the world telecom companies aggressively eyeing the Indian market.

The cabinet approved unanimously, and the cabinet secretary switched over to the next subject.

December 2002

THE CHEERS IN Oriont India were loud. They had done it. They now had two papers in their hand that had made them truly international. The GAVA Oriont contract that gave them ten transponders with 50 MHTz capacity, and the cabinet decision which had approved the construction of GeoS 10 to give them the transponders.

There was a huge party, again at the Taj Colaba, given by Oriont India. No one from ISA was present, as that would surely have been imprudent. Those who were present were from the leading telephony companies of the world—Sontag from Germany, Euripides from Sweden, Alaskom from the US.

This was a great beginning. It was now just a matter of time, and Oriont India would become a great multinational communication company.

The ISA lot was also extremely exhilarated. New slips had arrived from the Liechtenstein Bank with similar ten-digit numbers for everyone except Manal Kumar. He was the only person in the secretariat who was unaware of what was going on—the fly in the ointment, but also the potential fall guy of the deal, should the need for a fall guy arise. Any questions if they arose later could all be dumped on him. It was good to have a guy like him around.

THERE WAS AN atmosphere of furtive, joyful secrecy within the four walls of the GAVA offices. They had done it. Fortunately, the GAVA offices were a little distant from the main ISA building, which also housed the secretariat. They functioned in complete seclusion; there was never any corridor chatter or gossip, and most scientists normally walked around with grim, preoccupied expressions as a habit.

Karmaswamy would never come to ISA headquarters. He either had his meetings at the GAVA board room with all his other board members who were former employees of ISA anyway, or in his own office in Colaba. They worked out the future steps that had to be taken for construction of the satellite. But most importantly, with the contract in their hand, they had overnight become the hottest telecom item.

Oriont USA started its deal making in right earnest. Meetings were held with their bankers. Investment bankers were invited to plush parties at the Waldorf Astoria; business development officers were completely occupied with creating presentations, SWOT analyses, Gantt charts, you name it. Scientists were preparing technical proposals, and financial officers were preparing projections of costs and profits, rates of return over the next 10 years.

Dr Martin Georges would go through them very carefully, but was still not satisfied. He wanted to know the progress of the research that was going on in Winston Labs, and was worried about how much longer it would take. He called his director communications, and asked him to visit Winston Labs in Massachusetts to check on what was going on. If worst came to worst, they would have to buy the technology from Sontag or Europides, at enormous cost, and offer them a large stake in Oriont. The collaboration with Leon Mercurius, the Canadian company which was experimenting with DMR technologies fell through, as the company suddenly went into insolvency.

Anyhow, risks had to be taken when they were planning such an ambitious venture. That was the history of how all big deals were done, how wealth was created, and how millionaires become billionaires.

The communications director made a visit to Winston Labs and met the research team. He saw their work on the unfurlable antenna and the digital multimedia receiver design. There had been considerable progress in the development of the DMR prototype, but it still required a good deal of testing in controlled and simulated conditions. Another four months at least. But that was not too bad.

Dr Martin Georges was pleased. The presentations for the investment bankers were finalised, and a meeting with them was scheduled in his office for the next week. It was quite a crowd of their marketing, scientific and business development executives.

Dr Georges was impressive and eloquent. He presented the investment opportunities that flowed out of the agreement that he held in his hand, being owner of ten transponders of 50 megahertz of spectrum, and the vast market of India and other lands that he saw before him.

The presentations were perfect, and the questions were many. Mostly about delays that might happen in the construction of GeoS 10. ISA's record of constructing satellites within stipulated time limits was not too good.

Georges replied, "Yes, I agree. Delays do happen, but this is something that happens in all scientific organisations. But Oriont India is positioned right there, to monitor the time lines. And besides, the record of ISA in constructing satellites is not bad either. They have already built satellites for major service providers over the last ten years, some international, and they're doing quite well."

Then there were questions about the technology—

would it be ready in time when the satellite needed it? The answer given by the director communications was optimistic. "Yes, I expect that it should be ready within the next four to six months, which is quite in time for integrating it with the satellite system."

Of course, most of the questions were regarding the financial returns. The financial officers had prepared well and answered all the questions convincingly—about expected markets, service providers, connectivity in India. India had by now more than twenty mobile telephony companies covering about 80 million end consumers, and with higher incomes and aggressive marketing the number was expected to increase exponentially. The profits shown appeared realistic and not unreasonably high.

The investment bankers seemed quite satisfied, and said they would return in the next couple of days with all their documentation. They were confident they would be able to bring in sound investors in Oriont USA.

They were right. Within the next three months, they had succeeded in bringing in sixty million dollars into Oriont, mostly from two of the most respectable world telecom giants – Alascom from the US, and Sontag from Germany.

GEORGES WAS JUBILANT. Oriont had done it. From a medium size telecom company of the US, it was on the way to becoming a multinational.

He immediately transferred 20 million dollars to Oriont India, and asked them to transfer 10 million to set up Oriont Singapore, which had simple rules for setting up companies, and no questions asked about source of the money. Oriont India was able to get the permission to transfer the funds, through their contacts in the finance ministry. Everything was perfectly legal.

In ISA too, the mood was jubilant, but subdued. They had plenty of work to do. They had to start the construction of the satellite and the rocket launcher. Chairman Maharshi personally coordinated both the constructions—the rocket launcher, the unfailing geostationary launch vehicle, which was to be done at the Rocket Research Centre in Thane, and the satellite which was to be done at the Satellite Research Centre at Hyderabad. Things seemed to be going well, and there was no doubt that this would be a great success story for all, for ISA and GAVA, for Oriont, for the minister and all his cronies, with plenty of wealth generation for all concerned.

The usual *pujas* (prayers) were performed at both centres, with prosperous looking priests chanting *shlokas* (religious verses), no one knew what; blowing conches, smashing coconuts, and scattering an abundance of vermillion, camphor and incense during the *aarti* (prayer ritual).

December 2002

THE MINISTER FOR telecommunication was one Mr Shankar Raja, an exceptionally enterprising gentleman from Hyderabad. He owned several telecom companies in Andhra Pradesh and had a sizeable presence in the booming telephony market of India. He also had many collaborations with other South Asian communication companies, and was a wealthy man.

Presently, he was in his constituency talking to his representatives, discussing the problems of the people, summoning officers from various departments to redress their grievances, and to find out for himself the progress in development programmes since his last visit.

He was to have a meeting that afternoon with his chartered accountant and the MD of his companies, who were none other than his brother Mahesh and his nephew, Jeevanraj, to try and work out strategies for making his private empire expand, now that he was the telephone lord of the country.

He went through the accounts and profits, and also discussed the future road map for the next four years, keeping in mind his new position as minister for telecommunication.

His brother Mahesh collected his papers and returned them to the brief case. He was itching to tell his brother what he had heard in the telecom gossip circuits.

"Shankaranna, why don't we, that is our company, may be Hydratel, approach the ISA for building a satellite for us, just as they have done for so many companies. With that, we could be among the biggest leaders in the telecom market of India, and may be in other countries too."

"But how could I possibly do that, Mahesh? My ownership of our telecom companies has been declared to the government. And if I should try anything like that, there'd be a big scandal, conflict of interest, nepotism, misuse of power, all that and more."

"That's okay, Shankaranna, but our party, the Dakshin Prajasangha Party, is a major partner of the present coalition. You cannot simply be brushed aside."

Shankar Raja looked at his brother curiously. "Tell me clearly Mahesh, what exactly are you trying to say?"

"Shankaranna, surely you know that a company called Oriont India has got cabinet approval for giving them a satellite GeoS 10, through the benevolence of the Indian Space Agency."

"No, I really don't know. When did this happen? How did I miss this?"

"This was at a cabinet meeting last week, or the week

before. Did you not attend it? You would have received the papers."

Actually, Shankar Raja had not attended the cabinet meeting. He was away at a conference in Paris regarding cyber security in the telecom sector. And he had not yet read the decisions of the last two cabinet meetings that had been sent to him by the cabinet secretariat.

"You mean the cabinet has approved a communication satellite for Oriont India? I don't remember any such thing in the cabinet papers sent to me. Yes, there was something about a communication satellite, but I don't remember any Oriont India. By the way, who is Oriont India? Never heard of them."

"Yes, that's what is interesting. Oriont India did not figure in the cabinet note. Only construction of the satellite GeoS 10 did. But the news in the telecom market is that all ten transponders of the satellite, about 50 megahertz in all, had already been leased out to Oriont India in a separate contract with Gagan Vayu, GAVA."

"And this was not informed to the cabinet?"

"No, I believe not."

Shankar Raja scratched his cheek. This was incredible. He immediately phoned his PS in Delhi and asked him to pull out the cabinet notes and cabinet proceedings of the two weeks, particularly the ISA cabinet note. He was returning to Delhi late in the night, and wanted to see the papers first thing in the morning. He chided himself—it was rather careless of him not to have read the cabinet meeting proceedings.

"Let me see the papers," Shankar Raja said, "if what you say is true, then there's definitely something terribly mysterious about it. And here we are, trying to be proper about everything. And the minister for scientific development never stops giving us lectures about integrity and transparency."

"Shankaranna," replied Mahesh, "there's the 2 S spectrum auction coming up in the next few months. That's our big chance and opportunity. And there's no great risk. There's this shady ISA sale of spectrum that has happened without any bidding, to an unknown company, which has retired or dismissed members of ISA as shareholders, and a whole satellite dedicated to them. You can always throw this at them."

"Hmm, that's something," Shankar Raja was still in a bit of a daze. "But first, let me see the papers when I return to Delhi."

"And further," Mahesh continued, "the telecom grapevine is talking about some rumours that actually Oriont India, with all its fake scientist investors, is actually a front for a large business house in India which is operating behind the scenes."

"Which business house?"

"That nobody was able to tell. Could be any, I shall try and find out."

"Hmm, that's interesting. Yes, try and find out and let me know. We should be well armed, and keep our powder dry."

Shanker Raja reached Delhi late that night. The first thing that he did next morning after his walk in Lodi Gardens and saying his prayers was to go through the papers of the cabinet meetings that he had missed, and the decisions.

Yes, his brother Mahesh was right. A communication satellite was indeed being built for multimedia telephony, but there was no mention about whom it was being built for.

Good, he thought, he now had an ace of trumps in his hand; no one could accuse him of nepotism or corruption if he dished out spectrum the way he wanted.

But first, he needed complete verification of the information that his brother had given him. He phoned Mahesh and asked him to come over as soon as possible.

Mahesh came the next day and they had a long meeting mulling over the cabinet note.

"Now Mahesh, use all your contacts, and try and find out as soon as you can whether the information of the satellite transponders being leased out to Oriont is correct. This is dynamite. It can help us greatly in our own strategy for improving our companies, and becoming bigger in the telecom world."

"Yes, Shankaranna, I am already doing that. I have

an old friend, the lawyer Satyanadan, who I believe was pretty involved with the drafting of the Oriont contract with GAVA. I tried to contact him, and it was just luck that he's in Delhi right now. In fact, I'm meeting him this evening. You may remember, he's the same person who helped us draft our agreement with Mactel in Malaysia. I will somehow get the conversation to this subject and ask him about it."

"Good, meet him and try and find out. Let me know, even if it is late this evening. This is really dynamite. Of the most welcome kind."

SHANKAR RAJA WENT on to attend to his day-to-day matters in the office, his routine files, and the procedures that were to be adopted for the sale of the 2S spectrum. There were persistent calls from the Indian Democratic Party office, from the prime minister's office, which to a large extent everybody knew was really run by the prime minister's widower son-in-law, Rajeshwar Rana, who was popularly called Raja Bhaiyya. Rajeshwar Rana came from a rich land-owning family in Nepal, which had also set up hotel businesses in Mauritius and South Africa. Shamlal Kanwar had lost his only daughter in a terrible car accident in Cape Town about five years ago. Shamlal and his wife were devastated, and insisted that

Raja Bhaiyya and his young son who had survived the crash, continue to stay with them to bring some solace into their lives.

Mahesh and Satyanadan had a dinner meeting at the Taj Vivanta, a nice, comfortable, mid-cost hotel, where no celebrities or people from high places were ever found. It was mostly tourists and families, so all the more it would be discreet. And most importantly, Satyanadan was staying there.

They started dinner with a few drinks—Johnny Walker Black Label, and discussed the current political affairs of the new government—the equations of power between the prime minister and Raja Bhaiyya, which were the current favourite business houses, who were the most influential power brokers.

Satyanadan was loosening up and his speech was becoming freer.

Mahesh thought the time was now right to ask. "I say, Satyanadan, I believe you helped Oriont draft its agreement with GAVA for lease of transponders of some new satellite to be built by ISA. That must have been a very prestigious job. And I am sure, no one could have done it better than you." Mahesh had to flatter him a bit, too. "But, Satyanadan, was it a completely fair and proper deal?"

Satyanadan looked a little perplexed. Why had this subject suddenly surfaced?

"Yes," he replied, "it was a very proper job. Completely in conformity with all the rules and regulations. I saw their template. But why this question, Mahesh?"

"No, no special reason. Just picked up some chatter in Shankaranna's home office. That some questions were being asked about the propriety of the contract. Nothing concrete, just some talk among some telecom companies who thought that it wasn't a proper deal. And your name figured. So, I thought, as your well-wisher, especially since you have been so helpful to us, that I should inform you about it."

Satyanadan was now alert. "Inform me? About what?"

"No, nothing really, I'm just telling you what I heard in Shankaranna's home office. I'm sure the deal is absolutely sound if you have drafted it. And even if there's some problem later, you can always count on us."

Satyanadan was now worried. If there was indeed something wrong with the contract, his name would crop up, and he would be censured. And if things became serious, he would be blacklisted, and his practice would be badly hit.

"No, Mahesh, I'm absolutely sure, there was no irregularity, or violation of any law in the contract which was given to me by GAVA. I can sense these things, even from a distance. I'll show it to you, if you want."

Mahesh was secretly euphoric. He didn't even have to ask to see the contract. But he said casually, "Yes, please do. If I see it, I can vouch for you if the subject crops up again. You have a copy here?"

"Yes, on my computer. The final contract which was cleared for signing after both GAVA and Oriont had agreed. It is not marked confidential, though of course, I am pledged to confidentiality to GAVA in a sense."

"No, I don't think it is confidential any more. Actually, this contract should really be in the public domain."

They were veering away from production of the document, Mahesh thought, and he returned to the main topic.

"Anyway, let me see it," Mahesh asked casually.

Satyanadan went to his room and returned with his laptop. He turned it on and searched for the file. Finally, he found it—GAVA Oriont Contract—Final copy for signature. He opened it and handed over the laptop to Mahesh.

Mahesh was looking for only one thing. Had the transponders of GeoS 10 been leased to Oriont?

He pretended to read the file in dead earnest. He saw the name of Oriont India in the first paragraph. His eyes scanned the page and then the next page until he finally saw what he wanted to see—that ten transponders of 50 megahertz capacity of a satellite called Sat 1, to be built by ISA, had indeed been leased out to Oriont for the entire life of the satellite. He read those lines again to memorise them, and then went down the screen, pretending to read the remaining pages with equal interest. He spent some time doing that and returned the laptop to Satyanadan.

"It seems good. I find nothing wrong with it. No violations of law of any kind. I don't think we need to be worried about anything. So, let's toast to that."

Satyanadan had not touched his glass ever since the subject of the Oriont contract had cropped up. Both he and Mahesh clinked their glasses and ordered dinner. A nice simple dinner with roti and dal and chicken curry and rice, with ice cream to follow.

Mahesh rushed back to his brother's bungalow. It was not too late, just 10.30 pm.

Shankar Raja was sitting in his study. There were two other people in the room with him, a man and a woman, who also seemed to belong to South India.

"Ha, Mahesh, come, come. Meet Mr and Mrs Sanjiva Reddy. They're from Vijayawada, but presently residing in Singapore. Sanjiva Reddy works in a big telecom giant there with which we have had some dealings earlier. Remember Simha Com? A lot of excitement going on there. We've just finished dinner. What about you?"

Mahesh did a polite *namaskara* (greeting) to all of them. "Yes, Shankaranna, I've finished dinner too."

"We must leave now, sir," Sanjiva Reddy and his wife rose. "Thank you so much for your time and hospitality, sir. We shall be ever grateful and will remain in touch."

"Yes, and if for some reason it is not possible for you to get across to me, you may contact my brother, Mahesh. It's as good as contacting me."

Mahesh bowed his head with another *namaskara* to the couple. They exchanged visiting cards, and then the Reddys left.

"Well, Shankaranna, I have some news for you. Dynamite, as you would call it," Mahesh said.

"What?" asked Shankar Raju, as he went to the cabinet to pour himself a shot of Remy Martin.

"Some for you?"

"Yes, definitely. And we have cause to celebrate."

"Aha, what?"

"Well, I had dinner with Satyanadan, and he showed me the final contract to be signed by GAVA and Oriont. And yes, it definitely contained the leasing of transponders of a satellite called Sat 1 to Oriont, and the satellite is to be built by ISA. I saw it, read it, reread it."

"But, how do you know it is authentic?"

"I know, because he downloaded the file from an email to him from the MD, GAVA. I was able to see that. And the file had a heading 'Final draft for signature'."

"Can you not get a hard copy of it?"

"I'm sure I can. I did not want to demand too much at the first meeting itself. I'll ask him tomorrow. I'm sure he will give it. I frightened the hell out of him, telling him that we had received some feedback that the contract was going to be controversial, and that he might be in the soup. That's how he showed it to me. Shall I call him over now?"

"No, no, don't do that. He might get uneasy. Go and see him at his hotel tomorrow and ask him to give you a hard copy so that we can shield him, should there be any complaints about him later."

Mahesh said exactly the same words the next morning at Satyanandan's hotel, and he returned after breakfast with the hard copy of the contract in his hand. On the left corner of all the pages were the initials of both MD GAVA, Vidyasagar, and MD Oriont India, Dr Karmaswamy.

Shankar Raja was ecstatic. He now really held dynamite in his hands. It was well known that though the minister for scientific development was the favourite of the prime minister, he was held with suspicion by Raja Bhaiyya, the real power in the prime minister's office. Shankar Raja was now free to dish out the second stage 2S spectrum under his control to whoever he wanted to, on whatever terms he wanted to, with whatever benefit to himself that he wanted. And no one could do a thing. He would make sure that Raja Bhaiyya would share the spoils.

GAVA WAS NOW a hive of activity. Numerous meetings were happening between Oriont and them. Roadmaps and milestones were being drawn up. Oriont India deposited its first tranche of money, Rs 49.25 crores, and instructions for constructing the launch vehicle and satellite were issued to the Rocket Research Centre in Thane and the Satellite Research Centre at Hyderabad to complete the construction of the launch vehicle and the satellite in record time.

Shankar Raja, meanwhile, started his own grand plans for the sale of 2 S spectrum. He had an able secretary, one Vaidyanath Ravi, who had minutely studied all the shenanigans and strategies that had been adopted by the previous ministers for allocation of spectrum—the public tender notifications, invitations for bids, and the juiciest bit of first come first served, and deadlines for the same. They decided to opt for this method, got Raja Bhaiyya's blessings, and thereafter, all other clearances followed swiftly.

His personal assistant, Shashikala Palineer, was more than equal to the task, and proved her efficiency beyond measure. The bid receiving office was located on the seventh floor of the Doorsanchar Bhavan near India Gate. Her contribution to the entire 'first come first served' procedure was the most practical and ingenious that one could think of.

There were just two lifts and five lift operators in the Doorsanchar Bhavan. Shashikala summoned all the lift operators a day in advance of the last bidding day, and gave them envelopes with a fortune of rupees ten thousand each, with clear instructions that on the next day, none of the lifts should work efficiently between 4 pm and 5 pm. They should not come to stop, but should work erratically. That would take care of the last-minute rush. And, if they performed well, they would get another envelope with a similar amount later. Shashikala also had a list of all the favourite companies that Shankar Raja had selected for spectrum allocation. They had all been informed of how much to bid, and the time at which bids should be received at the seventh floor of the Doorsanchar Bhavan, well before the last date.

The bids were trickling in, not too many. Some familiar names, some not. The lifts dutifully started misbehaving during the last hour, between 4 and 5 pm.

There were brawls in the corridors of Doorsanchar Bhavan, and loud arguments. Electricians were called in to repair a short circuit. The minister's office was receiving a never-ending spate of telephone calls, demanding that someone from there should come down to get some order into the mayhem happening on the ground floor.

The minister was not in the office. Shashikala called her assistant and the peons, and phoned the joint secretary. She was told that he was busy attending to the bid documents, and couldn't leave the office. All his officers were with him.

So, she decided to go down herself with her assistants. But when she went to the lift, she found that it was not working, and who could she blame for that? Obviously, the lift operators had done a *pukka* job. So, she decided to walk down from the seventh floor to take stock of the situation on the ground floor, her mind completely preoccupied with the next round of envelopes she had to prepare for the dutiful lift operators.

But just as she reached the third floor, a monkey sitting on an open window near the staircase jumped at her—it must have been her red saree. She screamed and fell, rolling down a few steps, with the monkey gnawing at her rather succulent right shoulder, before it was chased away by the peons and ran down the corridor of the record room of the Doorsanchar Bhavan.

The peons yelled for some women staff to lift Shashikala, and someone phoned the Safdar Jung Hospital to send an ambulance at once for a VIP who needed immediate first aid for monkey bites. Shashikala was in a state of shock.

Some of the more enterprising bidders decided to climb the steps. It was 4.40 pm, and they still had time. Some lucky ones reached the top. But one slightly elderly gentleman who had a lot to gain from registering the bid, was not so lucky. Like his younger colleagues, he had also decided to climb the steps. He had barely reached the third floor, when he collapsed, panting for breath. The remaining pilgrims to the seventh floor looked the other way and continued their upward march. This was no time for philanthropy—they had to register their bids before the deadline expired. The elderly gentleman's assistant rushed up to the corridor and screamed for help. But there was no one there. Everyone had gone away for the monkey hunt. The offices were empty, so the assistant ran downstairs to the second floor and screamed loudly. Two ladies came out from their offices. They had just heard about the delinquent monkey, and were a little wary. But they got some water for the old gentleman, still panting and slumped on the steps, rubbed his back, called for a peon and all of them lifted the old gentleman.

They heard the siren of an ambulance. It had been called for Shashikala, but they did not know that. They thought it was an act of divine providence for the old gentleman.

The elderly gentleman felt a bit revived, and immediately regained his sense of duty. He turned to his assistant, "Now Ramesh, I can survive for some time, but may not be able to walk. Please run up and give the bid documents. I will wait here until you return. And don't forget to bring the receipt."

He then thanked the two ladies profusely and politely declined to get into the ambulance which was still blaring away. "Thank you, ladies, I feel quite well now, thanks to your care. I'm squarely to blame for what happened. You know, I often forget my age. It happens to me all the time. God bless you," the old man smiled.

The ladies beamed with happiness. They had done their *punya* (virtuous act) for the day.

The bid office was getting stuffy with the room heaters at full blast. Ramesh barely made it in time. He was the last. Just after his documents were received, the superintendent looked at the clock. It was 5 pm, and the door to the office was closed.

Even though the deadline of 5 pm was over, the mayhem on the ground floor continued, with the electricians working on the two lifts, and the police personnel pacifying the agitated telecom companies.

The ambulance to take Shashikala to the hospital for monkey bites sped away, its sirens blaring louder than ever. Inside, the Doorsanchar Bhavan staff had formed little squads to search for the errant monkey, and had left their files and their other commitments with great abandon. But the monkey continued to elude them. A pall of fear descended upon the Bhavan and rumours started doing the rounds that a monkey once having tasted blood would want more of it. Women were afraid to go to the bathroom, just in case the monkey was hiding there.

Sashikala remained in Safdar Jung Hospital for the

day and got her mandatory injections for tetanus and rabies. She had her whole family around her, and her entire office and the minister visited her. She figured on page three in the next day's newspapers with her picture, which made her and her family very happy. The issue of the nonfunctional elevators at Doorsanchar Bhavan got just a small mention.

Shankar Raja was pleased. There was not too much criticism about the 5 pm deadline or the non-functional lifts in the next day's papers. There was much more comment about the monkey menace in government buildings and what should be the most humanitarian way to deal with them and relocate them to a more suitable habitat.

Shankar Raja smiled. He had heard this business of the monkey menace many times before. For some reason, the monkeys of Delhi loved government buildings, and hated to be away from them. They always returned to them, even if they had been taken far away to the Ridge to their natural habitat of trees and nature. Well, he thought, the Lord Hanuman had been sent to protect him and he should not complain. The bidding for the 2S spectrum was over, and now nothing could come between him and his spectrum.

However, it was just a matter of time. Editorials started appearing in all newspapers about the allocation of spectrum, that it was irregular, that it should have been auctioned and not given for first come first served; that unqualified companies dealing in real estate and software were allocated spectrum at the base price of the year 2000, with undue favours shown to a select few, such as, Peacock and Trustwell.

But Shankar Raja was not too perturbed. After all, enough money had reached Raja Bhaiyya and his cronies, and other important ministers. And this media hysteria would die down soon. He had taken care of them too. Most importantly, the money had kept pouring in. All the allottees had kept their promises. Honest, decent guys.

But then something unexpected happened. A public interest litigation was filed in the supreme court about his actions, led by a ferocious lawyer-cum-politician, Keshav Yadav.

Keshav was a wealthy, brilliant fellow—a maverick, thoroughly unscrupulous and opportunistic, with no morals whatsoever. But because of his brilliance, he could always succeed in bringing embarrassment to anyone he wished. There was a general belief that he was really an extortionist, but no one had really been able to bring any such specific charge against him on that.

Keshav's petition was taken very seriously by the court, despite the strong plea put forth by the telecom department. A Federal Investigation Board (FIB) enquiry was ordered against Shankar Raja, his secretary Vaidynath

Ravi, his PS, Shashikala Palineer, roping in also some of the favoured sprectrum recipients like Peacock and Trustwell.

Shankar Raja tried to contact both Raja Bhaiyya and the prime minister, but was rebuffed. Ungrateful devils, he cursed, after all that he had given them. He tried to contact the finance minister, who was also the recipient of a handsome bounty, but was told that he was abroad and could not be contacted.

Shankar Raja was shocked. Was this how games were played in Delhi? He felt humiliated, betrayed and abandoned. He knew he would not get public support from anywhere, but he did hold an ace in his hands. If nothing else worked, he was ready to play his Oriont card. His brother had been with him in Delhi the last few days to provide whatever moral support he needed. However, he too was in a state of depression and despair. This would impact so badly upon the growth of their companies which had just started to take off.

IT WAS SIX o'clock in the evening. Shankar Raja was in his home office.

"Mahesh," he called his brother to his room.

"Yes, Shankaranna," Mahesh was still in a state of depression.

"Don't worry about this," Shankar Raja told his brother. "This happens here all the time."

"But there's an FIB enquiry ordered against you. Suppose they come and arrest you."

"Then, they'll be in bigger trouble," Shankar Raja smiled and tried to look unperturbed. "Anyway, don't worry about that. I will handle it from here but I have some work for you."

"What Shankaranna? I will do anything for you."

"You remember that GAVA Oriont contract. Give it to our friend in *Deccan Times*. I forget his name, the one to whom we give a retainer. And here is a copy of the cabinet note and the cabinet approval. Fax them to him right away and tell him to carry a story tomorrow. He will do it. He is our man. And next month, send him double the amount."

Mahesh did what he was told. He spoke to his friend Amitabh in *Deccan Times*, and gave him the background of the mission. Then he went to a booth in Sarojini Nagar, and faxed him all the documents. It took an hour. Then he called Amitabh again.

"Got them all?" Mahesh asked.

"Yes, but this is a lot of pages. I need time to study them, only then I can do a story. I will need the whole of tonight and can give my story only tomorrow. So, I can't do it for tomorrow. I need another day."

"Okay, that's fair. But do a good story."

The next day's papers were a disaster for Shankar Raja.

Details of the scandal were being dished out along with the supreme court order and the FIB enquiry. There was a chorus of demands from the Opposition, from social activists, from integrity organisations, that Shankar Raja should resign. Of course, he wasn't going to. His party was a major partner in the government, and the life of the government depended upon them.

He was in touch with his party bosses, who had been terribly pleased with him for the huge revenues he was bringing into the party coffers, and to them individually.

"Don't worry," the party supremo said, "we are with you and support you. I will have a word with the prime minister and sort it out. No FIB man will come after you. The government's survival depends on us."

Shankar Raja felt comforted, but not reassured. This was a ruthless world. Even his party would weigh the pros and cons before going the last mile to support him.

"Thank you, sir. I depend upon you. You will have to prevail upon the prime minister to instruct the FIB to lay off."

"Don't worry, it will be done."

And it was done. At least for a while.

AMITABH STUCK TO his promise. He did not sleep that night. He read the papers that Mahesh had sent him, and he too felt he had dynamite in his hands. He read them over and over again—the email, the contract, the cabinet note and its approval. He had never dealt with such sensitive papers before.

He spent some time with his wife and children and said he should not be disturbed until the next day.

He sat up the whole night, wrote out his piece giving all the details—GAVA's contract with Oriont India without any bids, transponders with 50 mghtz of spectrum leased out for a song, cabinet approval of GeoS 10 by hiding the fact that the transponders and spectrum had already been leased out to Oriont, and the deal sealed with cabinet approval.

The next day he went to see his editor and showed him his piece and all the documents.

The editor was exhilarated. He needed a shocker like this to increase the coverage of his paper that had been slumping a bit in north India.

"I say, Amitabh, this is explosive. But I do hope it's all authentic. You have checked everything carefully, I'm sure."

"Absolutely, sir. Would I ever give you something I have not checked?"

"But how did you get all this? Brilliant." Amitabh remained silent and felt good.

"Yes, it must be in the papers tomorrow."

February 5, 2003

The next day, *Deccan Times* had a titillating front page headline. "Sleeping with Spectrum—Shankar or Pratap?" And the GAVA Oriont contract was out with a blast—how it had violated every rule in the book, and how the ISA chairman and the scientific development minister had cheated the prime minister and the cabinet.

Shankar Raja opened the *Deccan Times*, the first paper he would see every morning. The frontpage headline gladdened his heart. What would the prime minister do now? Minister for scientific development, Pratap Singh, reported directly to the prime minister, as there were so many security and defence issues involved. He smiled. It would be interesting to see how he would handle it.

Deccan Times, which did not have too much coverage in New Delhi became the bestseller for the day, and its demand surged. Television channels, both pro and anti-government had loud debates and shouting matches about the Oriont deal for two continuous days. The *Deccan Times* editor was extremely pleased, and instructed Amitabh that he should give regular updates to keep the interest alive. And Amitabh also got a raise in his pay cheque.

ISA WOKE UP with a shock. What they saw in the *Deccan Times* put them in a daze. They were the icons of India, untouched by scandal, only bringing glory to the masses of India every time they shot off a satellite into space. What happened on earth never touched them, for it was always subterranean. And here was this nasty, cantankerous frontpage article placing them at par with the most hardened scamsters of the land.

It was a bad day. Phone calls came from journalists from across India, from the minister, from the prime minister's office, demanding that a befitting rejoinder be issued.

But what sort of a rejoinder would they issue? Everything stated in the news report was correct. But how on earth did it reach the press?

Maharishi rushed to Delhi to meet the minister.

"Well, sir," he started, with no pleasantries, "the worst seems to have happened. And now we must think of how to get over it."

"And how would we do that?"

"Well sir, first of all we must deny all allegations of wrongdoing. We should say that this had nothing to do with sale of spectrum in the general sense, but is a commercial step towards innovation, which is the job of GAVA anyway. The new hybrid technology of the hybrid multimedia telephone is known to very few countries, and if we could avail of this new technology and provide this service to our people with lower costs, what is wrong with that?"

"But what about the fact that it was given without any bidding? How would you answer that?"

"Not too difficult, sir. There is no competition for this technology in India. Who would bid for it except by tying up with a foreign company? You would agree that this would not be acceptable in any bidding process. And finally, the objective has been to help build up an Indian entity."

"Hmm. But it might be said this new Indian company is nothing but a little ghost company with all your former employees."

"What's wrong with that, sir? If an Indian entrepreneur company wants to start an ambitious enterprise, we should encourage it. And former ISA scientists can only bring it the best knowledge and science. After all, all big companies start small. Why should we call it a ghost company and be on the defensive?"

The Minister was listening, but was distracted. He continued, "Well, you seem quite confident, but I'm not. The Dakshin Prajasangha Party will not stop attacking us. They are in deep trouble about their 2S spectrum allocation. They will not let this rest even for a moment. They need something to deflect attention from themselves and will push this to the limits. The prime minister is so embarrassed. And this has made it much worse."

The minister continued, "And this damned DPP knows that without it, the government cannot survive, and they will employ every blackmailing trick they can to get what they want."

"But we really have nothing to worry about, sir. No one is charging us with corruption. No money has changed hands." Maharishi continued casually.

"No, of course not." The Minister was equally casual. "But that does not stop anyone from making any allegation, does it? Well, well, the damned show has just started. And we must be prepared for the worst. I think you better get on with a good team of trouble shooters. Give a press release from ISA. Just deny everything and say all the things that you have just said, but make them as general as possible."

"Yes sir, you'll see it by tomorrow evening. I'll fly back to Mumbai now."

Maharishi flew back to Mumbai the same night. He was thinking hard. First, about the press release. That was the easiest of all the things he had to do. Just a paragraph of about fifteen lines. He had finished that even before he boarded the flight.

Next, he had to draw up a chronology of how this whole thing had started. He was really a late comer to the whole deal. He had to systematically study all the papers from the time his predecessor had stared the dialogue with Oriont US, Georges and Karmaswamy, and draw up all the links, mostly to gather information about everyone concerned with the deal, so that he could use anyone he wanted for the cover up. He listed all the things he wanted, and worked out systematically how he would get them.

He phoned the chief publicity officer, John Samuel, and Vidyasagar, and asked them to be in his office by 9 pm. He showed them the press release that he had drafted, and asked Vidyasagar to check it and correct it if necessary.

Vidyasagar said it was fine. John immediately got to work and within an hour every leading paper in the country had the ISA denial.

"ISA is deeply shocked at reading the false and misleading report that has appeared in the *Deccan Times* of February 5. ISA strongly denies all the false allegations made against it, and against GAVA and the ministry for scientific development.

"There has been no violation of any law, rules or regulations in any of the actions described in the news report. All actions have been taken as per well-established rules and procedures, and in accordance with the mandate of ISA and GAVA.

"The construction and launch of satellites are the prime objectives of ISA in accordance with the needs of the nation, in this case hybrid telephony, and the mandate of GAVA is to promote commercial ventures in space related enterprises, in the best interests of the country.

"Both ISA and GAVA have acted completely in accordance with their mandate and mission, in a lawful manner."

Maharishi was weary by the time he reached home. His wife, Radha, looked worried as she laid out the dinner. She had read the paper with her husband's name splashed all over it. All her relatives had been ringing up asking if all was well.

"Nothing to worry about, Radha. This sort of thing keeps happening in these positions. It's probably a lot of mischief being done by the telecom fellows who are caught in a terrific corruption scandal. It will all be sorted out by tomorrow. You will see. So, please don't worry about it."

She asked no more questions, and the exhausted Maharishi switched off his mobile phone and went straight to bed.

THE ISA DENIAL was the frontpage headline in all the newspapers next day. Some papers embellished it with pictures of Maharishi and Karmaswamy, some with Vidyasagar as well.

Maharishi woke early. He had so much to do. He had to strategise to combat this terrible leak that had happened from somewhere, god knows where. But before that, he had to look at the papers. He saw the press release. It was faithfully reported with a few journalistic twists here and there, the prerogative of the fifth estate, but nothing very damaging.

His personal phone rang. It was the agitated voice of Satyadev. "Hello, Maharishi, this is terrible. I was in Singapore for a lecture and just returned yesterday. But this is really bad. Who has done this?"

"I really have no idea, sir. But yes, this is really bad. In fact, I was planning to call you myself a little later."

"Listen, I must come over and see you. This is important. We have to stop this bad press immediately. This will ruin all our reputations, and of ISA."

"Yes sir, please come over at any time. I'm calling all the GAVA and ISA heads and the secretariat officers, only the two who know about the contract, and work out the strategy. I want to do this first thing in the morning. Why don't you come over at lunch time? We can have our discussions over lunch."

"That's a good idea, Maharishi. I'll be there around 12.30."

"Yes, sir."

Maharishi asked his PS to inform Vidyasagar, Gurupriya, his communications chief, Ashok Kumar Raina, and his publicity chief, John Samuel, to be in his office at 9.30 am.

He himself was in office at 8 am and had been browsing through all the newspapers, reading his mail, and all the other reports and files stacked on his desk.

Vidyasagar, Ashok and John came in early looking extremely agitated.

"Sir, this is quite shocking. How could this happen? I only hope there is no traitor amongst us." Vidyasagar was almost in tears.

"Well, John, have you been able to find out from your journalist friends how the leak has come about?" Maharishi asked.

"I did try, sir. I've been chasing one of my contacts in *Deccan Times*. He tells me that the news actually came from Delhi, from some political sources."

"Oh, I see," Maharishi showed no expression. "Well, the cabinet note could have leaked out from anywhere. It is circulated to so many ministers, and all their staff get to see it. But what about the contract? How did that leak out? Very few people had a copy of that. The soft copy is only available with me and Vidyasagar and the Oriont people. Who else would have a soft copy of it?"

"Sir, we've been trying to figure that out too. The only other people who might have a copy of the contract would be the legal people on both sides. But I don't think our legal advisor would have done it. He's been with us for so many years, and it has never happened before," Vidyasagar said.

"So, do you think it's an inside job?" Maharishi questioned, his face expressionless, but his eyes razor sharp.

"It could be anything, sir." Vidyasagar replied. "There are plenty of disgruntled people around here. Or it could be someone from Oriont. But that also seems unlikely. Why would they want to bring trouble upon themselves?"

Maharishi remained expressionless.

"Unless, there are some disgruntled people in Oriont too," Vidyasagar continued, wanting to deflect any suspicion that someone from his office had engineered the leak.

"Hmm, everything seems to be full of possibilities. Anyway, John, keep an eye on all the newspapers, especially the *Deccan Times*, and do a thorough check on their reporter and find out if he or his editor need anything special. The usual tricks that you know so well. And keep me updated of every detail."

"Yes sir," John Samuel rose and left the room.

Gurupriya came in at the appointed time, just before John Samuel was leaving. She looked extremely worried. Her *kumkum* (red dot on forehead) and *mangalsutra* (necklace of a married woman) were in place, and her sari pallu too seemed more secure, with the usual room for maneuverability, should the need arise. These were trying times, indeed.

"Good morning, sir." She was grim but tried to look professional. She was also worried as she had plenty to hide.

"This is so shocking. How can the papers write so much lies about us?"

She was also thinking of the little note she had received from Oriont with a ten-digit number, and of her son's education in Stanford. She had to ensure that whatever happened to the rest, no enquiry should reach her. She would figure out how to do that. Except for two or three of the top scientists who really did seem to possess sound knowledge of science and had high IQ, the rest were just a mediocre bunch of clones whose future lay with slavishness to the bosses. She could manipulate the whole bunch if she wanted, with all her intellectual and other assets.

Maharishi was reading a newspaper report very intently. It wasn't an Indian newspaper but a report downloaded from the space news of the US. There was a complete report about GeoS 10 and the on-going controversy. He threw away the report in disgust.

"Well, now let's get on with some work. Now you, Vidyasagar, Gurupriya and Ashok, please do a thorough check of all the old files that you all have, starting from the proposed joint venture that had been discussed between Oriont US and Dr Satyadev. I would like to see the entire chronology of events. Who were the scientists and bureaucrats who were involved in the meetings and negotiations? What was the correspondence that was exchanged between ISA, GAVA and Oriont and the ministry? We must have this information as soon as possible, even if you have to sit up all night. The minister wants it urgently. Can I have it by tomorrow morning? Remember, this is an emergency."

Vidyasagar had never looked grimmer. He was the one who had to collect all the papers, as he and his organisation were the ones that were being attacked most virulently in the media, as the central point of the scandal. GAVA and ISA would have most of the correspondence and record of meetings. The secretariat would have nothing much really, except for the cabinet note papers.

"Sir, please give us time till tomorrow afternoon. We do have to search quite a bit, both for papers and for emails etc. And after so much time, I don't even know how many emails would have been preserved."

"Yes sir, tomorrow afternoon, please," Gurupriya chimed in. Her sari pallu has started the process of displacement.

All the men noticed. It meant that Gurupriya was at their mercy now.

"Okay, but start right away," Maharishi growled.

EVERYONE LEFT THE room and Maharishi was alone. He wanted to clear his desk before Satyadev came at 12:30 for lunch. There were routine papers and reports, progress reports from several centres, some labour problems in Karwar. Most interesting of all was a letter in a confidential, sealed cover, which contained details of some terrible corruption allegations against Shukra Devi, the PS he had inherited from his predecessor. The petition contained details of the real estate business and extortion rackets that she and her husband were supposed to be running from right inside her little office which was just outside his own.

He remembered that the Minister had also mentioned this. Probably, he had received a similar letter. He wondered what Satyadev would have done with it. Most likely, just marked it down to the chief vigilance officer, who would have brought it back to him seeking his 'guidance' in the matter, before it was confined to the waste paper basket or to the shredder.

Maharishi chuckled. He would keep this aside and discuss it with Satyadev who was expected any minute now for his luncheon meeting. This would take care of any peremptory airs that he might put on to force his views.

Satyadev came, exactly at 12:30 pm. He looked fresh, but also quite tense. He knew that everybody knew that the whole episode had started during his time, and that he was really the father figure of this whole deal.

"I'm sorry, Maharishi, bothering you at a time like this. You must be completely bogged down with this absolutely nasty item that has appeared. Really, so demoralising. How can they write such slanderous things about an absolutely clean and pioneering agreement?" Satyadev was visibly agitated.

"Quite right, sir. They're nothing short of slander. Absolutely shocking."

"We've got to stop this bad press coverage." Satyadev's agitation was increasing. "It is so demoralising for the organisation. And this, after all our efforts and achievements to place India on the world space map."

"Yes, sir, I'm doing my best. You would have seen our press note which has come in all the papers today."

"Yes, I've seen it. But that's not enough. We have to preempt our enemies from doing further damage to us and to our great organisation."

"Yes, of course, sir." Hmm … thought Maharishi, so the bugger's scared.

"I hear you have asked for all the papers from ISA and

GAVA to be put together for you. That is good, because now we must sit together and work out a good defence."

Maharishi couldn't believe his ears. News from his office seemed to be leaking out to Satyadev, even within a few minutes. Clearly, Shukra Devi's presence as his PS was important for Satyadev. Nothing in this office would remain secret from him. Maharishi had to do something about that.

But he continued amiably, "Sir, you're absolutely right. We have to work out a credible, logical self-defence, which no enquiry or committee can find fault with. I'm already on the job."

"Yes, that's good. But please keep Shukra Devi informed of all the developments. She is a very loyal person. And very capable."

"Yes, sir. I'm already doing that, not that we have anything to hide."

"No, no. I didn't mean that at all. But even so, we've got to make sure that all our interactions and communications concerning Oriont, especially when the negotiations first started, are properly arranged and sanitised."

"You know best, sir, that I really do not know anything about this whole agreement, as I wasn't involved in it. Let me first see all the papers. They've promised to have everything ready by tomorrow afternoon. And then let us see how to go about it."

Maharishi asked for lunch to be served. A simple lunch with dal, vegetables, puris, rice and curd.

Satyadev was clearly anxious, as he could tell instinctively that this whole affair would not end with a mere denial. And most of all, he wanted to make sure that his name would not be dragged into the mess.

By now, Maharishi could also easily sense this. This was the time to strike, he thought. "Talking about Shukra Devi, I just thought it was necessary for me to tell you about some complaints I've been receiving about her. That she and her husband are misusing this office for some real estate dealings of a dubious nature. Actually, the minister also mentioned this quite emphatically during my last meeting with him, and just today, I have received a complaint against her about the same thing. Was this going around during your time too?" Maharishi went to his table and brought the letter and showed it to Satyadev.

Satyadev's eyes narrowed. "Absolute nonsense," he replied. "She's a fine lady. It's unfortunate that she has a no-good husband and she's the breadwinner of the family. Yes, I too received similar complaints about her. But I just junked them. We have to protect our women employees—women's empowerment and all that. Just ignore it. Complete rubbish." He wondered whether Maharishi was sending any particular message to him.

Maharishi smiled inside, but kept a straight face.

Satyadev lapsed into silence, thinking hard. Shukra Devi and her land deals be damned. He had to save himself. He had approved the Oriont contract as chair of the GAVA board and of the science council, which had led to the cabinet note.

The two men ate silently. Maharishi tried to make some polite conversation about the studies that were going on for global positioning satellites. But it didn't work. Satyadev remained silent and was thinking about how much he could trust Maharishi and how much he would have to fend for himself.

Lunch was over and Maharishi asked for coffee, but Satyadev declined, saying he had to leave as he had a flight to catch. He stood up, looked Maharishi directly in the eye and said, "Now Maharishi, check the papers carefully and see that nothing which can cause any trouble remains in them."

Maharishi was getting a little impatient and irritated, but kept himself in control. What on earth was Satyadev expecting him to do? Burn up all the papers which he had signed?

But he replied, "Let me see the papers tomorrow, sir. I'm sure we'll need your advice as we go along. Let's see how this develops. Perhaps, it will all quieten down."

"No, no, this will only become shriller, believe me. The government is getting caught up in too many scandals. This will just become another one. The

Opposition will make sure that it becomes one, even though it's completely clean and straight. They will not let it pass, especially since there is already a full-blown telecom scandal raging against one of its partners. No, they will not let it rest." Satyadev seemed even more disturbed.

He rose, taking his leave. "Anyway, thank you for the lunch, Maharishi. Let me know after you've seen the papers."

"Yes sir, I'll be in touch with you. Good day." Satyadev escorted Maharishi to the lift and Shukra Devi accompanied him down.

MEANWHILE, IN DELHI, a different scenario was in motion. Rajeshwar Rana, the formidable Raja Bhaiyya, who everyone knew was the real centre of power, and could move anything he wanted with a twist of his little finger, read about the ISA Oriont affair in the newspapers, the latest scandal about which he knew nothing. But how was this possible—that a scam of this dimension could be hatched behind his back?

But here it was, another one, headlines shrieking all the details. The government was going through such a rough time, being bludgeoned by one scam after another. There was the lottery scandal causing headlines every day, where all his loyalists were seen neck deep in corruption; then a whole bunch of defence scandals, purchases of guns, planes and submarines; and the fiercest one reigning currently regarding the sale of spectrum, where their government partners were involved. And now a new one, where their own scientific development minister was making huge deals on spectrum while keeping him completely in the dark. How could a deal of this magnitude happen behind his back? How was his express writ to the ministers being disobeyed—that he had to be kept informed about every major deal or lucrative contract that was being negotiated inside the government?

The Dakshin Prajasangha Party had proved itself an honest and reliable partner. They had kept their word and made regular remittances to various agreed off-shore accounts in Switzerland and other places. But this was incredible. Pratap Singh, a minister from their own party, had committed the ultimate treachery. No doubt, he was a powerful politician, considered very close to his father-in-law, both being from the same state and community. But even so, coalition rules regarding negotiating of contracts, especially of the lucrative kind, and an equitable and rational administration of kickbacks were sacrosanct, and could not be violated under any circumstances. What had happened with the GAVA Oriont contract was scandalous.

Raja Bhaiyya immediately summoned his political advisor and close confidante, Darius Bhatt, his anger writ large in his gestures and speech.

Darius Bhatt was originally a small-time politician in Mumbai from the Indian Democratic Party, born of Parsee and Saraswat parents. He rose to power in the 1990s, when there was a great division happening in the party. Darius Bhatt infiltrated the side that was opposed to the ruling Prime Minister Shamlal Kanwar, Raja Bhaiyya's father-in-law, and just in the nick of time, informed Shamlal Kanwar of the conspiracy that was going on against him.

The conspiracy was nipped in the bud and Darius Bhatt became part of the inner circle of the Shamlal Kanwar family. His influence rose after Shamlal Kanwar tragically lost his only daughter in a car crash, and his son-in-law, Raja Bhaiyya, developed complete trust in him, and made him his political advisor. Today, Darius Bhatt was the most powerful man in the Indian Democratic Party, after Raja Bhaiyya himself.

A tall lanky man, he entered Raja Bhaiyya's study and sensed the fury on his face.

"Good afternoon, sir. You sent for me."

"Yes, I did. What is all this I'm hearing about some huge contract being signed in the scientific development ministry? Something about a satellite and sale of spectrum which is even worse than the telecom affair. How is it you never kept me informed?"

Darius kept standing, because he hadn't been asked to sit.

"Yes, sir. I too have read about it in the papers. Believe me, I had no idea about it. All we had seen in the cabinet note was that a satellite was being built for some new kind of mobile telephones. The cabinet note didn't say anything about sale of spectrum."

"Well, go and find out all about it now. How much money has charged hands? And to whom? I've always distrusted that Pratap Singh. But he's too close to the prime minister. How can they cheat us like this? After all, it is we who made him minister. And you've failed miserably. Go and find out all about it and let me know. I am so disappointed with you."

"I'm really sorry, sir. Please forgive me. I'm equally shocked that he could deceive us like this. I will try and get all the information."

Raja Bhaiyya's face was still angry and he gestured him to leave. A bunch of deceivers these were. He could trust no one.

DR KARMASWAMY, MANAGING Director, Oriont India, was also extremely disturbed and agitated. How could such a leak happen? Anyhow, there was no use wasting time about it at this point. It had happened, and what was to be done next was more important. He immediately asked for appointments with both the GAVA chief and the ISA chairman. Both replied that the appointments would be given during the next week. He followed the request with detailed letters informing them of all the investments Oriont had made for the ground stations and satellite construction and wanted to discuss some technical issues for which Oriont needed some guidance.

Maharishi called Vidyasagar to his office and told him, "Tell Karmaswamy to stop telephoning our officers. Doesn't he know that all our phones are heavily tapped? We can meet in some place in Delhi, in some guest house. Much safer."

"I'll tell him, sir. He's coming to see me tomorrow."

"Be careful and don't talk too much. It's going to become more and more his interest versus ours."

DARIUS BHATT, MEANWHILE, got cracking. He had enough moles in the ministry for scientific development, and some in ISA headquarters. First, he contacted his moles spread across the ministry and asked them to meet him in a guest house in Sainik Farms.

The first mole was a senior scientist called Prabhakar, whom he had helped to get over a departmental enquiry relating to some corruption matters about ghost science parks for women. The second was a lady, one Manorama Francis, an assistant director in the same ministry. Darius Bhatt had helped her out in getting admission for her children in the prestigious Presentation Convent, and she was ever grateful for that. She was also a close confidante of the private secretary to the scientific development minister. The last and the most important mole that Darius Bhatt had was the additional PS to the minister, Aslam Yunus, who had close links with Shukra Devi, the inherited PS of the ISA chairman. Shukra Devi was indebted to Aslam Yunus for chucking all the allegation petitions against her, particularly about the real estate business that she carried on right inside the heart of ISA, into the shredder.

Darius Bhatt invited all his moles to a dinner that night at the Lotus guest house in Sainik Farms, saying it was urgent. The guest house belonged to an industrialist, Ramnath Jain, who had expressly designated it for the use of Darius Bhatt and his friends. Prabhakar and

Aslam Yunus said that they would be happy to attend. Manorama Francis said she would have to make some arrangement for picking up her children from tuition, but assured that in all probability she would be there. How could she refuse Darius Bhatt who had been so kind to her always? Finally, she asked her husband to organise the picking up of children and attend to dinner, saying she had an urgent meeting which might run late, which she couldn't miss.

Darius Bhatt came to the point straight after asking the guest house staff to serve the drinks and snacks. Whisky and soda for the men, and fruit juice and white wine for Manorama Francis. Manorama opted for the fruit juice. She didn't want any give away on returning home.

"Friends, thank you for coming, especially you, Manorama, for having sacrificed your home time. But this matter is important, and I need some information as soon as possible. A contract has seen signed between GAVA of the Indian Space Agency and a company called Oriont, based in the US, but with an Indian entity, gifting away a whole satellite GEO S10, and all its transponders and spectrum at rates which are even cheaper than what Shankar Raja gave off in his Telecom Ministry. That was bad enough, and is causing enough headaches for the government. But at least that was a different political party. This is our own minister for scientific development who has done a worse thing. The papers are full of it, and a bad name is coming to us for something we were not even aware of. The scientists have done it all by themselves, and most probably with the blessings of the minister."

Darius glanced at all his guests. By now, the snacks had arrived—finger chips, hot *samosas* and *seekh kebabs*.

Prabhakar spoke first. "Yes, sir. We saw it in the papers and were quite surprised. This isn't the way our ministry works."

Aslam Yunus, the additional PS, did not want to be left behind in audience with the second most powerful man of the ruling party. Besides, he owed him a debt of deep gratitude. It was Darius Bhatt who had helped him get this position in the ministry, just when he was about to be sent back to Madhya Pradesh Bhavan without a job. Of course, he had to use a lot of influence from his brethren, but nevertheless, the job was done by Darius Bhatt without payment of a naya paisa.

"Sir," he said, "we were also shocked at what we saw in the papers. Please tell us what you would like us to do? We will be most happy to do it."

Manorama Francis, feeling a little left out, chipped in, "Anything I can do sir, please let me know."

The formalities being over, Darius Bhatt was at his bluntest.

"Yes, there's something I want all of you to do. Not

just for me, but for our party and our country. I'm told a lot of money has been paid by Oriont to the minister for scientific development, and maybe to others in ISA and GAVA, in this whole deal." He took a sip of whiskey and munched a piece of *kebab*.

"I want you to find out who in ISA and GAVA got paid, and how much. Our party is very concerned that such things are happening without their knowledge. Can you do that?"

Aslam Yunus was the first to reply, "Yes, sir, I will try. But I will have to make a trip to Mumbai for that. Shukra Devi knows everything that happens in ISA and GAVA and I can get it from her. I protect her here in the ministry."

Prabhakar was not too far behind. He was in close contact with the scientists from Oriont, all former ISA employees, and was certain that he could get some information from them.

Manorama Francis promised that she would use all her back room influence with the PS to the minister over an informal lunch at the office or on some other pretext, and gather some authentic information.

It was a comfortable dinner with mutton curry and rice, dal and mixed vegetables, and ice cream and mixed fruit to follow. The evening was getting over.

Darius Bhatt thanked his guests for the trouble they had taken to come. "Thank you, thank you so much for sparing your precious time for this evening. But I didn't want you to come to my office. It would not have been good for you. People would have noticed. But what is important is that I want this information as soon as possible. Who has been paid in this deal and how much? And I repeat, I want this information as soon as possible. Within a week?"

"And Aslam," he continued, "if you have to make a trip to Mumbai to contact Shukra Devi, please do so. I will pay for the fare and the stay. Just get the information from her. She is supposed to be the eyes and ears of all the ISA chairmen for decades."

"Yes sir," said Aslam, "let me speak to her tomorrow and I will let you know how we will work it out, and if I have to travel to Mumbai."

"Yes sir," said Prabhakar, "I will contact my friends in Oriont, and try and find out as much as I can."

"Yes sir," said Manorama Francis, "I will try as much as I can with the PS to the minister, and see what information he can give me."

"Good," said Darius Bhatt, "this evening has been a success. But please remember, this is an emergency. The newspapers are hammering us about a scandal which we do not even know about. I want this information as early as possible. Within a week? Is that okay with all of you?"

Darius Bhatt's three guests looked at each other, and nodded in assent.

"Yes sir," said Aslam Yunus, "I think that's okay. We should have the information by that time."

"Good," said Darius Bhatt, "so we shall meet here next Tuesday evening, which is a week from now. And let us see what we get."

THEY ALL MET the next Tuesday at the same place. And the result of all their findings was pretty much the same—the information from Oriont, from ISA, and from the minister's office. That a sum of rupees five crore had been paid directly to the minister, and an amount of rupees three crore paid to past and present chairmen ISA, MD GAVA, and Director Satellite Research Centre, and rupees one crore to senior officials, Gurupriya and Sushil Ramu. The versions of all three officials more or less matched, with the Oriont information getting the highest credibility rating.

Darius Bhatt was pleased. He had carried out Raja Bhaiyya's wishes faithfully. He excitedly asked to meet him and report the information to him.

Raja Bhaiyya frowned when he saw him.

"So, Darius, have you been able to make amends for your past inefficiency?"

"Yes, sir, I have made enquiries from several quarters and the information is the same. An amount of rupees five crores has been paid to the minister, and another rupees four crores to the ISA chairmen and GAVA, and ISA officials." He rattled off the names and amounts, as had been given by Prabhakar, received directly from the Oriont representatives and more or less confirmed by Aslam Yunus from ISA and by Manorama Francis from the minister's office.

"Oh," said Raja Bhaiyya, "so our own ministers are trying to rip us off and giving such a bad name to our government. Day after day, there are such scandalous reports coming out in the newspapers about this Oriont contract and there's hardly anything the government is doing to defend itself. And all the abuse is hurled towards me. I have spoken to the prime minister, but he says he knows nothing about it. What a traitor this Pratap Singh is."

Darius Bhatt listened without saying a word. He was trying to gauge Raja Bhaiyya's mind, which was engaged in nothing other than totalling up how much he had lost in the Oriont deal.

"Sir, if I may suggest, the whole deal seems so irregular. Using a cabinet decision to build a satellite without informing that the spectrum of the satellite has already been sold at a dirt-cheap rate to a fake company without any bids. I think you should use your position to order an enquiry into the whole affair. At least, then we will get our fair share from the deal."

"You know, Darius, sometimes you do come up with good ideas. I think I will do just that. Call my secretary, Prakrit Nayyar immediately. I will ask him to get the papers ready for ordering an enquiry and send them to the prime minister."

"Yes, sir, I will ask Prakrit to come here right away."

Prakrit Nayyar hardly took ten minutes to reach, and both he and Darius entered Raja Bhaiyya's office. He looked surly and angry.

"Prakrit, there's this terrible scandal happening in the scientific development ministry about which we had no clue. You would have seen it too. Something about satellites and spectrum and transponders with some company called Oriont. Imagine, no one from Oriont has even come to see me. Go through whatever information we have and call for papers from the ministry. I want an enquiry ordered into this whole business immediately. Get whatever information you want from Darius."

Prakrit looked a little nonplussed, and turned towards Darius Bhatt for support. He had read about the GAVA Oriont stuff, but that was the scientific development ministry's affair.

Darius merely nodded and said, "Sir, let's just sit for a while and discuss this and then we'll work out how to do the enquiry."

Raja Bhaiyya continued his rant, "And the enquiry officer should be selected by me. He should be our loyalist. Preferably, a retired IAS officer who is looking for a job…a little pliant…may be, with some hidden dirt…who can be arm twisted."

Both Prakrit and Darius looked at each other a little amused, and both said, "Yes, sir."

"Ah, I just remembered. There's this retired IAS chap, I think his name is Ashutosh Prasad. He's come to see me once or twice, but keeps sending people to plead on his behalf for a Rajya Sabha ticket or a governorship. Yes, I think he'll be good. And he comes from a loyal political family. His father-in-law was chief minister of Bihar, many years ago. Prakrit, just find out where he is and let him know that we want him to do this enquiry."

MARTIN GEORGES HAD a lot on his mind. He had seen the news about the various exposures of the ISA Oriont contract in the papers sent to him by Karmaswamy. This was not good. Georges had seen the meticulous work done by Satyadev who had literally shepherded the agreement from the start. Of course, there was always the unseen presence of the international company TerrAkash International, providing the umbrella of protection. But really speaking, Satyadev had to be given full credit for transitioning the deal successfully from the old government to the new.

Karmaswamy sent Georges an urgent message saying that he must come over to India soon, and meet the minister and his principal secretary. Besides, Oriont US had received large investments from Alascom and Sontag, and it would only be appropriate to monetise their token expressions of confidence to the minister and his principal secretary.

Karmaswamy had enough contacts in Delhi to fix up Georges' meetings with the minister. Besides, the helping hand of Prabhakar, right inside the ministry was always there. He did not have to bother the ISA for any help on this.

But Karmaswamy did have to contact Vidyasagar about one small technicality. What would be the best way that the tokens of gratitude to the minister and his principal secretary be handled. Vidyasagar asked Karmaswamy to just wait for a while, as he had to consult the chairman and his contacts in the minister's office regarding this. After all, Georges was expected in Delhi only during the next week, and the appointment was yet to be confirmed.

Vidyasagar performed his responsibility with diligence. He spoke to his usual contact, the minister's officer on special duty, whose major responsibility was to track the payments coming from several sources. He was advised that the times were bad, and they should wait for further instructions.

Maharishi, on the other hand, became hyperactive. He

was a great devotee of a god lady called Sri Sri Om Amma, who ran an *ashram* (spiritual retreat) in Raigarh, and several other charitable schools and colleges and hospitals. Her *ashram* was a hub of great charity and contributions from the rich and famous, and corrupt, as she went around with a beatific face and form, spraying holy water and chanting secret *mantras* (sacred chants) into the ears of the multitudes of her devotees. Her *mantras* clearly had a great deal of power because the multitudes kept returning for more of them, each time making even greater charitable contributions.

Maharishi got in touch with Om Amma's secretary, Ramanna Madhav, and alerted him. He told him that a large contribution would be coming in shortly in cash, but it would be there only for a while, as it was required for higher charitable purposes elsewhere.

Ramanna Madhav replied with great sincerity. "Yes, surely. Sri Sri Om Amma is aware of your great devotion and charity. This would not be a problem."

"Good. Good. Then we shall do so accordingly."

Maharishi had been reading about several crackdowns happening on the hawala dealers and on some foreign banks as a result of the huge debate on black money that was going on in the country. It would be risky for the minister and the rest of them to use the offshore accounts route or the hawala route to lodge their confidence money. No, this would not be good for the minister or his secretary.

Maharishi suggested to Karmaswamy that the confidence money could be deposited in the Sri Sri Om Amma *ashram*, and that Karmaswamy should keep the minister's office informed about it.

MEANWHILE, AMITABH WAS placing a new piece of news everyday about the ISA Oriont deal. On one day, it would be a long interview with Karmaswamy that the deal was perfectly legal as far as Oriont was concerned. On another day, he would extract some conditions from the contract, commenting how they favoured Oriont to the detriment of the government. On the next day, it would be about comparing the price of spectrum given to Oriont with the price of spectrum given by Shankar Raja, being investigated in the 2S spectrum auction.

Newspaper articles, opeds, and editorials about the GAVA Oriont deal and its several implications became a periodic feature. Attacks against the government persisted and the minister was confronted with at least five parliament questions every week. Fortunately, he never had to answer any of them, because parliament was hardly ever allowed to function.

GEORGES WAS ALSO worried about many other things. There had been a great crackdown on offshore accounts, after some leaks had happened in Le Revieran Bank, where one of the bank employees had sold the names of all the offshore account holders to the Dutch Government. There were a lot of investigations happening in the US on companies which had salted away their monies in various accounts in offshore havens. No, this was not the time for foreign remittances. The transfers would have to be done through Oriont India, on the basis of percentages and payments.

Investments kept pouring into Oriont US—from Russia, Mauritius, Singapore and Dubai. Georges transferred a handsome amount to Oriont India, with directions that the money must be used for payments to ISA, in accordance with the payment schedule and for research. Ten percent of the amount was to be discreetly removed in stages as an expression of good-will for the minister, his secretary, and all the well-wishers in ISA and GAVA.

The chartered accountant hired by Oriont India was smart and well connected. Through his contacts in the Indus Bank, he was able to retrieve the designated ten percent amount in cash, on the basis of assorted fake bills. It took about two weeks to do so, and by the end of it he had rupees six crores in cash. The amount was placed in the vaults of Sri Sri Om Amma's *ashram*. It was the responsibility of Maharishi to ensure that rupees three crores was delivered to the minister and his secretary, before the visit of Martin Georges, and the remaining to the scientists, friendly bureaucrats and lower staff, strictly in accordance with their order of precedence.

Maharishi did ensure that the amount was delivered through the Delhi network, specifically designated for this work. But Maharishi made an additional request to Georges for rupees one crore which he told Georges was urgently required for some new requirements that had emerged in New Delhi. The amount was withdrawn in the same manner during the next week.

BUT MAHARISHI WAS also a worried man. After his officers brought the papers from various divisions of ISA and GAVA, he knew he had much to be worried about in the present circumstances.

There was no way anyone could justify why Oriont had been selected. But more than that, the fact that the Oriont contract had not officially been informed to the cabinet could certainly be used against him and the ISA. He would have to find a way of getting around it.

But the person most worried about it was Satyadev. He barged into Maharishi's office one day, without prior information or apology, and sat down at the table.

"Maharishi, I must inform you, an enquiry is in the

offing. Very soon. You have to get your papers in order."

"Yes sir, I have taken a cursory look at them. All your meetings in the US and here. How it all started. Must look at all of them again." A slight amount of sadism surfaced in Maharishi. He was enjoying Satyadev's discomfiture.

"You must segregate that lot of papers and keep them aside. Just show all the papers where I am not present. Anyway, we ISA scientists are lousy file keepers, so it won't matter. And the secretariat papers have hardly anything from our side. Let the bureaucrats handle their own problems."

"But what makes you think there will be an enquiry?" asked Maharishi.

"Just take my word for it."

Maharishi knew that Satyadev was strongly supported by the US establishment and also by the most influential sections of the scientific community in India. But judging from the panic in his voice, it was quite evident that the information he had about the enquiry was a certainty.

Well, if there was an enquiry, Satyadev would be the first one to be found culpable for approving the contract in the GAVA board and in the science council, both of which he chaired. But what Maharishi did not know was that Satyadev was using every channel of influence that he could muster, to reach Raja Bhaiyya, and make sure that his name would not figure anywhere in the enquiry.

For the next two days, the trusted officials of ISA

and GAVA sat in seclusion, segregating the papers which should be shown for the enquiry from those which should not, and for preparing replies to the expected questions that the enquiry officers would ask.

MARTIN GEORGES ARRIVED in New Delhi on April 11, 2003. Karmaswamy had organised his meetings with the minister and his secretary. Georges had been assured by Karmaswamy that the payment schedule through the new route had been completed.

But it could not have been a worse time. The next day as he woke up in his grand suite at the Indraprastha International, Georges reached for the newspaper. There they were—the front-page headlines, splashed in bolder letters than usual—that the government had ordered an enquiry into the GAVA Oriont deal, with column after column regurgitating the same old stuff.

Dear god, Georges wondered. Now what was all this about? Karmaswamy had told him nothing about any enquiry. And who was this Ashutosh Prasad, who had been appointed to do the enquiry?

He phoned Karmaswamy immediately.

"Hey, Karma, what's going on? What's all this about an enquiry? Against us? What on earth is going on?"

"Yes, Martin," Karmaswamy replied, deeply distressed

and embarrassed, "I've just read the papers too. We had no idea about this. This is such a jolt. When can I come and see you?"

"In an hour. I'll be down for breakfast. Damn."

Karmaswamy was waiting in the breakfast lounge when Georges entered.

"You must believe me, Martin, I really had no idea about any of this. Must have been a real hush hush thing in the prime minister's office. Even people in ISA and GAVA are in a state of shock. They spoke to me in the morning. Of course, there's been a lot of bad press, despite our best efforts. And a lot of commotion in parliament, but we never thought it would come to this. It's the telecom ministry chaps who are facing an enquiry ordered by the supreme court. And they are organizing this attack on us just to divert attention."

"That's all very well. But how do you intend to handle this?" Georges sounded a little irritated. "Anyway," he continued, "let's get on with breakfast."

Georges helped himself to some orange juice, fruit and cereal, and then ordered some fried eggs, sunny side up, and coffee, and returned to the table.

Karmaswamy, an early riser, had already finished breakfast, and joined Georges with a cup of coffee.

"So, tell me, Karma, does my meeting with the minister stand?"

"Yes, it does. That's the first thing that I checked on

after I read the newspaper. The meeting is very much on, at his home office at 10.30 am. And then just after that, with his secretary."

"Good. Small mercies. I wonder what I should tell him."

"I left the brief with you last night. Here's another copy." He handed it over to Georges.

Georges went through it while eating his cereal. "Seems okay. The usual stuff, but I like your future projections for Oriont India. I can see that my guys back home and your team have worked pretty hard. But I am a little worried about this enquiry. Is it to be taken seriously, or is it just another of those pointless things that dies down after a while?"

"Well, my information—of course it needs to be further reconfirmed—is that the real power behind the throne, Raja Bhaiyya, that's the PM's son-in-law, is pretty upset that ministers are signing contracts without informing him. I'm told he was very upset when our contract became public, and that he had been left out of everything. And that's the reason for this enquiry. It is meant to be a message to all the ministers that any contract with potential benefit has to be informed to him. That's what I've been able to gather so far."

"Oh, quite a deadly character, I must say."

"Yes, that he certainly is."

"By the way, all the stuff meant for the minister

and his secretary, has it reached them? And there was an additional requirement as well."

"Yes, I believe it has. Through a rather circuitous route. But I believe it has. So I'm told by Vidyasagar."

"Good. So, what time must we leave here for the minister's meeting?"

"Say around ten minutes after ten o'clock. The minister's house is just about ten minutes from here, but let us keep another ten minutes for bad traffic or any delays with security, etc."

The eggs and coffee had arrived. Georges ate them quickly, sipping his coffee alongside, and then rose.

"Okay Karma, I'll be down at ten."

"Fine. I have a nice case of Black Label and some boxes of Godiva chocolate to take along."

"You can handle all of that, Karma. I'll be down at ten."

Georges had a frown on his face. He was wondering where all this was leading to.

PRATAP SINGH WAS devastated when he read the headlines in the morning newspapers that an enquiry had been ordered into the Oriont contract. How could the prime minister have done this without consulting him? Or had Raja Bhaiyya done this, and forced it over the prime minister's head? But then, these things happened all the time. He was sure the prime minister would sort it out.

But this morning, he had to meet the chairman of Oriont US, and it would not be proper to call it off, especially since he had been so generous in his gratitude. Also, it would betray a sense of weakness. He thought it was best to meet him and speak in the usual pleasant, diplomatic language, and assure him that nothing had changed. And after that, he would seek an appointment with the prime minister.

Martin Georges and Karmaswamy reached the minister's home office exactly at ten thirty. Karmaswamy discreetly requested the PS to carry the case of Black Label from his car to the house, but making sure that the minister had heard him. Georges carried the hamper of Godiva chocolates and presented them to the minister.

They shook hands. They were meeting for the second time. "Thank you, thank you so much, Mr Georges. Godiva chocolates! They are the best. Except that I should not be indulging in them. Growing old, you know." Both men laughed.

The minister continued, "Well, I'm really sorry, Mr Georges, that you've come at a rather unfortunate time. Just when everything was going so well. You've been reading the papers, I'm sure. And your staff in India would have briefed you."

"Yes, yes, minister, my staff has briefed me. And this is really unfortunate, especially what I read this morning in the newspapers about the enquiry."

"Well, this is a democracy, and anyone can say anything he wants. What they're saying about us is so malicious, and so false. But I have full faith that this will be over soon. As a matter of fact, I will be briefing the prime minister about this, probably today or tomorrow. I'm sure it will pass over soon. Let not our work suffer on account of this."

"Minister, let us assure you that I have no doubt that this is merely a passing storm that we will all overcome. It happens in my country too. As you said, we both live in democracies where anyone can say anything he wants."

"Rest assured, Mr Georges, we are committed to our relationship. Our association will continue. I am informed that the construction of GeoS 10 has begun, and I am also aware of the work and investments that have been done by you."

ISA WAS IN panic when the news hit them, even though the top brass had been preparing themselves for such an eventuality.

Maharishi remained cool. Fortunately, he had been able to pull out all the related papers, and by now, all the offending ones had been removed. They mostly related to the long period of negotiations dating back to Satyadev's time, and a lot of them dealing with GAVA correspondence with Oriont, led by Vidyasagar. Fortunately, a lot of email correspondence had been copied to the secretariat at that time. Gurupriya's name was always prominent. That was good. And in all the subsequent committees, some bureaucrat or other was always present, like in the Haridas committee and the GAVA board meetings.

Original documents which had not been copied to outside offices were replaced with fresh signatures and sanitised content, and new documents were created to show that copies had been sent to someone or the other in the secretariat.

The newspapers had started devoting at least one column for this subject each day. It became something like a serialised crime thriller, and many readers got completely hooked on to it, searching for the column every morning waiting to read the next episode.

Maharishi put on his leadership role to dispel the sense of gloom that had overtaken his organisation. Now that the papers had been cleaned up, he felt slightly more comfortable. Satyadev, who by now had also acquired an office in the building as a distinguished scientist emeritus, would pop in every now and then. They waited in suspense for the enquiry officer, Ashutosh Prasad, to announce his arrival. But before that, Maharishi had to meet his minister.

Maharishi did a quick background check on Ashutosh Prasad. Well, he was a retired IAS Officer, the son-in-law of a former chief minister of Bihar, and known to be rather close to the Raja Bhaiyya's side of the ruling party. He had just completed his tenure as chairman of the national economic advisory commission, and was presently without any assignment.

Maharishi did not have to wait long. The very same day he received a secret communication from the cabinet secretariat, announcing the enquiry into the ISA Oriont contract, the procedures that had been followed, the selection criteria, the technology involved, etc. The communication stated that the enquiry would be conducted by Shri Ashutosh Prasad, a retired IAS officer, who would be assisted by two officials, and requested that a secretariat be provided to them in the ISA building.

A separate letter came from Ashutosh Prasad with his tour programme and flight details, saying that he would be arriving two days later. He requested that a fully furnished office with computers and other office equipment be provided, and accommodation for at least a week should be made available for himself and his two assistants.

That was good. Maharishi had two days within which he could make a trip to meet the minister and read his mind. He summoned Vidyasagar immediately.

Vidyasagar entered his office looking gloomy and depressed.

"Vidyasagar, come on, don't look so downtrodden. These things happen all the time in government. And if you keep looking like that, you will infect everybody else too."

"Yes, sir. But how could they do this to us? After all we have done for the nation. How could they disgrace us like this? Look at the plight of our families. All our neighbours and friends look at us so strangely. And my wife can't even go out anymore."

"Oh, come on. We've all got to face this. It will be over soon," Maharishi continued, hiding his own anger at the establishment which had used them and was now victimising them. But anger was the last thing he could indulge in at the moment. He had to organise the enquiry as smoothly as he could, and then use the minister and, if possible, the elusive business magnate to quieten it up.

"Now, Vidya, this Prasad chap will be coming over the day after tomorrow. Get the smaller conference room on this same floor organised as his office. Put in the computers, printer, photocopier in the adjoining room for his two assistants. You can book a suite for him in the Emerald Green, or if he wishes, he can stay in our own guest house here in the VIP suite. Have both ready, and rooms for his assistants."

"Yes, sir, it will be done."

He asked his PA to bring a copy of Ashutosh Prasad's tour programme. He handed it over to Vidyasagar and asked Shukra Devi to type out a memo from him to all the ISA division heads and the secretariat officers to remain in headquarters for the entire one week that Prasad was there.

Satyadev did not drop in that morning. He was in more important places, negotiating and buying goodwill and protection.

The same afternoon Maharishi left for Delhi to meet his minister.

ASHUTOSH PRASAD, MEANWHILE, had been called by Raja Bhaiyya for a special briefing the same day. He entered through the high security maze and was led by a plain clothes security man to his office waiting room. He saw that Prakrit Nayyar was in his office in the adjoining room, so he dropped by to say hello.

"Hello, Prakrit, and why have I been selected for this honour?" Prasad smiled.

Prakrit returned the smile. "Well, the boss so desires, sir." The PS came running to inform Prasad that sahib was calling him.

"I'll see you after the meeting," Prasad went towards Raja Bhaiyya's office.

Raja Bhaiyya was reading some letters on his table and signing them, one by one.

"Good morning, sir."

"Ah, good morning, Ashutosh. Please sit down," he said with a rather dull face. He looked pale and tired.

Ashutosh spoke his opening line. "I must thank you, sir, for selecting me for this assignment, and for the trust you are placing in me."

"That's alright, that's alright. You have always been a good, loyal officer. I always remember loyalty."

"Thank you, sir."

"Now, about this assignment that I'm sending you for. There are a lot of underhand dealings going on in this ISA and their scientific development ministry. I was shocked to read about them in the papers. You must have read them too. It is giving us all such a bad name. You must get to the bottom of it and expose their corruption."

"Anything particular you have in mind, sir. I mean, any particular person or persons you have in mind."

"Yes, the whole bunch of those wily scientists. All of them have betrayed me. All of them. Of course, they would have all been led by their minister, that traitor, Pratap Singh, but we can't bring that in. Let him get the message, anyhow. Making deals behind our back, indeed."

"What about the bureaucrats? Any particular ones you have in mind?"

"No, I don't know any of them, and I don't care. Do

whatever you want with them, based on your enquiry."

"Yes, sir."

"And I want the enquiry report soon. This is just too much. Within ten days, or maximum two weeks. Go to Mumbai. Sit tight there and complete the job. Prakrit will give you all the details."

"Yes, sir, that should be possible."

The meeting was over. Raja Bhaiyya buzzed for his PS, and gestured that Ashutosh could leave.

Ashutosh Prasad realised that this was no time to remind Raja Bhaiyya about his earlier requests for a Rajya Sabha seat or a governorship. He would claim his reward later, after the enquiry report was ready. He returned to Prakrit Nayyar's office and narrated a summary of the meeting.

"Well, I will be off the day after tomorrow. Just need to send a few letters to the ISA chairman. I know they have a liaison office here. In fact, they've been in touch with me asking me if there's any assistance that I need. I think I should go there today and send off my letters."

"Yes, it's better you send all your letters from there. Those guys should give you whatever assistance you need."

"By the way, the boss said you might have some details you would like to give me."

"None that I can remember. I'll let you know if there's something."

Ashutosh Prasad called up the liaison officer whose

name was Amit Priyadarshi and told him that he would be coming over within the next half hour.

Amit was there at the entrance of the ISA liaison office at the CGO Complex on Lodhi Road. Prasad nodded at everyone rather superciliously and straightaway asked for the services of a stenographer. He dictated a letter to chairman ISA, telling him that he must have all the papers ready for examination by the time he arrived the day after tomorrow, and requested him to be personally available to brief him regarding the history of the case. Thereafter, he would summon the officials, depending upon the facts that emerged from the papers. The liaison officer firmed up the air tickets, the car, the reception at Mumbai airport. He asked whether Ashutosh Prasad would prefer to stay at a hotel, but Prasad replied that the ISA guest house was fine, that he would be there definitely for at least a week or more, depending on how much time it would take to complete the enquiry.

Coffee and a variety of snacks were loaded on to the table in the ISA liaison office, but Ashutosh just had the coffee. The official car was placed at his disposal, but he declined the offer. He asked for it to be sent to his residence the day he was leaving for Mumbai. After all, the right message had to be sent to ISA—that he was the standard bearer of justice and fairness and didn't accept favours from the organisation against whom he was conducting an enquiry.

MAHARISHI'S MEETING WITH the Minister was not very encouraging, though on the face of it, it was cordial and polite.

The Minister was deeply preoccupied and appeared worried. Maharishi also detected a streak of somewhat latent hostility, something he had never seen earlier. The recording devise on his fountain pen was on.

"Well, sir, you are aware that Ashutosh Prasad is coming over to Mumbai the day after tomorrow to start his enquiry. We have got all the papers ready. We have prepared the answers to the questions that he is expected to raise. This is most unfortunate, sir. But we will make sure that everything goes off smoothly and to his satisfaction."

"Oh, really? I wish I could be that optimistic. Anyway, I'm sure you will do your best and see that everything is settled at ISA, and that no one else from Delhi is dragged into it."

The message was clear. The Minister was distancing himself from everything in ISA.

"Yes sir, you may rest assured. Delhi will not be dragged into this."

"And be prepared for some shocks," the Minister continued, "it's much more complicated than you think."

"I understand, sir," said Maharishi, not even trying to

understand what the Minister was saying, "all the more we will ensure that the enquiry goes off smoothly."

"You must understand Maharshi, Prasad has instructions from none other than Raja Bhaiyya himself. He somehow feels he was left out of this whole thing and that's the reason he's doing all this."

"We will answer everything, sir. Any other instructions?"

"No, just try and see that minimum damage is done. It won't be easy."

"Right, sir. I'm returning to Mumbai tonight, and will take charge of everything. I will report to you daily."

The Minister did not give even an oblique hint that he had come to know about Maharishi's neat little kill behind his back from Oriont. Maharishi had committed the worst breach of trust, and would pay for it. But this was not the time for any confrontation.

"Okay, Maharishi. All the best. And keep me informed of what's going on. It could have very serious consequences for all of us."

"Thank you, sir. Goodnight. I shall keep you informed of everything." Maharishi took his leave.

But he left with a sense of disquiet. There was a hidden, ominous meaning in the minister's words. He had made it clear that he would do nothing to help and support ISA, even though it was part of his ministry. ISA was now left unprotected, and was expected to defend itself, even though the entire project had been executed according to directions from Delhi.

ASHUTOSH PRASAD ARRIVED in Mumbai as scheduled, late in the evening. There was a high-level reception for him at the Mumbai airport. Gurupriya, representing the chairman, was designated as the escort officer and led the delegation. Vidyasagar, MD GAVA, played the role of master of ceremonies with a flourish. Several senior scientists with hordes of assistants added volume to the reception party.

It was felt that strategically it would be good to place Gurupriya in proximity with Ashutosh Prasad, being a member of the same service. They could speak the same language, recall common comrades and friends, and make small talk about subjects that they were both conversant with. Gurupriya was particular about her *kumkum* and *mangalsutra* being completely prominent, and the sari pallu could be adjusted according to the demands of the moment.

Ashutosh Prasad was a short, stocky man, with a rather cheerless and bland face, and slow, ponderous movement. Gurupriya tried all her welcome jargon to cheer him up, but nothing worked. The man just refused to stop looking grim.

His luggage was collected and they went towards the

car. Gurupriya sat with Ashutosh Prasad in the back seat, and Vidyasagar sat in front. But Ashutosh Prasad still would not speak.

So Gurupriya started on her act. She had to say something. "Sir, we are so pleased that you're visiting us. Of course, the circumstances are unfortunate, but then, this is also part of public service." Ashutosh Prasad looked at her with his smileless face, and merely nodded his head with a completely disinterested expression.

However, Gurupriya continued undeterred, "Sir, I was in a training programme in the academy when you came as a guest lecturer and spoke to us about globalisation and its impact on the Indian economy. I think it was around 1996. It was such a fabulous lecture. I remember, our group kept talking about it for days together. I've never forgotten it." Of course, she was bluffing like hell.

Finally, Ashutosh Prasad's face turned towards her and showed some interest. And Gurupriya realised it was the right time to handle her sari *pallu* and *mangalsutra* appropriately. Ashutosh Prasad showed a little more interest.

"So, what batch are you?" he asked, his words emerging like bubbles.

"1982 batch, sir, Union Territory cadre."

"Oh, so you are of Krishna Nair's batch. He was my Joint Secretary, when I was Home Secretary. A wonderful officer. I believe he's now somewhere in the World Bank,

I think." He kept speaking in bubbles.

"Yes, sir," Gurupriya replied, "actually, we're pretty good friends. He keeps in touch with me." Her sari pallu was playing wonderful manipulations, of which Ashutosh could get a peek from the corner of his eye. Not a bad place, he thought, this ISA. More interesting than those dull and demanding desert-stone buildings of North Block.

They were reaching the guest house. Gurupriya demurely remained at the reception on the ground floor and wished Ashutosh Prasad goodnight, while Vidyasagar escorted him to his suite upstairs.

She waited for Vidyasagar to return. She then phoned Maharishi, "Sir, everything went off well. Mr Ashutosh Prasad is in his suite. So far, so good, and we will all meet in your office tomorrow at 10 am. Goodnight, sir."

The scientists had taken care to plant their bugging devices strategically in the VIP suite.

ASHUTOSH PRASAD HAD a light dinner. It was nice to be waited upon like a king after a long time. There was a bottle of Black Label whisky and cognac placed on the cabinet, but he did not touch it. And this girl, Gurupriya, she seemed nice, quite attractive and professional in a rather carnal way. Anyway, to hell with the nonsense that he had to attend to. He wondered why Raja Bhaiyya was so perturbed about this contract… as if any multi-million dollar contract passed through without huge packages being dished around. Perhaps, Raja Bhaiyya had not got his fair share. Anyway, he'd have to handle it tomorrow, something he was not looking forward to at all. With these thoughts, he retired to bed.

He was to have breakfast with Maharishi the next morning in the guest house. It really was a sumptuous breakfast—the usual south Indian fare with *dosas* and *appams* and *idlis* and *upma*—then the continental with the best fruit, cereal, eggs and cheese. Ashutosh chose the South Indian menu, and enjoyed the delightful authentic tastes that could never be produced in Delhi.

"Sir," said Maharishi, while Ashutosh Prasad was relishing his appams and slurping the stew, "I hope you had a good rest. Would you like to discuss how you would want to go about this enquiry? I have all the papers ready. My officers have all been asked to remain in headquarters for the entire duration of your stay here."

"Okay, let me first take a look at the papers. The allegations are that you signed a contract with Oriont giving away an entire satellite and spectrum to them, without calling for any tenders. Now, that's serious, considering all the flak the government is facing over the spectrum auctions by the telecom ministry." He remembered the instructions from Raja Bhaiyya that all the scientists were to be branded, and as for the bureaucrats, he could choose whoever he wished.

Maharishi gave a short simple answer, "Sir, you will have answers to all your questions." Coffee had arrived. They finished it and walked over to Maharishi's office, which was two buildings away. Vidyasagar was waiting outside along with some other senior scientists of ISA and GAVA. He introduced them all.

"Call Ms Gurupriya and her team from the secretariat," Maharishi asked his inherited PS Shukra Devi, who was all decked up for the occasion. Her greatest ambition was to outdo Gurupriya's *mangalsutra* and cleavage machinations. Though she was aware that there was a fairly serious conflict of complexions between them, with Gurupriya holding a distinct edge, Shukra Devi tried hard to overcome that with expensive facials and bleaches.

Gurupriya and her team piled in, and she introduced them all—her deputy financial and administration officer, Sushil Ramu, and her chief administration officer, Manal Kumar and several other assistants.

The formalities being over, Ashutosh asked Maharishi to take him to the room where he was to conduct the enquiry. Just as he was moving to the room, his mobile phone rang. It was Prakrit Nayyar, so he had to take the call. He requested to be alone in the enquiry room and said, "Yes, Prakrit, I was just about to start the enquiry. What is it?"

The bugging devices were in active mode.

Prakrit from the other end was saying, "Sir, just wanted to pass on some instructions from the boss. Satyadev is not to be touched, and neither is Gurupriya. Do what you like with the others."

Ashutosh Prasad replied a little curtly, "Oh, anyway, I'm just starting the enquiry. Shall talk to you in the evening."

By now Ashutosh was losing interest. Just what sort of a ramshackle enquiry was this? His reputation was at stake if he gave a distorted report. But then again, there was the possibility of the two coveted initials of MP coming within closer reach, if he did the enquiry as per Raja Bhaiyya's wishes.

Ashutosh Prasad started the enquiry in a most indifferent way. He knew what he had to do, and what he did not have to do. Hang the leading scientists, and for a balancing act to keep the scientific community silent, book one or two of the bureaucrats, and be politically correct.

He started reading the files and papers presented to him. The same boring nonsense that he had already read in the papers. He asked his assistants to start listing the files and numbering the papers, and he started reading and studying them in a resigned, apathetic fashion. He sat there the whole day till eight o'clock in the evening, had some sandwiches and fruit for lunch by himself, and swallowed his blood pressure and prostate medicines at the appointed time. He didn't need any other assistance. There were still some more files to go through, and he would be able to complete that by the afternoon of the next day.

Clearly, the origin of the contract lay with Satyadev, though not too many files of his negotiations with Oriont were available. Just some presentations made in Canada and in the US and then in ISA Headquarters. Some odd emails to the scientists talking of term sheets to be finalised, copies of all of them marked to Gurupriya. But as for files—there was not a single file relating to this era. It all seemed so fraudulent. But Ashutosh remembered Prakrit's last telephone call—neither Satyadev nor Gurupriya were to be touched. What the hell was this all about? He ruefully realised that if there was indeed a scam, then he was part of yet another one. So be it, he reasoned philosophically. The initials M and P danced before his eyes.

He did ask a few questions, however, to Maharishi that evening, after he had been through the whole pile of files that had been provided to him.

"I say, Dr Maharishi, where are all the files of the period before the Haridas committee? I hardly find anything here, except for some presentations and emails."

"Sir, that's the way we function here. It's mostly by emails and presentations, discussions and decisions. We're scientists, not bureaucrats. We capture the essentials, then decide, then start working. I'm sure you've seen enough files after our decisions have reached the secretariat. You would have observed that, I'm sure,"

Maharishi continued, "The Haridas committee report has been well documented, and then carried forward to the contract, to the science council and the cabinet."

"Yes, but there are several important procedures that appear to have been completely disregarded. Why did you not at least ask for bids from other companies or organisations? You know the rules regarding public tendering. And how did you choose a new, insignificant start up with no credentials or experience or proprietary technology, even though several of your erstwhile staff are part of Oriont India? It just doesn't make it legitimate."

"Sir, with due respect, we don't quite function like other departments. As you know, we're reeling under sanctions imposed upon us prohibiting any technology transfer which can make GAVA grow. Besides, except Sontag or Europides, no one else has this proprietary technology ownership. So, if Oriont India, through its research and scientific networks has this technology and is willing to partner with GAVA on that, why should we refuse it? Had we refused it, we could easily have been accused of making unwise and unsound business decisions, of being risk averse, just like a typical public sector undertaking. You'd agree with this, I'm sure, with your rich experience in the public sector." Ashutosh kept listening. He nodded once or twice. It was all so terribly boring.

"And besides, sir, the bureaucrats, who are custodians of the rules and procedures, were present in each and every one of the meetings with Oriont. Email copies regarding every development, and every stage of progress were marked to them. You have seen all the papers. It is their job to advise us if we have missed out on some rules or procedures. What I'm trying to say, sir, is that we're here to make a product which is in the interest of the nation, and of course, the organisation, and all our energies are concentrated upon that. It is for the secretariat to give us the information and guidance regarding what procedures we must follow. I'm sure you would have seen in all the papers you have examined, there was not one word from anyone in the secretariat about that, even though they were always involved at every stage of the negotiations." Maharishi had made his point.

Ashutosh smirked to himself, but nodded with that supercilious and expressionless face that powerful bureaucrats often assume. The same old story, he thought, blame it all on the bureaucrats, who are your captives anyway. The only bureaucrat whose name appeared right from the start of the negotiations till the end was Gurupriya, and she was not to be touched. What the hell was he doing here, anyway? But there was Raja Bhaiyya who had to be pleased, and hopefully, a Rajya Sabha nomination not very far away.

He returned to his room and remembered that he had to return Prakrit Nayyar's call. "Hello Prakrit, I'm sorry I couldn't speak too much to you this morning. I was just about to start the enquiry and was surrounded by everybody. But I do remember what you said. That Satyadev and Gurupriya were to be kept out. Is that right?"

Prakrit replied, "Yes, sir, that is what the boss wants."

"But they are the ones who are involved in the deal from beginning to end. How do I absolve them?"

"Sorry, sir, I'm just conveying to you what the boss wants."

"Aha, let me see how this can be handled," Ashutosh Prasad replied.

The bugging devices were listening.

Ashutosh Prasad spent the next day making notes from the papers he had studied, and drafting a factual report regarding the chronology of the GAVA Oriont Contract—what was right with it, what was wrong with it, the various policies that had been disregarded, the rules that had been flouted, the role of the bureaucrats, (Gurupriya excluded), their acts of omission and commission. It didn't matter whether what he had written was correct or not. What was important was Raja Bhaiyya's orders.

Ashutosh Prasad then requested all the scientists, foremost being Maharishi, Vidyasagar and Haridas, the whole bunch of bureaucrats, ranging from Gurupriya, Manal Kumar, and Sushil Ramu, down to the assistant director and section officer who had typed the draft cabinet note, to make a statement in writing if they so wished. He gave them three days for it and said he would return the following week to receive them, and maybe call them personally, if he had any doubts or further questions.

That evening Ashutosh Prasad called up Prakrit Nayyar, and briefed him of what he had done. He assured him that both Satyadev and Gurupriya would not be mentioned in his report. The ISA bugging devices were listening.

Ashutosh returned to Delhi with a large file box full of papers, and his staff. He would start finalising his report. The comments of the ISA and its secretariat officers were a formality for the record, which would not interfere at all with the report he would present to Raja Bhaiyya, before he submitted it to the prime minister.

He persevered for the next two days, indicted all the scientists, except Satyadev, indicted all the bureaucrats, expect Gurupriya. He then started planning his second mission to Mumbai to create appearances of having done a fair and judicious enquiry.

Before leaving, he phoned Prakrit Nayyar and asked

for an appointment to meet him and Raja Bhaiyya to show them the draft report he had prepared.

He first met Prakrit, and presented him the draft. Prakrit was extremely preoccupied regarding several allegations being made against Raja Bhaiyya personally about some highly irregular appointments recommended by him in some nationalised banks. One of his nominees to chair the prestigious National Chambal Bank had just been arrested for massive hawala trading. Prakrit had to do a huge amount of backend management to ensure that Raja Bhaiyya's name would not figure anywhere in the newspapers, and that the whole issue should not reach his doorstep.

"Sir," said Prakrit, still terribly preoccupied, "I don't think boss is meeting anyone today. He's busy with his political advisors and the Goa politicians. You know, the Goa elections are coming closer."

"Okay, I'll leave a copy of the draft with you. Go through it whenever you have time. And brief the boss. And if there are any questions, you can phone me anytime. I'm leaving for Mumbai tomorrow evening."

Ashutosh was disappointed. He had hoped to meet Raja Bhaiyya and give him an exaggerated account of his achievements at ISA, even in the face of the stiffest resistance from the scientists, about the hostility that he had faced, and how he held his ground because of his loyalty to Raja Bhaiyya. The chances of getting a nomination for MP in his home state of Madhya Pradesh would have strengthened. Anyway, he would keep that for another day after his return from Mumbai.

MAHARISHI TOO, MADE a day trip to Delhi and briefed his minister about what had gone on during the enquiry. The minister listened impassively, and didn't say a word. Let the bastards stew, he thought. A bunch of cheats breaking all the sacrosanct norms and doing what was most unethical. Clandestinely receiving money in his name behind his back. What sort of an idiot did they think he was?

"Sir, I have ensured that nothing of the enquiry reaches Delhi."

The Minister nodded, but remained silent. Both men had their recording devices on.

Maharishi tried to interest the minister in the progress of some ongoing projects, and the upcoming launches, including the moon mission, but the minister still paid no attention.

Maharishi was nonplussed. This behaviuor was most unusual. Could he have found out about the money that he had received on the side? Not possible, he thought. The money he had kept was an additionality which he had obtained directly, over and above the amount committed to the minister by Oriont. The minister had received his promised amount—he would not have known of the additional amount that went to Maharishi. Or could he have known? Did he have his own information network? But no one knew about this except Georges and Karmaswamy, and they did not have the network to reach the minister without going through him. Or did they? He would have to figure that one out. Little did Maharishi realise that the information about the additional amount had come to the minister from Raja Bhaiyya's office.

Maharishi rose and took his leave and drove straight to the airport. Something was terribly amiss. And this Ashutosh fellow would be landing up again tomorrow evening.

THE ISA SCIENTISTS and bureaucrats were busy the next two days writing out their statements—the scientists blaming the bureaucrats that they were just not being advised properly and the bureaucrats blaming the scientists, that they kept everything so hush hush and only informed them at the last minute, or after the event, or not at all. Everyone, except the newcomer Manal Kumar, had been involved in the deal at some stage or the other.

They held a secret meeting after office hours and chalked out a common strategy. That everything was done in good faith, that there was no question of anything even remotely illegal in the deal; that there was no rule that every case of leasing of spectrum from a satellite to a private vendor had to be informed to the cabinet or the science commission; that there were enough precedents for this, including the leasing of the satellite to the telecom giant TerrAkask, (who were currently great favourites of the government) where no details of the vendor had been given to either the science council or the cabinet about the leasing of the transponders. As for getting permission from other telecom authorities, their view was that this was a new hybrid technology, a combination of the space and ground segments, and there were no rules at all regarding this. And if there were no rules, what kind of permissions would they ask for? It was a reasonable interpretation that the question of permissions did not arise.

The odd man out was Manal Kumar, who was anyway not a part of the secret meeting. He drafted his reply logically and systematically, that he was not aware at all regarding the deal, and if anyone had hidden the facts, it was the GAVA MD or the Chairman ISA. Besides, it was not within his powers to question either of them, either technically or administratively. He added that he was just four months in the organisation, and was not personally involved in any meeting or negotiations that took place before the cabinet note was processed.

Maharishi wrote his standard note justifying the agreement and how it would benefit GAVA and the country by entering the market in a big way and giving lower prices to the telephone using public, with state-of-the-art technology.

Ashutosh Prasad arrived for the second time, and was received again by Gurupriya, her *kumkum* blazing and her *mangalsutra* and cleavage discreetly covered. So, you're quite an item, thought Ashutosh, as he returned her greeting and *namaskar*. They made small talk about the weather and climate change, the fast urbanisation happening everywhere, and the rising costs of fruit and vegetables.

The next day, Ashutosh Prasad received the written statements from all the scientists and bureaucrats. He did ask all of them whether they wanted to say anything else in addition to what they had written. Some of them muttered a few sentences that nothing irregular or illegal had been done.

Manal Kumar requested a personal hearing and emphasised that he had processed the papers for the Cabinet note soon after taking charge four months ago.

"Sir, you can see from the Cabinet Note file that I have not been kept informed of the Oriont contract by anyone from GAVA or from ISA or from the secretariat.

I have processed the cabinet note on the basis of whatever information I had been given by MD GAVA, and in my position, I have no powers to question the information supplied by GAVA, whose chairman is none other than the chairman of ISA and also our Secretary."

"You had no knowledge of the contract you say?"

"Yes, sir. I had no knowledge. The first time I heard of it was from the newspapers. I'm sure you've seen in all the files and papers that I was not part of any of the committees or the GAVA meeting where the contract was approved."

Ashutosh nodded and said, "Anything else you want to say?"

"No, that is all sir, thank you." He rose and left the room, swearing to himself.

What a den he had landed himself into. His mind went back to his school days and his knowledge of Hindu mythology. Yes indeed, he had no doubt he was surrounded by the *asuras* of *antariksh*.

ASHUTOSH ASKED HIS assistants to compile all the written statements. Later, he dictated some notes to the stenographer, making a synopsis.

What a criminal waste of time, he thought. His draft report was already with Raja Bhaiyya. All he had to do was to add this junk to it.

Maharishi Nath spent an hour with him alone, stating his case forcefully and speaking in defence of his organisation and its dedication as convincingly as he could. He remembered the information from the listening device in Ashutosh's room that Satyadev and Gurupriya were to be let off. Smart cats both of them, and sly as hell. But he still did not know that he was a doomed man even before the enquiry had begun.

That evening, Ashutosh Prasad had been invited for dinner by his batchmates who had retired and settled in Mumbai. The next day, he returned to Delhi with another box of papers. He added some nonsensical stuff to the report that he had already sent to Raja Bhaiyya and sent it off to Prakrit immediately.

He telephoned Prakrit but was informed by his PS that he was not available as he was in important meetings throughout the day. Ashutosh Prasad could understand as yet another scandal was creating headlines in the papers about some purchase of radar systems from a South African firm, which again led to the doorstep of Raja Bhaiyya.

With great difficulty, Ashutosh Prasad managed to get an appointment with Raja Bhaiyya and Prakrit Nayyar after two days.

Prakrit had merely glanced through the report but had read the recommendations carefully. The chairman

ISA, the managing director GAVA, and the heads of the communications and satellite divisions were held responsible, and all senior bureaucrats, deputies and above, except for Gurupriya, were guilty of dereliction of duty and lack of due diligence. No details or reasons were given, but then, how did it matter.

Ashutosh Prasad met Prakrit, and had some perfunctory discussion about the recommendations of his report. They then went to Raja Bhaiyya's room. He looked unhappy and unwell.

"So, Ashutosh, what did you find? Prakrit has briefed me but I wanted to hear from you."

"Well, sir, what a tough job this was. In my entire career, I have never had such a challenging responsibility. There was so much hostility. No one was prepared to show me the original papers—neither the scientists, nor the bureaucrats in the secretariat. I literally had to bulldoze my way through and threaten them with dire consequences. Anyway, I was able to secure the most crucial files and papers, and have given the report to Prakrit. If you give the okay, I will sign it and hand it over to the prime minister's office."

"Prakrit, have you studied it carefully?" Raja Bhaiyya asked.

"Sir, I've gone through it, but will do so again more carefully this evening. May I discuss it with you tomorrow morning?"

"But Ashutosh, what did you find in your report?"

"Sir, all the senior scientists—the chairman ISA, the MD GAVA, the communications and satellites heads are involved, and all the bureaucrats have connived. I've recorded it all in the report."

Ashutosh briefly ran through the recommendations, one by one. Raja Bhaiyya glanced through them and said, "Yes, but what about corruption and money changing hands."

"Well, on the face of it, it is a corrupt deal, no doubt. But for making an allegation of corruption, according to the law, we would have had to do a thorough study of the books of Oriont and the personal accounts of the officers, which of course I couldn't do, according to my terms of reference. For that, we would require a regular enquiry by the Federal Investigation Board, the FIB."

"Prakrit, show me the report with your comments by tomorrow morning. And after that, I want it to be sent to the prime minister, and ask him to order an enquiry by the Federal Investigation Board. They must all be booked by FIB. Doing deals like this by themselves and bringing shame to our government, with us not knowing a thing about it."

"Yes, sir. I'll have my brief ready by tomorrow morning for discussion."

Both Prakrit and Ashutosh left Raja Bhaiyya's office.

"Well, Prakrit, now the ball is in your court. Let me

know as soon as boss has given the nod. I'll present the report to the prime minister's office after that."

"Yes sir, you'll hear from me by tomorrow afternoon." Ashutosh Prasad took his leave.

SHUKRA DEVI WAS despondent. It was almost four months that the new chairman Maharishi Nath had taken over, and he had not shown the slightest bit of interest in her.

She would go to the beauty parlour near her house, would get her face bleached and threaded, get her eyebrows shaped, but it seemed to make no difference. Maharishi still paid her no attention. He would just call her for some dictation, or ask her to fix some meetings or appointments, and that was it.

And then, there was also something else bothering her… the information that she had given to Aslam Yunus in the ministry about the money that had changed hands between Oriont and the ISA. Of course, the chairman did not know about this, but it could land her in a big soup if the whole affair snowballed into a more serious enquiry. She could even be called as a witness, and that would spell doom for her. Betraying the trust of her masters. Unpardonable.

Shukra Devi became even more despondent. She decided to phone Aslam Yunus and ask him what was going on about Ashutosh Prasad's enquiry. She called him up on his private phone and requested him to get approval from the minister for some important appointments that had to be made for the Russian delegation which was visiting ISA during the next week.

She continued with a studied casualness, "And Aslam sir, what is the latest on the Ashutosh enquiry? We haven't heard anything about it."

"Oh, that? Nothing official has come to us yet. But a lot of rumours are flying around that it is a matter of time that an FIB enquiry would be ordered against the scientists including the chairman. Now, keep this to yourself. They may just be only rumours."

Shukra Devi was stunned. How could this happen? ISA scientists were sacrosanct. This had never happened before, even though deals much more scandalous than the Oriont deal had sailed through so smoothly, right under the nose of the government.

"Sir," she said to Aslam, "I don't know what is going on, but only you can protect me. I am a poor woman who must work hard to support my family. You know my husband only drinks and squanders money and doesn't do any work. Please see no harm comes to me. I am only a humble PS."

Aslam raised his eyebrow over the phone—yes,

indeed, only a humble PS, he thought, who runs a whole underworld down there in space, and keeps all the chairmen hooked on to her bed. But he also thought—she's a trustworthy and generous woman. Enough money reaches me every month for my family to have a decent life. She doesn't cheat on that. Of course, he would help her.

"Yes," he spoke, "I will keep you informed if I hear anything, and also try and help you, particularly about the FIB enquiry."

The mere sound of FIB terrified Shukra Devi further. She had to act fast and she had to act now.

Maharishi Nath had just finished his lunch. She buzzed him on his telephone and asked him if she could come in to discuss something important.

He replied, "Yes, of course. If it's really important."

Meanwhile, she had looked at herself in the mirror in the bathroom to make sure that her hair was in place, her eyes lined conspicuously, and her sari tight around her waist. She just had to make Maharishi notice. All the more, as he was perfectly aware of what his entitlements were from his inherited PS.

She entered the chairman's office bringing in a whiff of jasmine. She had rubbed some jasmine oil on her arms just before entering his office.

Maharishi looked up without showing any interest. "Yes, what is it?" he asked, and returned to his computer.

"Sir, please forgive me, but there is some news I have heard from one of my colleagues in Delhi which I must share with you."

"Yes, what is it?" Maharishi replied, his head still fixed on the computer screen.

"Sir, I am told that an FIB enquiry will be ordered into this whole Oriont contract."

"Yes, so let them go ahead and order," he said, his eyes still on the computer screen, "how does it matter?" knowing fully well that it mattered plenty.

"Sir, with your permission, may I suggest something. You will be going to Raigarh on Saturday to lecture at Sri Sri Om Amma University. May I come with you?"

"Why do you want to come?" he asked, finally looking up.

"Sir, there's a temple around twenty kilometers away from the university, a *Shakti* temple (temple dedicated to goddess Durga), very powerful. We could ask the temple head who knows very powerful *mantras* to do a special *homa* (ritual with fire) for us. They follow the South Indian tradition of *mantras,* which I believe are very powerful."

"A special *homa*? What for?" he asked with slight irritation.

"Sir, to protect us from the evil designs of all our enemies."

Maharishi was now looking at her with some curiosity and Shukra Devi decided to extend her heavily lined eyes, with lids half closed, something which used to have an almost immediate effect on her previous bosses.

But Maharishi remained disinterested, or pretended to be so.

"Please go ahead, Shukra Devi, if you have the faith. I'll give you the leave if you want."

"No sir, it's you who has to be present at the *puja*. It's you they are trying to harm. I'm only your PS and I'm willing to take any risks or blame to protect you." Shukra Devi extended her half-lidded eyes further.

This time Maharishi noticed, and his irritation increased. Surely, this was no time for seduction. His organisation was in deep trouble and he had to do everything to see that he was not attacked personally. But a *puja* in a temple? Was it not supposed to be inauspicious to refuse one, even if it was a *Shakti* temple, probably *tantrik*? (esoteric ritual, sometimes occult) According to the tradition he was brought up with, refusal of a *puja* was never a good thing to do, so he gave in.

"Okay, Shukra Devi, go and arrange it. I will come after my lecture in the university. But remember, complete confidentiality."

"Sir, I have worked with Dr Satyadev and you over the last ten years. Can you point out a single instance when I have betrayed any confidence?"

"No, as a matter of fact, I can't, but I am still new here."

"Thank you, sir. So, I will fix it for the afternoon of

Saturday after your lecture is over."

Maharishi looked at her and nodded.

Shukra Devi started work immediately. She called up the temple priest, one Vaidyacharya, a master of *tantric* rites, and told him that she was coming with a very eminent national figure, her chairman, and that a special *puja* had to be performed to protect them from the evil designs of some enemies who were trying to harm them.

"Any particular *puja*, ma?"

"Yes, the one that destroys the enemies and protects us from all harm."

"Then we should do the *Mahakali puja.*"

"And don't worry about the money. I'll give you whatever you want."

"I never asked for any money from you, ma. It's enough for me that you are coming here with your high officer."

"But, *panditji*, this should be kept absolutely secret. No one should know."

"Certainly, ma. All our *pujas* are kept secret."

Shukra Devi took leave on Friday and went off to Raigarh and stayed the night at Om Amma's *ashram*, taking part in all kinds of prayer ceremonies and *bhajans* (hymns). Next day, she drove off to the *tartrik's* temple to arrange for the evening *puja*, and to ensure that there was complete secrecy maintained at the temple. She also reserved two rooms at a fairly comfortable hotel near the seaside, because she knew that *tantrik pujas* went on for quite long, and in all likelihood, they would have to spend the night there.

Maharishi gave a good lecture to the students of Sri Sri Om Amma University regarding the basics of India's space programmes, and their importance for the country's development. The students loved it, and he was besieged for photographs and autographs. He then had a long *darshan* (audience) with Sri Sri Om Amma herself, and she blessed him with *mantras*, doing *aarti* over his head, and then with some more *mantras* into his ears. He touched her feet and then went on to check the finances with Ramanna Madhav, keeper of funds. Yes, part funds were here intact, and others had been secreted to their destinations.

He remembered he had this *homa* to attend after this. Why had he agreed to this nonsense, he wondered… must have been that ingrained belief in him that one never refused a good *puja*….

And so he was spirited off to the *Shakti* temple in one of Om Amma's luxurious cars, the latest Mercedes Benz, which Shukra Devi had arranged. Shukra Devi was waiting for him at the temple door. She escorted him inside and led him to a private room where he could bathe and dress in the temple attire with *angavastra*, and prepare to meet the head priest Vaidyacharya. Maharishi obediently did what he was told by Shukra Devi.

He emerged with his *angavastra* and sacred thread, and was escorted by Shukra Devi to the head priest Vaidyacharya. He bent and touched his feet.

Vaidyacharya muttered a *mantra* and addressed Maharishi, "Fear not. God will protect you. We will begin the *puja*."

He led Maharishi through several dingy corridors to a hall where there were pictures of the mighty *Durga* (warrior goddess who destroys evil forces), wearing a garland of skulls, slaying demons, with blood dripping from her mouth and hands. Piles of fruit and flowers were arranged around the goddess. The place was flooded with lamps with soothing little flames. There were circles and triangles of them in various places, and lines of them in strategic corners.

Two other priests were sitting near a central place surrounded by burning lamps, where a fire had to be lit. Vaidyacharya started on a never-ending chant of *mantras*, propitiating various gods and goddesses which Maharishi could make little sense of. He started admonishing himself for coming here, but consciously corrected himself. He had to be positive and in harmony with whatever the priests were doing and do whatever Vaidyacharya asked him to do.

Vaidyacharya's *mantras* continued. He handed Maharishi a can of *ghee* (purified butter) to pour over the sandalwood pieces stacked in the urn, and then bade him light them with burning camphor, spray a jet of vermillion over them, then cut a few lemons and fill them with vermillion and place them in certain strategic places around the urn.

The flames were rising higher. The priests went on with their chants, god knows what, but it went on endlessly with Maharishi being ordered every now and then to stand up, walk around the fire, first clockwise, then anti clockwise, sit down, throw some more *ghee* and incense into the fire, sprinkle some more vermillion, cut a few more lemons, dress them up with vermillion, place them in certain locations, and so on.

Shukra Devi sat on the ground with her eyes tightly shut, her hands folded and her bosom generously covered.

The *mantras* went on and on, with Maharishi being ordered every few minutes to repeat some of them, bow before the deity, light some more lamps, touch various corners of the room, and then pour more *ghee* and incense into the fire. He went through the whole ritual for three hours. Finally, it was time for the conches to shout loud, the fire to be enhanced with more *ghee*, the coconuts to be smashed, the lemons to be crushed, and the final *aarti* and *purnahuti* (final ritual).

The demons threatening Maharishi and Shukra Devi had been annihilated by this *Mahakali puja.*

Maharishi gave his *dakshina* (contribution) and Shukra Devi did the same. The *prasadam* (religious offerings), vermillion, turmeric and betel leaves were packed into a bag and given to both.

Both Maharishi and Shukra Devi touched Vaidyacharya's feet and sought his blessings.

"Have no fear, the almighty will protect you," were Vaidyacharya's last words to them.

SHUKRA DEVI ESCORTED Maharishi to the car waiting outside, and they drove to the hotel. She had already done the registration and had the room keys in her hand.

"Sir, I knew it would get late, so I booked two rooms at the Seaside Hotel. It's the best one here," she said, as she led him up the lift to his room, "please let me know if you need anything."

"Thank you," he said, as he went into his room exhausted, with Shukra Devi following him.

"Sir, may I order dinner for you? It's been a long day for you, sir."

"Okay. Order anything. I'll come down."

"Sir, you could have it here if you wish. There is a nice sitting room in your suite. You would be tired. I could order your dinner for you here."

"Okay, that's fine. Just order a simple dinner. Some chappatis, dal and vegetables."

"Yes sir, I'll see that it is served here," she said. But she was disappointed. Maharashi had not invited her to join him for dinner. But anyhow, she would be popping in soon to supervise the dinner service. That would take care of a few things.

Shukra Devi ordered the chairman's dinner—a good green salad and vegetable soup, chappatis, dal and vegetables as he wished, curds, and some nice *kulfi* for dessert.

She thought she would go to her room and freshen up and then supervise the arrangements for dinner, which would take about twenty minutes to serve according to the chef.

She entered the bathroom to wash her face and apply some make up, especially around her eyes. But, first, she badly wanted to use the commode.

She sat on it, and at the very second that she was about to expel, she experienced a huge explosion, like a high velocity jet of steam escaping from her....

She froze in a state of shock. Oh god, the *tantrik's mantras* were rebounding upon her... a rocket was being shot off through her... her insides had burst and she would die, right here in this bathroom.

She jumped up from the commode, still in shock and frozen with fear. She jumped yet again, but the jet of escaping steam continued. Her heart was pounding and she was breathing very fast. She turned still for a moment, her ears straining.

It was an exceptionally robust pressure cooker spouting steam, in the neighbouring house, just outside her open window.

She almost collapsed with relief.

Badly shaken, and still quite breathless, she rushed through her makeup and called room service to check how much more time the service would take. She was informed that dinner was on its way.

She decided she would wait outside his room until the dinner was brought. She ran down the steps and stood outside Maharishi's room.

Soon the food trolley appeared and the waiter pressed the doorbell.

Maharishi opened the door and she entered the suite along with the waiter and supervised the laying of the dinner. Maharishi returned to the bedroom. The food was laid, and she gently knocked at the connecting door informing him that dinner was served.

Maharishi emerged again and sat down. "What about your dinner? Have you finished?"

"No sir. I wanted to make sure it was served to you first."

"Well, that's a lot for me to eat. There's enough here for two. I hate wasting food. Unless you want to eat something else."

"No sir, I'll be happy to share this with you."

So, the first obstacle was overcome. They had dinner, the two of them. Shukra Devi was still terribly shaken by her commode and pressure cooker experience. She was sure it was a bad omen.

Maharishi was experiencing a terrible headache. It must have been a result of those fumes of camphor and ghee and wood that he had to inhale for three hours.

They started their dinner. There was the vegetable soup that Maharishi did not want, so Shukra Devi had it. Maharishi merely nibbled at the food, and went straight for the curds. His headache was getting worse.

"Sir, but you've not eaten anything."

"I have this blasted headache and I find that I have left my aspirin behind. Well, it's past ten o clock now. I suppose all the shops will be closed."

"Sir, if its aspirin you need, I have some. I always carry it too. And I also have a wonderful ayurvedic balm that works miracles for a headache. I will get it right away."

"Yes, I think I need it. Thank you, Shukra Devi."

She stayed until the waiters had cleared up, and then went to her room to fetch the aspirin and the special ayurvedic balm.

Maharishi was clearly in a bad state. His head was splitting and his mind disoriented. He lay down and covered his eyes with a sheet.

Shukra Devi knocked on the half open door, "Sir, I have the aspirin and the balm. May I come in?

"Yes," Maharishi shouted in irritation and disgust at his vulnerability.

Shukra Devi entered, poured a glass of water and administered the aspirin.

"Thank you," he muttered.

"Sir, shall I now apply this special balm on your forehead?"

Maharishi did not answer. So Shukra Devi went ahead, starting from his forehead to the crown, down the nape of his neck, his shoulders, his clavicles.

It felt good…there was great relief… and he growled in comfort. The massaging continued, and he was about to doze off. And then he felt fingers going down his back and chest, massaging up and down. He was just half-awake. The pain in his head was receding, and he was uttering some sounds of relief and pleasure.

Shukra Devi was beginning to sense some satisfaction. She was now kneeling beside him on the bed, her hands alternating between the massage down his chest, going lower towards his abdomen and down his back, as far as she could go inside his shirt. She knew it was just a matter of time.

Maharishi's comfort was increasing, and the pain in his head was reducing. His eyes were shut and he was drifting into orbits of the most pleasurable kind.

He opened his eyes. There were some levers moving up and down his body, and he felt an inflatable sort of a payload, probably made of silicone, which was disturbing the aerodynamics going on somewhere around him....

He tried to calculate the drag force... the lift force... the torque and centre of gravity... but they were all wrong and working at cross purposes... not what was required for a perfect lift off... he tried to locate the unfurlable antenna... but saw instead Marilyn Monroe's full blown, unfurled skirt, the iconic picture that he would stare at as a young lad....

The levers were going beneath his clothes... he removed his shirt and felt his hands accelerate the levers, their force and momentum, and led them further down... he muttered something and thought lovingly of his phallic rockets, and sighed in pleasure... his headache had almost disappeared.

Shukra Devi was triumphant. Maharishi felt the inflatable, silicone payload rolling over his face. He pulled it down towards himself, thinking of his grand rockets and their satellite mates.

It turned out to be a perfect launch.

The seduction was over, and Shukra Devi added one more point to her score board.

WHEN MAHARISHI RETURNED to his office on Monday, the atmosphere wasn't exactly comfortable.

There were repeated calls from his predecessor, Satyadev, asking for an urgent meeting. Repeated calls from journalists asking for appointments, and repeated calls from the minister's office asking for status reports on the implementation of the Oriont contract.

He asked his scientific secretary to prepare a note on the Oriont contract implementation for the minister, and gave Satyadev time to meet him the next day.

Satyadev came over and sounded rather high pitched and worried. "I must inform you Maharishi, that I have reliably learnt from my sources in Delhi that an FIB enquiry will be announced any day."

What's your problem, Maharishi thought, looking benignly at Satyadev... you've already bought yourself immunity… But he feigned an expression of surprise and realised that Shukra Devi's information was correct. Wisely, he had turned his recording device on.

Satyadev continued, "You are aware that the government is facing serious allegations not only in the telecom affair, but also in our matter. So, before it reaches the minister's doorstep, they want to scuttle it by ordering an FIB enquiry. That will deflect attention and keep everybody quiet for the next parliament session. By then, everything will be forgotten."

Maharishi remained silent. Did Satyadev think he was such a fool that he would believe him?

"Well, sir, from what I have seen, once enquiries

start, they go out of everyone's hand. Besides, wouldn't starting such an enquiry harm the government much more? What will it do to our organisation? To the morale of the scientists? There would be serious repercussions."

"Do you think the PM or the minister think of these things when they are being attacked? They are just looking for scapegoats, and ISA, you and I, will be the scapegoats."

What Maharishi did not know and had not yet guessed was that Satyadev had already got his powerful American contacts to inform the prime minister that he was not to be touched in the FIB enquiry.

"So, what do you suggest we should do?" Maharishi asked.

"First, we should get all the papers together, right from the start. Then, we should check what are the potentially incriminating papers, if any. And after that, decide how we should deal with them," Satyadev replied firmly.

He continued, "You know, these FIB chaps are a bunch of illiterate clowns. They will just pick up everything they can find and call it evidence of corruption or a conspiracy. But we will have to deal with them too. Can't escape it."

"Okay, we already have all the papers. They had been put together for that Ashutosh fellow. When would you like to see them?"

"I think tomorrow would be a good idea. It's a holiday. So, there will be just you and me. Vidyasagar should also be here. No one else. We shall handle this among ourselves. No one from the secretariat. They are not to be trusted. Not even Gurupriya. We could meet at 9 am right here."

The next day, Vidyasagar had assembled all the papers starting from the Oriont negotiations and meetings before the Haridas committee was constituted; papers relating to the cabinet note, both from ISA and the secretariat; all the correspondence with Oriont; and some stray papers and letters from ISA, GAVA and the secretariat.

The papers were neatly piled with as much cataloging as was possible.

They assembled the next day at 9 am. There were no PAs—only Satyadev, Maharishi, and Vidyasagar.

Satyadev started examining the papers of his time. He removed all those where he had individually signed any Oriont correspondence, including the memorandum of understanding he had signed with them, and kept them aside.

Only those papers of his time that also bore signatures of Gurupriya or other bureaucrats or Vidyasagar were retained.

Maharishi was watching carefully, but chose to remain silent. He was beginning to see Satyadev's game. No papers individually incriminating Satyadev would remain in the pile. Papers relating to the Haridas committee were allowed to remain as they already contained the involvement of all the bureaucrats. So too, the papers relating to the GAVA Board meetings.

The cabinet note papers had a problem because too many pages had been switched by Maharishi in Delhi, and the remaining pages did not match. But Satyadev was not interested in them, as they were well after his time. They were Maharishi's problem.

Satyadev bundled the sheets he had removed and placed them in a file. Maharishi stared at him.

"What do you plan to do with them, sir?"

"Tear them up. What else did you think?" he replied without concern. "Now, none of you can talk about it, you know that. Our loyalty to each other and to our organisation is paramount. And you know that I'm not doing this for myself, but only for ISA and my brother scientists."

He flung his arms on each side and tried to look *satvik* (virtuous), and then he returned to his bundle of papers and started tearing them up, page by page.

Maharishi and Vidyasagar looked at each other in shock, in disgust, and in awe. Here was their senior, their guru, committing a criminal act right in front of them.

Satyadev finished tearing the pages, stuffed the pieces in a plastic bag that he pulled out of his briefcase, and then put it back inside the briefcase.

"Now, I've sanitised my bit. You do yours."

He looked at his watch.

"I can be with you for another half hour. Well, I've been through the cabinet note papers. I know we did not show all of them to that chap Ashutosh when he came, but when the FIB fellows come, it will be different. They can search and seize anything they want, which Ashutosh could not do. And these pages that you have switched in Delhi where you added that bit that you had been approached by several companies and were negotiating with them, those need to be built up through the bureaucrats."

"And how do you propose we do that?" Maharishi asked with his impassive face, wondering how the hell he knew about the switching of papers in Delhi. Clearly, Satyadev made it his business to know about everything that happened at ISA on an hourly basis.

"Simple. Just do some distorted overwriting on it with the same colour ink used by the chap, cut out the 'approached by a reputed company' bit, and write 'approached by several reputed companies' over it."

"Who will do that?"

"Any of you."

Now the bastard wants us to become forgers, thought Maharishi, after he's torn up all his own incriminating papers.

"Which bureaucrat do you have in mind?"

"Manal Kumar. A little too cocky, isn't he? Very arrogant. Always so condescending. Never cares about anything we say. Even disobeys us. He's the real danger. So, fix him before he gets too dangerous."

"But it's the others, Sushil Ramu and Gurupriya, who have suppressed the facts of the contract. And there are plenty of papers to establish that. We cannot burn up all the papers, can we?

"Don't worry about that. We'll handle that when the time comes. But, do the over writing, so that Manal Kumar becomes the person who inserted it. Otherwise, you can be in trouble over the switched note. And if Manal Kumar is the one who is fixed, the whole case falls flat, doesn't it?"

Satyadev looked at his watch again. "I must leave now, I have to catch a flight to Delhi. There's a reception at the American Embassy that I must attend. The ambassador called me personally." He picked up his briefcase and started to walk towards the door. Maharishi accompanied him down to his car and then returned to his office.

As soon as he returned to his room, Maharishi broke into the loudest, most uncontrollable bout of laughter he had ever had in his adult life.

Vidyasagar, himself recovering from shock, didn't know what to do. He thought Maharishi was breaking down under stress and getting hit by a hysteria attack. He poured a glass of water for him. "Sir, are you all right?" he asked.

"Yes, yes, I'm all right, bloody all right, Vidyasagar. Never been better," and he continued laughing.

"Oh, my god," he said, "I've never seen anything like this in my life." He placed his hand on his fountain pen on the table, and laughed some more.

"Come on, Vidyasagar. We are going to enhance our criminal skills. Start practising. You are the most qualified and experienced. Try and get Manal Kumar's handwriting, and finish the damned thing. I'm sick and tired of it."

Vidyasagar started practising the words in Manal Kumar's handwriting, and after several rounds, was satisfied with the result. It had taken six sheets of A 4 paper. Finally, he pulled out one of the drafts of the cabinet note from the file, struck out the words 'approached by a very qualified company' with a blue ball point pen with the same colour of ink that Manal Kumar had signed with, and scrawled the words 'several very qualified companies' above it.

The deed was done. He stared at his work with intense concentration. It was pretty good. At a cursory glance, there was enough resemblance.

"Well, how does this look, sir?" Vidyasagar asked Maharishi.

Maharishi stared hard at it, "Not bad. Not bad at all." He stared some more. "Pretty good, in fact. You should be running a counterfeiting business," he laughed.

They then removed several drafts with Manal

Kumar's corrections on it, which had been sent to other offices. The entire ISA file on the subject was recreated, retaining just a few letters to the secretariat which meant nothing at all. Drafts sent to the finance ministry and cabinet secretariat had already been switched earlier, so there was no harm leaving them there.

The bundle of papers was quite huge, and it would have taken a long time tearing them manually. So, they were pushed into the shredder and the remains collected in a plastic bag to be cremated later in Vidyasagar's home.

The place now felt pure and sanitised. Both Vidyasagar and Maharishi felt tired, hungry and relieved.

The FIB goons could come whenever they wanted.

THE NEXT DAY, Maharishi made a quick trip to Sri Sri Om Amma's *ashram*, and sought a darshan with her.

She saw him almost immediately. He touched her feet and sought her blessings.

"Om Amma, mother, I need your protection in the PMO. I hear they are determined to falsely implicate me in an enquiry to be done by the FIB, to save some others. It's all dirty politics. I need your protection."

Om Amma's beatific expression became a little perplexed this time. "Strange, just a few days ago, one of your officers, Sushil Ramu, who has become my devotee also, was here. He said the same thing to me. Of course, I blessed him and promised to protect him. And I bless you and will protect you also. Why are they doing this to all god-fearing people, all my good devotees? I will speak to them. Go in peace and without fear."

Maharishi touched her feet, and she blessed him, and chanted her *mantras* into his ear.

Not bad, he thought, his deputy administration officer had beaten him to it. These IAS chaps did indeed have very strong information networks.

MEANWHILE, NEWS ABOUT an impending FIB investigation had spread like wildfire throughout the organization. The media too, once again started reporting it on television channels and in newspaper columns and editorials, and the entire chronology of the Oriont deal was brought back to the forefront.

Raja Bhaiyya decided to take the Ashutosh Prasad report to the prime minister. "See what they're doing in the scientific development ministry. Signing multi-million-dollar contracts which they don't even inform us about. In fact, they go out of their way to hide them from us. Here's the report by Ashutosh Prasad on the GAVA Oriont deal which has given us so much trouble. See what they did and caused such a scandal, for which we are being held responsible. We must refer this to the FIB. As for Pratap Singh, he deserves no mercy, even though he's your favourite."

The prime minister handed over the report to his principal secretary, Pushpendra Vedi, an eminent and respected retired civil servant from Bengal. "Pushpendra, go through this. It is serious. Very serious allegations have been made against us. All because of some nefarious goings on in the scientific development ministry, which the minister has done behind our back, for which I am being held responsible. Let there be a strong message in this so that they can learn a lesson, and others too. An FIB enquiry immediately."

Pushpendra Vedi dutifully took the file and replied, "Yes, sir. I'll go through it immediately and then let you know the best way to proceed."

The prime minister did not even look at him, and Pushpendra Vedi left with the file.

Later Raja Bhaiyya met the prime minister in the house. "This is scandalous, papaji. The money that Pratap Singh has made on this—I have it from credible sources from many sides. At least a hundred crores for starters, and shares and benami companies in Mauritius and Virgin Islands. And we have to bear all the blame. A real traitor, this Pratap Singh. Don't spare him."

"No, we won't. The FIB enquiry will take care of him."

Pushpendra Vedi went through the file in a cursory manner. The prime minister wanted an FIB enquiry. That was it. He called his senior secretary and asked him to go through the papers in detail, and prepare the note for sending the Ashutosh Prasad report to the FIB for further action, through the scientific development minister.

The next day, the prime minister took him aside and said, "Pushpendra, let me know the day on which the case is sent to the FIB. There's bound to be a lot of press coverage on that. Just spread the word that the government is considering cancellation of the deal. It will be good for us. And by the way, you may also start looking at the options we have for cancelling the contract. It's not good for us to have it hanging over our heads with so many state elections coming up within the next one year."

"Yes, sir, but for that, I'll have to call the same chairman ISA who has steered the contract stealthily to the cabinet. That may not work. We'll see what we can do. I will talk to the scientific development minister."

"Yes, we must talk to him, that's true, but that doesn't have to be done now. He's the one who's behind it all, so there's no point in telling him this now. He'll surely scuttle it. First, call the FIB director and tell him what we want. Make him issue the enquiry orders, and only after that go and inform the minister with the best bureaucratic skills that you have. But first get the FIB to take up the enquiry. After that, we'll talk about cancelling or annulling the deal."

"Okay sir, as you wish. Let me first take a look at it."

Pushpendra Vedi recalled the file from his senior secretary and studied it more carefully that night. It was a complex issue with a lot of technicalities that he couldn't quite understand. He needed some help from a trustworthy source. The next day, he summoned a retired scientist, Dr SK Ghosh, whom he knew from his days as Defence Secretary. Dr Ghosh had started his career in ISA, but left after a few years to join the Aeronautical Research Institute in Calcutta, from where he retired as director. He was now advisor to a global telecom company, Mercury International.

Professor Ghosh was received at the entrance of the prime minister's office and was escorted into Pushpendra Vedi's office. He felt very good at the prospect of advising none less than the prime minister's principal secretary.

"Ah, come in, come in, Professor Ghosh. Good to see you again. You are badly needed. I need some advice urgently. It's about the GAVA Oriont affair. I'm sure you would have read about it in the papers."

"Yes, sir, I have followed it in the papers. Such a pity that ISA is going through rough times."

"Well, everything goes through good times and rough times. I'm going to give you a copy of Ashutosh Prasad's report. You must have read about it in the papers too. Please go through it and tell me what's right with it and what's wrong with it."

Professor Ghosh looked at him silently. Pushpendra Vedi continued, "There's one problem though—the report cannot leave this office. So, you may use my anteroom and study it. I am out of this office till evening. I will be in the PM's home office and then there's a cabinet meeting. So, please make yourself comfortable here. My PA is at your disposal, should you need to make any notes or dictate anything. You just have to buzz for him. They will serve you lunch here too. I should be back here only around 7 pm. If you haven't finished by then and need to come again tomorrow, just let me know in the evening."

"Perfectly fine, sir. This is a great honour," said Ghosh, eyeing the thick file.

Pushpendra left for the prime minister's home office and Prof Ghosh wondered what he was getting into.

He started reading the report, page by page. What had happened in ISA was nothing unusual. They had done it all the time, flaunting every rule in the book, building up an image for themselves based on obsolete technology, fooling the nation with the backing of the politicians and media, and more recently, a string of godmen and women. He knew them too well, their questionable financial dealings for which the line between corruption and themselves was very narrow, their bluffs which the politicians and ordinary people swallowed with gullibility and pride.

He read the report painstakingly. There was plenty wrong with it. But when he read the recommendations, he was astounded.

There was no doubt that Maharishi and Vidyasagar were guilty of concealing the facts from the cabinet, but the report conveniently buried the role of Satyadev, the real father of the deal. And the role of the main bureaucrat, Gurupriya, who had steered the deal from the time of Satyadev to the present day, was not mentioned anywhere in the report.

He went through the contract and its technical content. The technology that Oriont claimed they possessed seemed highly ambitious, and he was doubtful whether Oriont really possessed it. Just one of two companies in the world had it, to the best of his knowledge. However, he thought he should not comment about that now without studying it carefully.

Professor Ghosh buzzed for the PS and gave his dictation. The gist of it was that while the contract may be good, the fault lay in the concealment of it from the cabinet when building a satellite for Oriont. And for that, all those who were in the know of it and had concealed it while processing the cabinet papers, had been exonerated by Prasad.

True to his word, Pushpendra returned to his office

around 7 pm.

"So, Professor Ghosh, how was it? I'm really grateful for all the trouble you've taken."

"Sir, I have gone through the papers and made my note. Here it is."

Pushpendra glanced through it and went to the last para.

"Hmm. This is serious. So, Prasad has left out the main culprits. Interesting."

Professor Ghosh was getting a little tired.

"Anyway, let me go through this tonight, and if I need your assistance further, I will request you to come over. My sincere thanks."

"Not at all, sir."

"And professor, someone will call you tomorrow regarding your consultation fee."

"No sir, that's not necessary. This is an honour."

He felt good, sitting in this office, passing judgment over his former colleagues who had been the cause of so much humiliation to him when he was in ISA.

The next day, Pushpendra Vedi called the FIB director, Paul Jacob, to his office to instruct him about the enquiry. Paul Jacob was a through gentleman from the Tamil Nadu cadre, who spent an enormous amount of time on humanitarian activities and conservation and environment through his NGO called *Jai Prakriti*, and during the remaining time he indulged heavily in physical fitness and golf. After becoming the FIB director, a large part of the spacious grounds around his office were converted into a nice little putting and practice range. The nitty gritty and turmoil of the FIB was handled very efficiently by his deputy Prashant Sardana, a politically savvy man about town, who took orders directly either from Raja Bhaiyya or the prime minister's office, or from some favoured business houses. He had no interest in finding out what was right or wrong, ethical or unethical, or even what was legal or illegal, in the investigations that he supervised.

Because of his astuteness and ability to read the political mind, Paul Jacob always carried him to all his meetings. Sardana would handle all the pleasantries and politics, while Paul Jacob would visualise himself hitting his next birdie.

Just before leaving the FIB headquarters for the meeting, Sardana got a call from an eminent godman from Rishikesh who was very influential with Raja Bhaiyya, one Sri Raghavachari.

Sri Raghavachari started speaking in a tone of benediction, blessing Sardana and his family, and seeking divine grace for him to perform his duty like Arjuna in the *Bhagawad Gita*.

Sardana thanked him for his blessings and waited for the catch. The godman continued, "You are going to be asked to perform a very difficult duty very soon about the Oriont deal. I just wanted to advise you for your own protection, do not be misled by what others tell you. There are two people who must not be harmed under any circumstances. They have done so much for our country, and instead of honouring them, we are trying to disgrace them. Satyadev, who is also my devotee, has been one of our greatest scientists, a god-fearing man who has brought much honour to our country. And his officer, Gurupriya, she is also my devotee, a fine god-fearing lady, so kind and helpful to everyone. There are many evil forces trying to harm them. You must not allow it."

"*Guruji,*" said Sardana, "I hear your words with great respect. But I really don't know too much of the details except what I've read in the newspapers. Let me see when I get the papers."

"But remember my advice. There is a grand design to destroy our most respected scientists," the guruji persisted.

"Of course, *Guruji*, I will remember your words." The conversation ended, and Sardana walked over to his boss' office. He wondered whether Paul Jacob had also been asked to play Arjuna's role. He smiled to himself. He would probably be thinking of his evening game of golf.

The two of them drove together to Puspendra Vedi's office. Paul Jacob was speaking eloquently about a very erudite article he had read that morning in the papers about the porcupines in the wooded areas of the Ridge which were attacking the monkey population, which was in turn migrating to the office spaces of New Delhi. He was planning to commission a series of research papers as to how to protect and conserve the wild life in the entire Ridge area which cut through all sections of Delhi. He had already sounded his NGO about it and was hopeful that the work would start soon.

Prashant Sardana bent his head downwards and held it in despair. Clearly, he had to handle whatever lay ahead alone.

They reached the entrance to the PMO and walked through the various gates and scanners to Pushpendra Vedi's office.

"Come in, come in," Pushpendra was saying, as they entered his room, sharp at 10.30 am. Both of them straightened their chests and pushed back their shoulders as a mark of respect to him. Paul Jacob had no paunch to hide, but Sardana, who had been neglecting his workouts ever since he had landed in FIB, had to pull in and tighten his stomach extremely hard to make it look smart.

They sat across his table. Pushpendra spoke impatiently. He had already received his briefing from Raja Bhaiyya in the morning.

"Well, you will be getting the Ashutosh Prasad report on the GAVA Oriont contract and its recommendations from the ministry for scientific development. An enquiry is to be instituted immediately."

"Let it come, sir, and we will do what is necessary," Paul Jacob replied, concentrating hard now on the business at hand, steering his mind away from the monkey-porcupine conflict across the Ridge, and his evening game of golf.

"Good, but remember, two people are not to be touched for some reasons which I cannot disclose to you right now. Dr Satyadev, the former ISA chairman, and Ms Gurupriya, the present financial advisor. Please remember this."

"Yes, sir. But, of course, we'll have to study what sort of evidence there is in the report and work according to the law," said Paul Jacob.

"Evidence? What are you taking about? Evidence is what you decide is evidence, in any way you want, isn't it?" Pushpendra Vedi sounded irritated and intimidating.

Paul Jacob was again dreaming of his evening golf. Sardana was thinking of what risks say ahead of him. This government still had a good two years to go, and he would wiggle his way out before he was through.

"What about the courts, sir?" Paul Jacob continued. He had to say something.

"Courts? What courts? The trial court where it will go first? Come on, everyone knows you are the masters of the trial courts. They dare not do anything against your command. How much of your secret service amount do you spend on them? So, don't give me all those lectures. Just do what needs to be done, and...."

While he was speaking, Pushpendra Vedi's PS came in and whispered something to him.

Pushpendra Vedi rose. "Please excuse me," he said, as he went towards his anteroom.

His PS connected the phone. Raja Bhaiyya was on the line. "Vediji, I'm speaking about that Oriont enquiry. The FIB must be told that Sushil Ramu should not be touched. He is a great devotee of Sri Sri Om Amma, and now with the elections coming up in Goa, Om Amma's support is vital for the party. She has a huge following there. Please note this."

"Yes, sir, just let me take a look at everything. I'll see how this can be done."

Pushpendra Vedi had to suppress his irritation. What on earth was this enquiry all about, and who was it to be conducted against?

He returned to his office table.

"Yes Paul, what were we talking about before I went inside?"

Paul was still thinking about how to improve his swing for the golf game in the evening. His back swing was just not wide enough, he believed.

Sardana quickly responded, "Sir, you were saying that Dr Satyadev and Ms Gurupriya were not to be touched in the enquiry."

"Ah, yes. There's one other person who is not to be

touched, and that is Sushil Ramu." Pushpendra Vedi's words had a finality to them.

"But then who does one book, sir?" Paul Jacob asked.

"Well, you have Maharishi, Vidyasagar and Manal Kumar. And those Oriont chaps. That's a good number, isn't it?"

"Sir, can we just take a look at the evidence first?" Sardana added.

"Don't give me all those lectures about evidence, young man. I've seen enough of your evidence in four and a half decades of my service. As if evidence has ever been a concern of yours."

The meeting was over. Paul Jacob and Prashant Sardana returned to their offices, awaiting the communication that they were to receive.

Next, Pushpendra Vedi asked his office to fix a time to meet the minister for scientific development, Pratap Singh. He was informed that the minister was in his constituency and would be back only the next day. He dropped into his office the next day at noon to inform him of the impending FIB enquiry into the GAVA Oriont deal.

"Sir, I'm here on a rather delicate mission. The prime minister has ordered an FIB enquiry into that GAVA Oriont deal, which as you know has been causing so much trouble for the government."

The Minister's face remained impassive. Pushpendra

Vedi was waiting for a response, and since he got none, he decided to continue.

"It appears that the Ashutosh Prasad report has given some severe findings against Maharishi and Vidyasagar, and some bureaucrats."

"Oh, I see," was all that the minister said.

"Sir, here are the papers for you to send on to the FIB for starting the investigations. You know how much embarrassment this has caused the government, with all kinds of allegations of corruption flying around. The prime minister believes we must take action urgently. Otherwise, it would appear as if we are all party to the corruption."

"Corruption? Surely there are no allegations of corruption against the government. ISA may have violated some procedures, which scientists do all the time. They are wedded to science, not to our useless procedures and rules. But anyhow, if the prime minister has taken such a decision, we are duty bound to abide by it."

"So, sir, if you could kindly forward the Ashutosh Prasad report to the FIB to institute an enquiry. Today, if possible."

"Surely I must be allowed to read the report and examine it before sending it to the FIB."

"Of course, sir, but the prime minister desires that it should be done as soon as possible."

"Of course. Rest assured, I will send it as soon as

possible." With that, Pushpendra Vedi left.

Pratap Singh remained alone in his room. He didn't even open the report. Pushpendra Vedi had spoken of an FIB enquiry against Maharishi and Vidyasagar. Let it remain so; they deserved it. God knows how much they had cheated him of. As for the bureaucrats, he couldn't care less—let them hang along with the scientists. How did it matter? This was divine punishment descending upon the deceivers. Let it go on.

He then flipped through the pages, saw what he wanted to see, and that was the names of Maharishi and Vidyasagar as those to be investigated. The bureaucrats didn't concern him. He would send the papers off to the FIB for a report to begin with, he decided. But not now. He would keep them for a while on the pretext of studying them, and then wait and watch. However, he asked his press secretary to leak out some vague information to the media that an FIB enquiry was being ordered.

THE NEXT DAY, every newspaper had front page headlines that the government was going to order an FIB enquiry into the entire GAVA Oriont contract. Though the press didn't include the names of Vidyasagar and Maharishi Nath, it was clear that it was directed against them. As for the bureaucrats, no names appeared. But the desperate scramble for protector politicians and god men and god ladies had started at ISA.

There was complete silence for a while from the FIB. Gurupriya, fearing for her safety, ran to her mentor, Satyadev. She met him in Delhi and pleaded, "Please save me from this, sir. You know I have done nothing of my own accord. I served you for whatever you wanted, and I continued to be loyal to you even after the government changed and you left. Sir, you must save me from this," she wept.

"Yes, Gurupriya, I know you have always been loyal to me. I've already seen to it that you will not be harmed. Do not worry."

"Sir, but these FIB chaps—who knows what they will do? And if they look at my role in the negotiations with Oriont, they will see that it was all done under your leadership. This must be stopped, sir. We'll all be in it together otherwise."

Gurupriya had sent her lethal message to Satyadev, veiled in helplessness and tears. Her *kumkum* was large but her cleavage was wrapped.

Satyadev got the message, something he had anticipated even before she had stated it. That is why he had taken pre-emptive measures to ensure that her name be left out—both in the Ashutosh Prasad enquiry and with the FIB.

"Don't worry, Gurupriya, I will see you are protected."

Gurupriya wept and touched Satyadev's feet.

Sushil Ramu rushed to Sri Sri Om Amma in Raigarh, taking two days leave. He was granted audience immediately.

'Holy Om Amma, save me," he wept. "An FIB enquiry has been ordered, and I'm so afraid they will nail me, even though I have done everything in accordance with orders from the bosses. I will always remain your most loyal devotee."

Om Amma converted her expression to one of benediction. "You don't need to fear. After you met me last week, I have communicated my desire to Delhi. No harm will come to you. Be assured."

Sushil Ramu wept in gratitude and touched Om Amma's feet.

Next, it was the turn of Maharishi. He had the privilege of speaking to her over telephone.

"Om Amma, my apologies; I cannot come to see you in person as I must remain in the office. As I told you, the worst has happened. You may be knowing that an FIB enquiry has been instituted into this Oriont matter. You would understand why I cannot leave this place. Please forgive me."

"Yes, I know. I have spoken to the prime minister's people after you met me. But they say they need time, and give no assurance. I have also spoken to the scientific development minister's agents. They say they will do their best to protect you, but they make no promises either. They say it has something to do with some Oriont accounts that were being handled by you."

"But they have all been sorted out. They are all clean and correct."

"This is what they are saying. It would be good if you clarify with Ramanna Madhava."

Maharishi was a worried man, no doubt. He had kept back an additional rupees one crore of Oriont money, which the minister did not know of, or so he thought. But, perhaps, he had his own sources and had found out. It appeared clear at the moment that he was without any protection from that end. Damn the greed that had overpowered him at that moment, and made him lose his balance and good sense, even though he had taken nothing from the minister's share. This was just a little extra something he had obtained for himself. Well, it was now becoming quite clear that he would have to fend for himself to face whatever lay ahead, and would have no protection from New Delhi.

Manal Kumar was unconcerned. He had not been part of any negotiations with Oriont and he was not part of the contract. All he had done, as per his charter of duties, was to steer a cabinet note provided by GAVA, over which he had no authority. He had committed no error and had performed his duties according to the letter and spirit of his responsibilities. He had nothing to fear.

AN EMERGENCY MEETING was held by Satyadev with Maharishi and Vidyasagar in a private guest house in Mumbai. Satyadev certainly looked a little disoriented. He advised Maharishi, "When the FIB scoundrels show up, just tell them exactly what you told that Ashutosh fellow, that you did everything for the larger interest of the country. That there are no rules that you have to inform the cabinet or anyone about who you are negotiating with or have signed agreements with. Cite national security and the threat of being scuttled by our enemies and competitors. Why should we publicly state who we are signing agreements with for a fast-emerging segment of the world telephony market? There is no rule that we should do so, especially in matters of national security."

"Yes sir, I agree completely with you. That is the approach we must take," Maharishi replied.

"So, when they ask for the papers, give them whatever we have left. And let the bureaucrats answer if there are any faults with the papers. And Maharishi, I suggest that you just take a look at all the papers again, and make sure that the bureaucrats are involved in every major decision that was taken in this affair."

"Yes sir, I'll do that. This evening itself, even if I have to sit late."

"No, do it tomorrow in the course of the day. Don't forget the intelligence wing bastards are watching you."

THERE WAS STILL no word from the FIB. Meanwhile, the papers meant for them were checked and rechecked, to ensure that the originals were destroyed and the remaining were those where the bureaucrats were as deeply involved as the ISA scientists.

The assault from the Dakshin Prajasangha Party grew louder after the announcement of the FIB enquiry into the Oriont affair. The contract should be cancelled, was the consensus in all leading newspapers. If the telecom agreements had been cancelled, so should be the Oriont deal. Each day, there was an editorial in almost every national newspaper and in the vernacular newspapers, about the double standards being employed for the telecom ministry and the scientific development ministry. The FIB enquiry would take generations to complete, and going by their record, would yield nothing.

Parliament was in session, and there were stormy scenes on this issue, with the house often having to be adjourned.

Finally, the prime minister got fed up. He was having to endure this calumny and allegations of corruption, all because of his scientific development minister who had struck this deal behind his back.

He called Pratap Singh to his office and informed him in no uncertain terms that the Oriont contract had to be terminated.

"Sir, but how do we do it? It's a perfectly proper agreement, in the interest of the country. How do we do it? It could well have serious international repercussions."

"I don't care how you do it—just do it, in accordance with whatever legal practices and rules there are. You have the law ministry to assist you. Do it and do it fast. This is costing the government too much, all because of you doing all this behind the government's back. I am planning to call for a meeting of the cabinet security committee to issue instructions."

There was no talk of the FIB enquiry, for which Pratap Singh had still not sent them any communication.

Pratap Singh had nothing to say. He summoned the chairman ISA immediately. They were both in the same soup—Pratap Singh betraying the prime minister, and Maharishi betraying his minister, Pratap Singh.

MAHARISHI'S MEETING WITH the minister the next day started on a sinister note.

"Listen, Maharishi," the minister didn't seem comfortable, "I know it's difficult for you, but I must tell you because of the regard that I have for you, that the situation about the Oriont contract is becoming very difficult for the government. We are finding it very hard to defend ourselves against the onslaught of the opposition, and even our partners like Dakshin Prajasangha Party. You must also be reading everything in the press. The prime minister now believes that it would be best to cancel the contract."

Maharishi couldn't believe his ears.

"But, sir, every step in this contract has been made with complete approval of the government. You were personally kept informed."

"Yes, I know, Maharishi. But sometimes political compulsions overtake everything else, even the most rational and national."

Maharishi was disgusted.

"I understand it must be devastating for you. And it would also be very embarrassing for you to continue in such a situation."

Maharishi felt his hair stand. He was about to be sacked, he sensed.

"You know, we were discussing this in the national security committee and we thought it best that the person who cancels the contract should not be you, but someone else—your successor perhaps. We could always appoint you as the scientific advisor to the prime minister, or if you wish to live abroad, as an attaché in one of our embassies where we have scientific partnerships, like the US, Russia or France. Think about it and let me know."

"Sir, why don't you tell me straight? You want to sack me."

"No, no, we don't want to sack you. We only want to make sure that you don't run the embarrassment of cancelling a contract that you are presently operationalising."

Maharishi was silent for a while. "That's fine, sir," he replied. "If the government does not want me, I should not be there. And no, I'm not interested in those fancy posts in foreign missions. I have plenty of offers for teaching assignments in several universities in India and abroad, where I can at least give knowledge to our aspiring scientists. I am ready to tender my resignation if the government so wishes."

"No, no, don't do that. We don't want you to resign. We just want to spare you the embarrassment of terminating an agreement that you are in the process of carrying forward. You may choose any other scientific assignment you want."

"Yes, I understand that sir, and thank you for your support. Let me think about it."

"How much time do you need?"

"Give me a month."

"No, that may not be possible. You may have a week. This must be done before parliament meets next month."

"Okay, sir, you give me no choice. But I would still require at least another two weeks to tie up all loose ends of this contract and so many other projects at various stages."

"Fine, that's reasonable. You may take two weeks. But remember, no resignation. Only another assignment."

"Thank you, sir," and Maharishi left, seared and angry.

The minister's plans for Maharishi were however dashed to the ground. The prime minister's office kept sustained pressure on the FIB to start the investigations urgently, but Minister Pratap Singh was showing no signs of parting with the file. Finally, they decided that they would themselves send the entire Ashutosh Prasad report file to the FIB for them to start the process.

The prime minister's principal secretary summoned the FIB chief, Paul Jacob, but was told that he was on leave that day. Prashant Sardana was then called personally and handed over the report officially.

The minister was taken unawares, as he heard about this from his informants. He was furious, but turned a little philosophic. Well, he thought, this was the punishment being meted out to him for making deals behind the prime minister's—and more so—behind Raja Bhaiyya's back.

NEWS OF THE impending termination of the Oriont contract reached Raja Bhaiyya through his personal secretary.

He had a discussion with his father-in-law and then called Pushpendra Vedi. "Vediji, I hear that the government is planning to cancel the Oriont deal. Please let me know the steps that are taken in the matter. I'm sure that cancellation of contracts, especially if there's so much of foreign investment, can have a lot of international repercussions. Please make sure that our country's interest is protected."

Touching indeed, thought Pushpendra Vedi, who could only reply in the affirmative. "Of course, sir, that would be of prime importance. I'm sure the scientific development ministry will study it carefully."

Raja Bhaiyya smelt gold. And he smelt it strong. Let the contract be cancelled, if it had to be, for political compulsions. But let it be cancelled right, so that the money keeps pouring in.

"On what grounds do you propose to cancel it?" he asked.

"Sir, we will have to study the papers carefully and also obtain advice from the law ministry. The scientific development ministry will study it and then send it to us."

Signals from the prime minister's office and Raja Bhaiyya started reaching the law ministry. The law minister, Peer Mulla, had great loyalty to the prime minister and to Raja Bhaiyya. Off the record, he sought advice from Raja Bhaiyya.

Raja Bhaiyya went ahead without any preambles. "Mr Peer Mulla, I am informed that foreign investment of at least Rs. 700 crores has already come into Oriont India from major foreign companies. Now, if we cancel the contract, let it be on grounds that we no longer have the spectrum to spare, that we need if for our national requirements that have suddenly surfaced."

"Sir, but that places us on a very weak footing. It would be better if we cancelled it on grounds that Oriont falsely stated in the contract that they had the technology for the hybrid telephony systems that they had committed to in the contract. This would make the contract null and void."

"Yes, but wouldn't that also embarrass the government that its ISA signs contracts without proper study and examination? And some more charges of corruption would be hurled at us. How would that look for the government?"

Peer Mulla remained silent. The man had a point. Raja Bhaiyya continued, "So, cancel it since it has to be cancelled for political compulsions, on grounds that because of changed circumstances, we need the spectrum for some very urgent national needs."

Peer Mulla heard, thought, and remained silent. The gentleman wasn't talking on his own. Was this the voice of the prime minister?

THE NEXT DAY, the ISA chairman received top secret instructions from the cabinet secretariat that the cabinet security committee was to meet shortly. A note was required with all the details regarding the usage of the X band spectrum that had been allotted to ISA for the last ten years, as there was need to review the same for the future, particularly in view of the commitments made in the GAVA Oriont contract. The hidden message was clear, that already there was serious thinking going on regarding cancellation of the contract.

Maharishi rushed to Delhi to meet his minister and had to wait for a day to meet him.

"Sir, we have received these instructions, one direct copy to us, and one to you. What do you want us to do?"

"Well, I hardly have a choice. Do what the security committee has ordered you to do."

"Start the process of cancelling the Oriont contract? That can have dire financial consequences for the country. There will be arbitration proceedings where we would appear very weak, with great cost to the public exchequer."

"Do as you are told. This is not the time for debate, either for you or for me."

"Sir, but please note, this is going to be a great disgrace

to our organisation. We would lose so much credibility, and won't be able to do any business for a long, long time. Besides, we'll be stuck in arbitration proceedings for which we will be in a very weak position, which will cost the nation dearly."

"Just do what you're directed to do. I'll be sending the instructions by tomorrow."

"Sir, we're all going to be so busy with the FIB showing up any day. And now, we're being asked to cancel the contract. This will cause complete chaos in the organisation. It will be very tough on us."

"Just handle it. That's all."

Maharishi left, disgusted and dispirited.

He stayed on another day in Delhi, alone and by himself. He did some serious thinking that evening—it was a do or die situation for him. He poured himself some whiskey and soda, thinking it might relax him a little. His thinking sharpened and he pondered seriously over his situation, and thought of several moves and maneuvers. Finally, he made up his mind.

The next morning, he phoned the minister's home office and said he had to meet the minister urgently on a very important matter. He was asked to come immediately, as the minister had to leave for a meeting at 11 am.

Maharishi invoked every god and goddess he knew before leaving his guest house. He was now in their hands, as every terrestrial hand was working against him.

He entered the minister's home office with his pen with the listening device perched in his shirt pocket.

"Good morning, sir. Thank you for this meeting. It was important. Forgive me, if it has inconvenienced you."

"No, no. Now, what is it? I thought we had discussed everything yesterday, what the PM wants, and what we need to do."

"Yes, sir. But I'm here to discuss a little about justice and propriety."

The Minister looked at him with some irritation and impatience.

"Sir, I'm somewhat disturbed that I alone am being held accountable for the Oriont deal. You have been informed of it at every stage. In fact, you have directed it from the very start. Nothing was done in ISA in respect of the deal without your instructions, knowledge or approval. This was started during the previous regime under the stewardship of Satyadev. You and I were mere inheritors."

The Minister was stunned. He had never heard this kind of language from Maharishi before.

"What do you mean I directed the deal and gave you instructions? How can you prove anything you're saying?"

"Very simple, sir. Just as you record everything, I say to you, I do the same. You know, we are a very high security organisation, so recording all conversations is the very basic rule of our working."

The Minister froze. Blackmail. But how much of his meetings with Maharishi over the last year had been recorded? He tried to think back and recollect what those meetings had been about. Yes, one of them was about concealing the name of Oriont. There were so many others, the exact contents of which he couldn't remember. He would have to check his own recordings.

The Minister regained his composure. "So, what is it that you have come to see me about?"

"Sir, I say this categorically—stop this FIB enquiry. If you allow this against me, you will go down too along with me. It's just good sense."

The Minister stared unbelieving at his ISA chief. No, this was not a bluff. He had no idea what Maharishi had recorded and where it was stored.

"But the prime minister has ordered the FIB enquiry. There's very little I can do about it."

"Sir, it's your own skin you have to save, not mine. You will do even the impossible for that."

Maharishi rose to leave.

"Just for my information, Maharishi, what sort of a recording device do you carry? Aren't you supposed to leave your gadgets behind before you come in here?"

"It's a special recording device, sir. A furlable antenna, specially designed by us. In my ass."

THE SAME EVENING around 7 pm, Pratap Singh summoned the FIB chief Paul Jacob to his office to discuss the enquiry into the Oriont affair. Paul Jacob was extremely irritated. He had organised a meeting of his NGO to discuss the proposals that had been received for addressing the porcupine menace in the Ridge and containing the monkey menace in Lutyen's Delhi in a humanitarian way. He asked his NGO secretary to cancel the meeting and then called his second-in-command Prashant Sardana to accompany him to the minister's office.

Sardana too was irritated. He was to attend a very exclusive and affluent party in a posh private restaurant in Gurgaon, with leading film stars from Mumbai. Well, he would tell his wife to go ahead, and he would join her later.

Sardana and Paul Jacob rode together to the scientific development minister's office in South Block. The minister appeared very distracted and sullen. The two of them stiffened their backs and chests and drew in their stomachs. The minister ignored them.

"Well, well, sit down, we have lot to discuss." The two gentlemen sat down.

The minister continued, "The PM's office informs me that they have discussed with you that an FIB enquiry is to be conducted into the GAVA Oriont agreement. Am I right?"

"Yes, sir," replied Paul Jacob.

"Just go through the Ahutosh Prasad report carefully. It looks to me that the real culprits have been left scot-free. Am I right?"

"Sir," said Paul Jacob, "we have still not received the report."

"What about you, Sardana, have you studied the report?"

"I'm studying it, sir. We got it just yesterday."

"Got it? Got it from where? I haven't sent it to you yet."

Sardana squirmed and kicked himself. He had goofed up. Must have been his anxiety about being late for the Bollywood party.

"Okay, I understand." The minister turned towards Sardana and continued, "So you already have a copy of the report which you are studying. Am I right? Where did you get it from?

Sardana continued cursing himself and his goof up.

"Sir, it was given to us by the prime minister's office, to just study it."

"But you know, for you to take any action, it must come from me."

"Of course, sir."

"Well, let me tell you Sardana, just tread a little carefully. I've really not called you regarding anything to do with the Oriont enquiry. What I've called you for is to inform you about a lot of your actions in your previous posting in the Mumbai Police Commissionerate, where your name appears in a lot of diaries of various big business houses for having received retainer amounts for protecting their interests."

This time Sardana froze. He was speechless for a while, but he gathered himself quickly.

"Sir, as public servants, we're accustomed to these allegations all the time. We pay no attention to them, and continue to perform our duty."

"Yes, but I'm receiving a lot of public complaints about you from my constituents, many of whom are being unjustly harassed by your organisation, which I'm duty bound to give serious attention to. Also, about some rather unsavoury connections you have with some big business houses, some of which operate in my constituency. I just called you here to sound you about this. Yes, and I must also warn you that some of my constituents have been wanting to file a PIL against you for your alleged misdemeanors of the past. I've tried to hold them back, but I'm not sure I'll succeed."

Paul Jacob was listening, with his mind going back and forth from the porcupines and monkeys in the Ridge, his NGO meeting that he had to cancel, and now to some strange allegations being made against Sardana of being a crook.

Crook, of course he was, he always knew. But then, he was the government's favourite crook, and that made him legitimate. Now, what was all this about his name being in some business house diaries for payoffs? He had not heard that before.

Sardana got the message. He was to go slow on the FIB enquiry. Otherwise, the business house diaries would be out. So far, they had been protected by the PMO, as it was those same business houses which were the government's biggest pay masters.

MEANWHILE, THE MINISTER'S establishment which was studying the references from the prime minister's office noticed that the files and annexures mentioned in the Ashutosh Prasad report were either missing or truncated. They sent a polite note to the PMO, requesting that the supporting documents and files cited in the Ashutosh Prasad report be made available urgently, before they could refer the case to the FIB.

It was a bizarre scenario. Even though his office had already sent the Ashutosh Prasad report to the FIB, Pushpendra Vedi had no option but to summon both Ashutosh Prasad and Maharishi and ask for the documents that the scientific development minister was requesting, quite legitimately.

Ashutosh Prasad feigned complete ignorance. He had worked on whatever documents that had been provided to him by ISA. He could hardly tell Pushpendra Vedi that he had finalised his report based on instructions from Raja Bhaiyya. Maharishi exclaimed in the tone of an injured innocent that his office was open to anyone who wanted documents lodged there. Of course, he couldn't tell them that all offending documents had already been destroyed.

The prime minister's office was flummoxed and frustrated. But on paper, they could find nothing wrong with what the minister had requested. The FIB deputy chief Sardana continued to be disturbed, but was pleased that the scientific development ministry had still not sent them any request for any enquiry. The newspapers could say what they liked. Everything was at a standstill for the moment.

MAHARISHI HAD AN important series of international meetings lined up which he had to attend during the next few weeks. The first was at Vienna on June 18, where orbital slots for satellites for the next two years had to be finalised. This was followed by two international meetings at the UN starting June 23, on International Space Law and Space for Development. Maharishi had been given permission by his ministry to attend both of them.

Maharishi did some serious thinking. For the first time he discussed the whole Oriont affair in detail with his wife. She, of course, had known for quite a long time that there was something very strange and worrisome going on in her husband's life—the horrible newspaper and television reports, his frequent visits to Delhi, the unusual bouts of silence, the mysterious phone calls at odd hours of the night. She had worried about it secretly, but this she did not expect—that he wanted to leave the ISA and take up a teaching assignment in the International Space Research Academy (ISRA) in Florida. Though, in a way, she was also happy. Both her children were in the US. Their daughter was a doctor in Dallas, and their son had set up his own software company in San Diego. Even though Florida was on the other side of the country, it still brought her much closer to her children and grandchildren. She vigorously supported her husband's decision to join the Florida academy. It would give them both a break from the nasty business appearing in the newspapers day after day.

Maharishi did not speak about the FIB or the Oriont contract at all during the week. He took stock of pending issues, gave necessary instructions and orders. Finally, when he was satisfied that he had tied up all loose ends, he took a trip to Delhi to meet the minister. There was still no word from the FIB or from the PMO about cancellation of the contract.

The minister met him in his office, his face cold and expressionless.

"So, have you decided, Maharishi?"

"Yes, sir. I will request for long leave and for permission to join the International Space Research Academy in Florida. I have a standing invitation from them to join their faculty. Just thought I would inform you before I give you my request. Their response may take about a week. So just bear with me until then. You may then place anyone you wish as ISA chairman and cancel the contract."

"Good, I'm glad you've decided wisely and maturely. Send me your letter immediately. I will approve it at once, and recommend it to the prime minister."

"I have it right here, sir, thank you." Maharishi handed over his request.

The minister immediately summoned his personal secretary.

"Put this in an urgent file, and put up a note from me to the PM with a recommendation that we may accept chairman ISA's request immediately. The next most senior scientist, Dr Nageshwar, director of the Hyderabad Satellite Research Centre, may be kept in charge until a regular chairman is selected."

"So, Maharishi, this is probably the last time we meet. Good luck to you for your new assignment."

"Thank you, sir. And good luck to you for your stay

here and your next election."

The rest was easy. Maharishi had already informed the ISRA, Florida, that he was now ready to take up the position. He required the appointment letter so that he could send it to the government for permission. The letter came within a week. He immediately sent it off to the minister's office, requesting permission to demit office and proceed to his new assignment.

The minister was delighted. He was well rid of his ISA chief with his sophisticated listening devices. He had selected the dumbest number two to remain in charge for ever, a guarantee for insecurity. The prime minister approved immediately. He was also immensely relieved. An in-charge entity was most welcome. He could be dictated to so much more easily.

Maharishi had taken every precaution. He didn't own much property. A few months ago, he had already transferred his house which was in the joint name with his wife, to his son. He and his wife had a joint bank account, and his few fixed deposits were already in the names of his children.

Maharishi and his wife made arrangements for their house to be occupied by her sister's daughter and son-in-law who had just set up an engineering company manufacturing solar panels for green energy. This would help them save costs during the initial stages.

Maharishi also informed the minister that since

he was in the process of winding up, he was deputing Vidyasagar to attend the Vienna Conference on June 18, and the UN meetings in New York during the next week starting from June 23.

Maharishi called Vidyasagar to his office the next day.

"Now, Vidyasagar, what I'm telling you is in the strictest confidence. I will be leaving soon. I'm planning to take up a teaching assignment in Florida. I am deputing you to attend the meeting in Vienna on June 18, and the UN meetings in New York starting on June 23."

Vidyasagar looked at Maharishi puzzled.

"Will your wife accompany you?"

"I don't know. I will have to ask her."

"In whose name do your properties stand?"

Vidyasagar was taken aback. Why was Maharishi asking him all these questions?

Maharishi continued, "Your children are in India, I think. Is that so?"

"Yes, sir. Both my children are in India."

"Okay. So, take my advice, and ask no questions. Transfer your property and your money, fixed deposits or whatever, to their names immediately."

"But why, sir? Is something serious happening?"

"Yes, obviously. Why would I be telling you this otherwise? You don't want your property or money to be seized by the FIB, do you?"

Finally, it dawned upon Vidyasagar. This was really

serious. His property and money could be confiscated.

"Sir, I'm grateful to you for your concern and your caring advice. I'll do so immediately."

"Good, and ask you wife to accompany you to Vienna. I'll issue the orders deputing you to attend shortly. And don't travel on a diplomatic passport. Carry your own passport. You have a long US visa, don't you?"

"Yes, another five years."

"Good."

The next day Maharishi sent a note to the minister informing him that since he was in a state of transition, it would be appropriate that Shri Vidyasagar who dealt with the subject be deputed to attend the meeting at Vienna on June 18, and the subsequent UN meetings in New York starting June 23. He received an approval from the minister's office within two days.

As far as Maharishi and his wife were concerned, all they had to do was pack their clothes and some other immediate requirements. ISRA would provide a fully furnished house to them during his tenure there.

Once again, ISA was abuzz. What in hell was going on? There were no signs of the FIB. There was nothing going on about cancellation of the contract which the newspapers had been yelling about. All that they knew was that Maharishi would be leaving and that Dr Nageshwar from the Satellite Research Centre in Hyderabad would be taking charge as a temporary measure.

The bureaucrats were anxious. Gurupriya tried her best to ferret some information from her colleagues in Delhi, but could get nothing. She tried her police sources, but drew a blank. Sushil Ramu was equally unsuccessful. No one seemed to know what was going on. Manal Kumar attended to his work as he always did, without any curiosity or concern.

A hushed silence descended upon the ISA, and nobody knew what was going on in the corridors of power.

THE WHEELS WERE now set in motion. Dr Maharishi received approval orders for joining the International Space Research Academy on June 6. He handed over charge to Dr Nageshwar, who was appointed as the in-charge chairman ISA. Though this was meant to be a temporary arrangement, no one knew how long it would last, with all the turbulence that had been going on in ISA.

There was a subdued but affectionate farewell for Maharishi and his wife, and a rather confused welcome for the new in-charge chairman, who seemed equally confused and perplexed about the whole affair. But then, this was the mighty government at work in its wisdom, before whom everybody had to bow their heads.

Maharishi had given standing instructions to the staff that they were not to give any presents of any kind, but both the scientist group and the secretariat group led by Grurupriya insisted that at least one memento was to be presented from each group. Gurupriya immediately organised a silver salver with Dr Maharishi's name inscribed on it, and the scientists purchased a beautifully carved sandalwood Ganesha from the state emporium for their chairman.

The newspapers went hysterical, with each of them carrying their own theories about Maharishi's departure. One said that he had been sacked for his disagreements with the minister. Another said that he was leaving in disgust because the government had failed to protect the scientists. Yet another said that it was all because the government wanted to scrap the Oriont agreement, and Maharishi was coming in the way.

Maharishi smiled at everyone and wished each one of them the very best. He exchanged a few jokes and assured everyone that he would be back soon after completing his assignment with ISRA.

VIDYASAGAR WAS TO leave for Vienna a week later. The Vienna meeting would last three days, after which he would leave for New York to attend the UN meetings on International Space Law and Space for Development on June 23, which would last the whole week.

The minister was waiting for Maharishi to depart. His presence weighed upon his conscience for executing the plans that he really wanted to execute for dealing with this ugly matter. The Oriont affair was like a serpent around his neck, and he had somehow to get rid of it before it killed him politically.

As soon as he heard of Maharishi's departure, he sought an appointment with the prime minister, which he got quite easily. He did not want anyone else at the meeting.

"Sir," he addressed the prime minister, "I'm grateful to you for your time. But this is a matter of great national importance. I'm referring to the recent controversies about the ISA and the Oriont contract. Your secretary, Pushpendra Vedi has briefed me about your views on the matter, mainly that you would like the contract to be cancelled, and that you would like the FIB to start investigations about it."

The prime minister listened impassively without any response or change of expression.

The minister continued, "Sir, with due respect, let me first express my deep concern about the FIB enquiry. It is commonly known by everyone—the scientists, the media, the bureaucrats—that it is your office that is ordering the enquiry. This is already having an extremely demoralising effect on the scientists, and the organisation.

I can sense it every day in the general feedback and the lack of interest that I'm seeing. There are already talks going on among other scientific organisations about this witch hunt against scientists by the government. I'm told they are enlisting the support of some eminent retired scientists to make a case for them and protect them, and it might become an ugly public issue very soon. You may have already received a report about this from the intelligence agencies."

The prime minister remained impassive and silent for a few more seconds. Finally, he broke his silence. "Yes, but don't you also see the damage that this deal is doing to the government and to our party? How do you expect me to defend myself and our party for all your ill-conceived actions?"

"Sir, with your permission, may I explain to you that there was no corrupt or mala fide intent in the contract. The approval procedure followed in this case has been going on for decades. It is just unfortunate that our routine activities got linked up with the telecom case, and we got a bad name for no fault of ours."

"So, what do you suggest? As I see it, I have no other option but to cancel the contract. Otherwise, we are all getting mired in allegations of corruption. Don't you read the papers? There are four state elections coming up in the next eight months. How do we answer the people?"

"Sir, as you know, I have sent Maharishi out of the

organisation. You yourself have approved it. There's a new in-charge chairman there now, who has no baggage. Let it start smoothly. Let the defence ministry approach us for our allocation of the spectrum for urgent needs. Let it be considered through the normal processes and then let us take a considered decision, after the advice of the law department. That will make everything look proper."

"What about the arbitrations that would follow?"

"Well sir, if the deal is cancelled in a legally proper manner, then we should be able to defend it legally in any arbitration proceedings."

"Yes, I see your point. What else do you want to say?"

"Sir, your secretary, Mr Vedi, came to me and briefed me about the fact that you wanted an FIB enquiry into this matter. My honest view is that this should be avoided. It would completely demoralise the scientists, something they are already going through. Our space programmes will get completely derailed. There are no charges of corruption against anyone. There are no charges of money changing hands. Okay, if some procedures have been violated, we can handle them departmentally. But an FIB enquiry would be unwise. It would take back the organisation considerably, and do greater harm to the government. Order a department enquiry if you wish, and the government can take credit for it. I repeat sir, there is no corruption in the contract, no charges of any kind, either in the media or by way of complaint. So, how can we order an FIB enquiry?"

The prime minister again remained silent and impassive. He smirked to himself. No corruption indeed... he was thinking of all the bank accounts operating on foreign shores, the ones which the minister and the ISA scamsters held under their control. And all this done behind his back. Now it was his turn to have the last laugh.

He spoke after a long pause, "Okay, let me see what I can do."

"Sir, I will send back the Ashutosh Prasad report. It has too many holes in it. Important supporting documents are missing. He's done a thoroughly incomplete and careless job. It cannot stand in any court of law."

"Okay, send it back, and then we'll see how we should handle it."

The minister returned to his office, not completely satisfied. He had made his points quite convincingly, he thought. But the prime minister had not given out his mind. He never did—that was his nature. Still and silent he was on the surface, and wily as hell beneath it. He had to keep a watch on what his future moves would be.

MAHARISHI AND HIS wife flew off to Miami on June 13. Their son Vijay had come all the way from San

Diego to receive them at the airport. A representative from ISRA, Tom Sargosa, was also there. They were to stay in Miami for the night, and drive next morning to the academy, which was located somewhere near Tampa.

Maharishi had a long, uninterrupted sleep on his flight from Paris to Miami, and felt quite good and refreshed on landing. His wife had a slightly worried look about her as she had to settle down to a new life here.

But she was overjoyed to see her son and couldn't wait to visit her daughter in Dallas, who was not able to come to Miami to receive her parents because of her hospital duties and looking after her two small children. However, she had a long chat on telephone with her parents and there was general happiness all around.

The next day Maharishi and his wife drove to the academy, along with their son Vijay and Tom Sargosa. It was just about four hours away from Miami, and they entered their new home, a well-furnished house with a pretty garden. There was plenty to do that evening, as there was a reception arranged for them at the academy club. Meanwhile, Vijay and his mother went out shopping for groceries and stocking up their immediate requirements. There were ever so many Indian shops and restaurants in Tampa, and pretty soon, a sense of transitory comfort descended upon the new lodgings of Dr Maharishi Nath.

TIME PASSED PLEASANTLY, and Maharishi enjoyed getting back to academic life and research, and most of all, to teaching. There was so much research happening here about inter-planetary systems and space stations, which he could never go into with enough depth, back home in ISA. He was truly happy to be here and get back to science, away from the useless, unproductive politics and intrigues of being chairman of ISA.

Shukra Devi continued to send him daily bulletins of what was going on in his old office. There were no further developments, she said, about the FIB enquiry or the cancellation of the Oriont contract.

That was good, thought Maharishi. Perhaps his threat to the minister had worked and he was able to convince the prime minister. But it was too early to draw any conclusions. Both the prime minister and the minister were known for their utter wiliness and cunning. They could lure anyone to complacency, and then strike at the most unexpected moment.

He had been in ISRA for about a week now, enjoying every bit of it. This Sunday, Vidyasagar would be in New York for about a week to attend the UN meetings. On Sunday morning, both Maharishi and his wife Radha, drove to New York to meet him. Vidyasagar was coming with his wife, and she would stay on for a while to be with her sister in New Jersey.

Maharishi had also been in touch with Dr Martin Georges and Dr Karmaswamy. They, too, were anxious and had been in touch with all their contacts in New Delhi for the latest news emanating from the PMO and the minister's office, but there had been none.

The prime minister had remained busy with parliament that whole week. There were chaotic scenes and direct charges against the government by the opposition for not acting on the Oriont agreement, and questioning the prime minister as to why he remained silent and was taking no action.

Enough was enough, the prime minister thought. Minister Pratap Singh deserved no mercy, and there was no further time left for dithering. He promised to make a statement in parliament. But, before that, he called for a meeting with the defence minister and the scientific development minister. He ordered the defence minister to write immediately to the scientific development minister requesting that the X Band spectrum with ISA be urgently allotted to the defence ministry for their unforeseen and immediate national security requirements.

He also directed the scientific development minister to immediately bring this subject before the cabinet security committee for getting the required approval. Information regarding usage of X band spectrum allotted to ISA had already been sent by ISA to the committee. The cabinet security committee met three days later and gave the approval. Thereafter, the in-charge ISA chairman was communicated the cabinet security committee decision and was directed to start the process of implementing it immediately, which meant first and foremost, cancelling the Oriont agreement.

This happened on June 23, the Monday that the UN meeting on International Space Law began.

FOUR DAYS LATER, on Friday June 27, there was an announcement from the FIB that they had started an enquiry into the GAVA Oriont Agreement, mentioning the names of Vidyasagar, Karmaswamy and Haridas in the first information report.

The UN meeting was over, and Vidyasagar who was expected to return to India thereafter, suddenly realised what had hit him. He recalled the words of Maharishi to sort out his property and money matters. What a wise and prescient man Maharishi was.

News from the Oriont lot was that the prime minister was baying for the scientific development minister's blood, and the scientific development minister was baying for Maharishi's blood. But since getting Maharishi was a rather difficult target at the moment, they would start with Vidyasagar and the Oriont India MD.

The Oriont information was correct. The next day

there were front page headlines in the newspapers that the FIB had filed a first information report in the case naming Vidyasagar, Haridas and Karmaswamy, along with unknown others from ISA and the secretariat. Some papers reported that the FIB had requested for custodial interrogation of Vidyasagar and some other officials from ISA.

The news shook the ISA like an earthquake. Vidyasagar thanked the stars he was here in the US, but the news really hit him hard. He suddenly felt huge panic attacks that were leaving him quite breathless, even while his heart pounded violently. His wife got immensely worried and the staff of India's permanent mission to the UN were contacted to take him to a doctor immediately. The doctor confirmed that Vidyasagar was suffering from acute cardiac distress and pulmonary fluctuation, and should be immediately hospitalised for treatment and further observation.

Maharishi and his wife rushed to New York. Georges and Karmaswamy rushed from Washington with an eminent lawyer. They were all in serious discussion about what should be done next.

"This is really quite scandalous, what the Indian government is doing. To do this in what is clearly a clean and upfront deal. First, they try to cancel the deal, and now to arrest everyone. What on earth is going on? What kind of a country do you live in?" Georges couldn't contain his anger.

Maharishi kept his cool. “Yes, but first we must attend to Vidyasagar. Let him be in this hospital until he recovers. And then, let him move to his sister-in-law’s house. We’ll take over from there.”

Georges took Maharishi aside. “Right now, he’s in this hospital with a referral from the permanent mission of India. Before they come for his release to send him to India, he must approach the court that he apprehends great harm to his body and person, and that he is being illegally investigated and apprehends arrest and that he would like to stay on in the US, until he feels safe to return. Let my lawyers handle this.”

Vidyasagar was given emergency treatment, and had to stay under observation for a week in the hospital. Finally, he was discharged and prescribed medication to stabilise his heart condition and blood pressure, and was advised complete rest for at least one month. In this situation, there was no need for the lawyers to step in.

His wife decided that they would stay with her sister until he was well enough to travel. This was conveyed to the permanent mission with all the medical papers, who in turn conveyed this to the foreign ministry, which in turn informed the scientific development ministry.

Pratap Singh read the reports with a smirk. So Vidyasagar would continue to stay on in the US. Maharishi was already there. The FIB would be in a spin. He smiled to himself in great amusement. The

PMO could rattle itself for all he cared. Well, the PM had done all this behind his back, so let him face further embarrassment. But what he was most worried about was the listening device which Maharishi could explode whenever he wanted. He would have to find some way to deal with that.

The furtive silence in ISA now became a permanent state. The scientists were too scared to talk to each other, or to express any views about the scandalous headlines that appeared in the newspapers, day after day. Public space became a free for all. There were speculations of all hue—that Maharishi and his wife had fled the country well in time; that Vidyasagar and wife were seeking asylum in the US; that Vidyasagar had suffered a massive heart attack and was in hospital, fighting for his life. And so on, it continued. Even Shukra Devi did not know what exactly was going on in the US. Her former boss and mentor Satyadev kept visiting and trying to get inside information, but there was hardly any available—and Shukra Devi, loyal mistress of both Satyadev and Maharishi, had no information to give. It was now just a matter of time that the FIB hoods would descend upon them.

The in-charge chairman Nageshwar wanted to have nothing to do with this murky business. He cursed his stars for bringing him here. The ISA affairs could run quite efficiently on auto pilot mode. Maharishi, to his credit, meticulous as always, had left enough instructions that would take the ongoing projects forward for at least the next three to four months.

Besides, Nageshwar hated the atmosphere at ISA. The scientists behaved liked trapped animals, too scared to speak about anything. The bureaucrats, correct to the core, showed nothing but politeness and disdain in all their interactions with him. How he longed to be back at his research centre at Hyderabad, where he was familiar with everything that was going on for the present and for the future.

He decided to go back to Hyderabad for some days, which he was well entitled to. He did not know whom to trust here. Shukra Devi was too engrossed in the affairs of her former bosses, and the constant appearance of Satyadev irritated him beyond measure. He could see that Satyadev wielded great influence in the organisation still. No one dared to question anything that he tried to impose on the organisation.

He was planning to go to Hyderabad the next day, when ISA received the huge jolt that they knew would happen any day. The FIB had arrived.

The deputy superintendent of the FIB, one Nishkam Narela, sent a polite communication to the in-charge chairman ISA that they would be coming over the next day for investigations regarding the GAVA Oriont agreement, and that they wanted to question Satyadev, Maharishi, Vidyasagar, Gurupriya, and all other scientists and bureaucrats, who were involved in the deal.

Nageshwar damned them all. His plans for Hyderabad were blown to bits. He immediately summoned Shukra Devi, who looked extremely tense and worried. She suggested that the chief vigilance officer, Sushil Ramu, should be made responsible for handling the whole affair.

Nageshwar thought it proper to phone the minister's office and ask to speak to him. He informed the minister what was going on. The minister remained silent, and then replied with a mere, "Okay, handle everything well, and keep me informed of what's going on," and hung up.

The FIB first wanted to question Vidyasagar, but were told that he was away in the US to attend a UN meeting. Thereafter, he had fallen seriously ill and was in hospital, and no one was sure when he would return.

The chief investigating officer, Gyan Prakash, then wanted to question Satyadev, but was told that he was attending a conference in Brussels, and would return only next month. Next, he wanted to know the whereabouts of Maharishi, and was informed that he was on a teaching assignment in the USA for the next three years.

He now turned to the examination of Gurupriya, but was informed that she was on one month's leave, and would return only after three weeks.

The FIB investigating team were now at their wit's end. No one seemed to be available for questioning. Nishkam Narela phoned Prashant Sardana and informed him of the situation. Sardana was furious. He directed them to start seizing the documents, and if things did not improve, they should ask the jurisdictional court for custodial interrogation of all of them.

The FIB team remained busy the next few days interrogating the minions in GAVA, and seizing the documents that had managed to survive the purge and cremation. Of course, they couldn't understand a thing about them. They also spent their valuable time in taking statements from the minions, after which they descended upon other senior scientists and junior bureaucrats and tried to make them talk about the conspiracy hatched by GAVA and Oriont to cheat the government. All of them honestly replied that they had no knowledge about any kind of conspiracy, and that such things never happened in their organisation.

The first important bureaucrat they had to question was Sushil Ramu, who was also the chief vigilance officer. But he suddenly took leave for the next one week, on grounds that he had to attend the wedding of his wife's brother's daughter, and disappeared. He produced a copy of the wedding invitation to convince the in-charge chairman. Nageshwar was exasperated. This is not what he had bargained for in becoming chairman ISA, even if only in-charge.

He handed over the FIB guys to Manal Kumar, the only other remaining bureaucrat. Manal Kumar did whatever he had to do, but he got the shock of his life when he saw the files. All important papers in them were missing.

"Hey, this is a doctored file," Manal Kumar told the investigating officer. "Where are the pages from 13 to 20? Where are the drafts that were sent on July 22, on August 2, and on September 4? Where is the original signed Cabinet Note dated September 13? None of them are in the file. Can't you see for yourself? You must try and find where they are. How can you investigate with this truncated, tampered file? Somebody here is trying to make a thorough fool of you."

The investigating officer said that this was all that the team had been able to find.

The investigation officer then showed Manal Kumar a draft cabinet note which contained a sentence that "GAVA had been approached by several very qualified companies..." The words 'several very qualified companies' were scrawled in ink and were written above the crossed out typed words 'a very qualified company', for providing the hybrid DMR technology. He asked Manal Kumar to identify the handwriting. Manal Kumar replied honesty that he couldn't, and suggested that they get the handwriting examined by a forensic expert.

The FIB interrogation team was clearly frustrated. They could find no incriminating documents except those that were already in the public domain. There was no evidence of any conspiracy or cheating or corruption, or any money changing hands.

They informed everything to their deputy chief Prashant Sardana in New Delhi. Sardana informed everything to the PM's secretary and to Raja Bhaiyya.

Raja Bhaiyya was furious. "What is going on in the FIB," he shouted, "that they can't even pin down the offenders in such a brazen open and shut case?"

He barked his orders, "Why are all the key scientists out of the country? Why are all the key bureaucrats out of Mumbai? These are enough grounds for asking the court for custodial interrogation. Get on with it immediately and don't speak to me again until it is done."

The FIB deputy chief replied, "As you wish, sir."

GURUPRIYA WAS TERRIFIED after she had read the first newspaper reports about the FIB custodial investigation. She took a month's leave, which was her entitlement. She first met her mentor Satyadev in Delhi, just before he was flying out to Brussels for a meeting, and asked him for advice about what she should do. She couldn't take any risks, especially since the papers of her involvement in the Oriont agreement were all available in the files that the FIB would seize.

Satyadev tried to remain cool, though he was certainly very tense.

"You know very well, Gurupriya, I have done all I could to inform the highest authorities that you should not be touched. But who knows what is happening. The best thing you can do is get anticipatory bail. I know a very good lawyer who knows a very good judge. I will put you on to him. Get the anticipatory bail."

"Thank you, sir. But you're sure, I'll get it?"

"One hundred percent."

He called someone on his mobile phone. "Nagaraj, I'm sending one of my officers to you. She must get anticipatory bail for this terrible FIB case going on in ISA. She's completely innocent, I assure you. Do it soon. She'll be in touch with you and explain everything. Her name is Gurupriya. She'll give you my reference, and be as discreet as you can."

Nagaraj replied. "Certainly, sir. Your word is a command."

"And Nagaraj, don't charge too much. She's an honest government servant."

"Of course, sir. Coming from you, I will not charge anything."

Gurupriya wept and touched Satyadev's feet. She had to spend a few days getting her papers ready. But true to his word, Nagaraj was able to approach the sessions court and was able to get her anticipatory bail, without any publicity.

She still had one week's leave before she joined her duties again. She thanked Satyadev, her mentor, and then spent a lot of time in meditation, trying to figure out what direction her life was flowing towards. She thought of her son being educated through the bounty of Oriont and prayed that no harm should come to him.

Sushil Ramu did, in fact, have to attend his wife's brother's daughter's wedding. He attended the ceremony in Chennai, and then took leave from his family saying he had an urgent summons from New Delhi to attend a meeting in the prime minister's office.

In actual fact, he was going to Sri Sri Om Amma's *ashram* in Raigarh to seek her assistance and blessing on how to handle the impending custodial interrogation.

He reached the *ashram* early the next day and sought an appointment with her. She saw him that evening.

He wept and touched her feet. "Help me, divine Om Amma. I'm in deep distress. I might be arrested. The FIB is investigating, and they will certainly find some papers that they will say implicate me. What should I do? They will arrest me."

Sri Sri Om Amma gave him her blessings by whispering something in his ear as he rose.

"Have no fear. No harm shall come to you. I have already spoken about you to the prime minister's office," she spoke as if in benediction.

"But this is beyond the prime minister's control. The

FIB is doing whatever they like. Help me, Om Amma," Sushil Ramu cried in terror.

"Have no fear. But there is no harm in taking some extra precautions to protect yourself. Go and get anticipatory bail. We have a very good lawyer here who knows a fine judge, who is also my devotee. He will do it for you."

She asked her secretary Ramanna Madhav to put Sushil Ramu in contact with the *ashram* lawyer Shreekaran.

Within the next four days Sushil Kumar was able to secure anticipatory bail. He returned to his office after his leave was over.

ON JULY 10, Manal Kumar received a telephone call from one of his batchmates, Akhila Sinha. She was presently a joint secretary in the cabinet secretariat, and had a reputation of being tough, honest and outspoken, always standing up for fairness and justice. She was about to complete her tenure in the Government of India and return to Tamil Nadu, the cadre to which both she and Manal Kumar belonged.

"Hello, Manal," she was speaking to him on his mobile phone, "this is Akhila. You'll be surprised by this call. It's been such a long time."

"Aah, Akhila, how wonderful to hear from you. Where are you?"

"Right here in Mumbai. I'm part of a committee to study something about Air India. Too boring to explain over phone. But we're having a small get together in our guest house in Nariman Point tonight. Please come. Sorry for the short notice, but you know how it is. Till the last minute, one doesn't know whether one is coming or not."

"Sure. It will be wonderful to see you again. What time?"

"Come by at 7.30 sharp."

"Will be there. Wonderful hearing from you. Bye."

Manal Kumar was at the Air India guest house at 7.30 sharp. He pressed the doorbell. Someone opened the door and he entered the hall. There was no one else there, though appetizing aroma of food being cooked was coming from somewhere. A little strange, he thought. Was there a mistake? He turned to the attendant, "There's a dinner here tonight, isn't there?"

"Yes *sahib*, the guests will arrive at 8 pm." Manal Kumar was intrigued.

Akhila entered the hall at that very moment. They shook hands affectionately. "Wow, you look greet Akhila. Just the same. Time makes no difference to you, obviously." Manal Kumar smiled.

"You look great too. A little thinner though."

"Thanks. Not such a bad thing, is it?" Manal Kumar laughed.

"Now Manal, you must be wondering why I called you earlier than the other guests. Just listen carefully. One of my very good friends, thoroughly reliable, from the PMO, told me that a decision has been taken that you will be accused in this ISA scam that's going on."

"Me? Why me? I'm not part of any of it. It was all over before I came. I've had nothing to do with it. Besides, why would anyone want to accuse me? And what would they accuse me of? This is just nonsense. Don't believe a word of it." Manal Kumar laughed.

"Will you please listen to me. This is true. I got it confirmed through my contacts in the FIB. Your other IAS colleagues are too well protected, even though they have been part of the whole deal. So, it's been decided to fix you. They've got to get a bureaucrat, and they've decided it shall be you. You've got no godman or politician, businessman or scientist protecting you. That's why."

"But what are they going to accuse me of?"

"Listen, Manal, I can't answer your questions. I'm just telling you what I know. Please do something about it fast. And sorry, the last bit of bad news I must give you is that there's every possibility that they may arrest you. I believe all the big-wig scientists have absconded abroad. Your other colleagues are too powerful and can't be touched. So that leaves only you. You must get a lawyer and get anticipatory bail immediately."

Manal Kumar laughed even louder.

"Manal, please listen to what I have said with the greatest seriousness. Take this." She handed him a slip of paper. "This is the phone number you must ring me at. It's my mother's number. She has gone to the US to visit my sister and has left her phone with me. But don't ring this number from your mobile or landline. I suppose you know, we're all being bugged."

Manal raised his eyebrow and gave her a questioning look.

"And being buggered," she added.

They both laughed. Manal slipped the piece of paper in his pocket.

"Thanks, thanks very much for this, and for your concern."

The doorbell rang. The guests had started arriving

It was an enjoyable dinner. Batchmates meeting each other after many years. Colleagues from other services. Good food and drink.

And then it was back to reality for Manal Kumar. What was it that Akhila was saying? She said she had heard it from a trusted colleague. She would never bluff. Perhaps it was true. But why on earth should he be looking for anticipatory bail when he had committed no crime?

He thought he would speak to his family lawyer who handled their businesses in Chennai.

But before he could do that, the next day he was informed by one of his junior staff who was very loyal to him, that there was talk that the FIB were going to approach the court and demand that Manal Kumar should be taken for custodial interrogation under the Anti Corruption Act, as there was no cooperation forthcoming from any of the ISA officers. The key scientists had already fled the country, and the key bureaucrats had fled their offices.

Manal Kumar remained cool, but knew that it was now time to act quickly. He immediately called his family lawyer, a very well-respected gentleman, Madan Mohan, who headed the law firm Chiragdeep Associates, with branches all over the country, and requested him to come over to Mumbai immediately. Madan Mohan reached by evening, and both he and his Mumbai partner Subhash Dave were with Manal Kumar by five o clock.

Manal Kumar explained the whole case to them. He then phoned his friend and batchmate, Ravindra Ahuja, who was an additional commissioner of police in the Mumbai police commissionerate, and asked if he could come over and see him urgently. They had met at dinner just the night before at the Air India guest house.

"Of course, come right away if you can. I'm in the office for another hour."

Manal Kumar and Madan Mohan were in Ahuja's office in the police commissionerate within the next half hour. Manal Kumar gave Ahuja the background and a gist of what was going on and asked for advice.

"This is preposterous," said Ahuja, "these FIB chaps have just gone berserk, thanks to the blessings of our great political bosses. This is crazy, but there's no way they can investigate you."

"Why do you say that?" Manal Kumar asked.

"I don't think our state government has given them the general consent to investigate All India Service officers. Let me just confirm that."

He picked up the phone and called someone in the home department.

"Hello, Kanwal, this is Ahuja. Just wanted to confirm something. Has our state government given any general permission to the FIB to investigate All India Service officers under the ACA?

He continued, after hearing the reply at the other end, "Yes, that's what I thought. Has any request come to the home department asking for permission to investigate any All India Service officers working in ISA?"

"Okay, just confirm this and let me know as soon as you can. This is urgent. Thanks." Ahuja hung up.

He turned to Manal Kumar.

"It's just what I thought. The FIB has no permission from the state government to investigate you, much less take you under custody. Have they turned so completely lawless?"

The phone rang. "That would be Kanwal from the home department."

"Hello. Yes, so no request has been made by the FIB… and there is no general permission… that's *pucca*… okay, thanks a lot… bye."

Ahuja looked at Manal Kumar, "Well, just as I thought. Confirmed. No request made to investigate and no general permission granted. That's good. So that should take care of them in the court. And if there's any further problem, just give me a call."

Madan Mohan, the lawyer, was listening intently. They all rose, and Manal shook Ahuja's hand. "How can I thank you enough for what you've done," he said.

"I've done nothing. Just given you some information. But remember, these FIB characters are a treacherous lot. Do not believe a word they say. Goodbye, and handle this carefully. Often, the judge is also completely in their hands."

Madan Mohan advised Manal Kumar exactly on the same lines as Akhila, that is to get anticipatory bail, and with the FIB acting against him with no legal jurisdiction, that would not be difficult.

Madan Mohan immediately went to the Chiragdeep Associates office in Mumbai, managed by his partner, and started preparing the papers. They would file them the next day in the special FIB magistrate's court located near Bombay Central.

At ISA Headquarters, the FIB staff were busy compiling papers and labelling them as seized. Of course, they followed no procedures. No witnesses were present for either the seizure of documents or for numbering them. The FIB was above all laws and rules. The only laws they were ruled by were the commands of their political masters.

The secretariat wore a haunted look. Except for Manal Kumar, there was hardly anyone there. Gurupriya and Sushil Ramu were still on leave. Dr Nageshwar, the in-charge chairman, locked himself in his room and didn't want to have anything to do with anyone in ISA. He told Shukra Devi he was not to be disturbed as he was working on an important project being prepared in his Hyderabad Centre for connecting the chief minister's constituency with tele-education. He had to complete the project proposal by the end of the day.

What he was actually doing was working on a lot of astrology charts, trying to figure out when he would get out of this hideous den that he had landed into.

The lower officers were at the beck and call of the FIB, recording statements, producing documents, or more often stating that they had none at all.

MADAN MOHAN ALONG with his partner Subhash Dave, prepared the application for anticipatory bail to be presented to the court the next day. Manal Kumar sat with them and gave the papers some finishing touches.

It was a strong case for anticipatory bail. First, that the entire process of signing of the agreement, and whatever elements of the alleged conspiracy it contained had been completed well before Manal Kumar had entered the organisation. Next, that the FIB had received no permission from the State Government to start investigation against Manal Kumar, who was an All India Service officer. Further, Manal Kumar's name did not figure in the FIR. And lastly, that he was holding a responsible position in the ISA as an IAS officer and was performing his duty as per law and the procedures laid down in his Department, with the highest standards of integrity. They then produced newspaper cuttings stating that the FIB had been directed to conduct custodial interrogation against Manal Kumar.

THE MATTER WAS listed for the next day in the Special FIB Magistrate's Court presided over by a lady, Ms Snehlata Maini. She had been appointed to this court very recently, and had earlier worked in the State Judicial

Academy, teaching subjects relating to trafficking of women and children, juvenile justice, and family courts. She had spent a good three years there, was quite popular, though her general reputation was that she was rather shallow and careless, and highly opinionated with rather crass opinions and a low knowledge base.

Her personal life, however, was a little complex. She came from a typical middle-class family. Her father taught law in a very prestigious college in Worli, and her mother taught statistics in a college nearby. They had two children, Snehlata and her younger brother Karan. Snehlata was a bright student but her mother noticed that even in early school, her performance would fluctuate quite inexplicably. For certain periods, it would be excellent and she would be at the top of the class. And then, suddenly, it would slump without reason, and her marks would drop drastically. This happened continuously for about six months when she was just eight years old, studying in the third standard.

Snehlata's mother was naturally concerned about her erratic performance, and being a teacher herself, realised that she must go and meet the school authorities to check on what was going on. She phoned the principal, Sister Cecilia, and asked for an appointment with her and also with Snehlata's class teacher, Ms Parvin Baltivala. The principal was glad that she had phoned because she and Ms Baltivala had also been discussing Snehlata's erratic performance, and they had planned to call her parents anyway, after they had come to a firm decision among themselves.

Mrs Maini met them both and explained to them that she wanted to discuss how her daughter was doing in class, and why her performance was so unsteady. They were most gracious and made her feel comfortable.

The class teacher, Ms Parvin Baltivala, took over. “Thank you for coming, Mrs Maini. We were planning to call you anyway. We are also a little worried about your daughter’s performance. Sometimes, she is very good. Her writing, her spelling, her arithmetic is perfect. And then suddenly, it just becomes terrible. We do try and ask her why she has done everything so incorrectly, especially since she was so good during the previous week. But she doesn’t say anything.”

“As a matter of policy,” Ms Baltiwala continued, “we do not punish children for poor performance. But we thought it was now important to discuss this with you. Do you supervise her homework?”

“Yes, I do. I have also noticed that sometimes she needs no help. Other times, I have to ask her to redo a whole lot of work that she’s done. I do try and explain to her what she’s done wrong in her spelling and writing, and I always get the impression that though she knew everything, she did it out of sheer carelessness, or as they sometimes say, to get attention. I really don’t know, but this has been at the back of my mind for a long time. And you know how it is, I don't want to raise an alarm and upset everybody in the family."

"Mrs Maini," Ms Baltivala continued, "we've been discussing this at our meetings also. We thought it would be a good idea to get some physical and psychological tests done. Vision and hearing. Sometimes, we ignore these very basic things and the children suffer. And also to rule out dysphasia, where there can be a problem with words and their understanding, or their expression into spelling and writing. I'm sure it won't be that, but there's no harm in getting some good advice from a trained psychologist."

"But from what little I know about dysphasia, wouldn't it be a permanent condition? Can it come and go like this?" Mrs Maini asked.

"We really don't know. She is quite an intelligent child. But there are periods where she just loses control of spellings, and sentences and writing, and proper expression. And she doesn't talk much during that time, not even with her closest friends. We have noticed that. But don't worry, we shall let her classes go on as before. We thought it would be good if you took her to a good psychologist for some tests and let's hope it's not dysphasia. Even if it is, I believe there are some excellent treatments for it. Please don't worry too much. I'm sure we'll be able to figure out what to do."

The principal asked, "What about her other qualities? Is she very quarrelsome at home, or disobedient? I believe she has a younger brother. How is she with him?"

Mrs Maini was now extremely worried and sad. "No, no. She's not quarrelsome at all. Of course, like all children, brother and sister do fight, but that's normal. Otherwise, I've not noticed anything unusual in her behavior." Mrs Maini could not bring herself to inform the principal about a rather crafty quality that she had been noticing in Snehlata, which she had not noticed before, about bluffing her way through some naughty act of hers, and blaming it on her brother or someone else. Maybe, many little children did that, she thought.

She continued, "Sister Cecilia, I must thank you for all your care and the interest you are taking in Snehlata. I know a good psychologist, and will take her to him. His name is Dr Thakre. You may have heard his name. He's very good with children's learning problems. He's dealt with some students in my college too. I'll try and get an appointment with him soon, but I'll have to ask permission for her to miss school on that day. Let me first get the appointment and then I'll inform you."

"Of course, don't worry about that, Mrs Maini. I'm sure everything will work out okay. We will pray for her," said Sister Cecilia, as Mrs Maini took leave with a heavy heart. Clearly, something was not fully right with her child.

The next few months saw a series of visits to the psychologist, Dr Thakre. Tests were conducted every week on Saturday to measure Snehlatha's verbal and understanding skills. On certain Saturdays, they were excellent, on certain Saturdays, abysmal. Her IQ tests were good, showing fairly high IQ. But her verbal understanding and expression for some periods of time was excellent, and for some periods inexplicably poor.

The doctors were perplexed. They had never come across such a case before. No doubt, this was dysphasia, but of a kind they had never seen before. It came and it went, and they were not able to determine what triggered it. The child had a good home, loving parents, went to a good school and was a contented child.

Dr Thakre contacted Dr James Otter, his colleague in the Harvard University, Department of Psychology, with whom he had a long research collaboration. Dr Otter replied that he too had come across some cases of recurrent dysphasia attacks, which would come and go. A new drug, Dystanova, for treating this rare condition had just been approved by the FDA, and had recently come out into the market. Dr Otter had treated some of his patients with it. The drug appeared to be quite effective and had provided immediate relief to his patients.

But how on earth could he get this drug here in Mumbai, Dr Thakre pondered. It would take years before it got the required approvals. He did some quick thinking.

He would try and secure a permission from his friends in the health ministry to get a supply for experimental purposes for a year. His friends obliged, and his institute was able to procure a year's supply, not for sale, but only for experimentation. But there was good news. Within one year, Kayzer, the global pharmaceutical, was able to get permission to market the drug in India.

The drug worked well on Snehlata. When the dysphasia attacks happened, she took the drug for about two weeks, and she was able to work out a fairly good balance. The dysphasia attacks would recede almost immediately, and her writing and expression would be back to normal.

She passed school with good marks, and then wanted desperately to study something that would enable her to compete for the highest civil services of the country, first and foremost, the India Administrative Service. This was the favourite profession that everyone in her group of friends aspired for.

Her parents suggested that she do a specialised degree in law, rather than a general BA degree, as a law degree held assured employment in some form or other, if the attempt towards the civil services did not succeed. Dystanova was working well and helping her overcome the dysphasia attacks.

She completed her law degree with a first class and then decided to compete for the civil service examination.

But she could only make it to the Class Two Services, which she did not take. A sense of failure hit her hard, and a bitterness against the world in general took hold of her, though she tried her best to conceal it from her parents and her friends. She did try for the second time, but gave up mid-way as she had a terrible nervous breakdown. She was hospitalised for about a week, recovered quickly, and seemed quite well and cheerful when she returned home.

Her mother, anxious as ever said, "Sneha, now it's time you gave up all these dreams that cause you so much tension and anxiety. You know, to get into the IAS, you must do your MA, and then prepare for at least a year. And there's no point in repeating the exam year after year until you make it. That's what most people do, but to my mind, it appears quite pointless. You've done well in your law exam. Start on an internship with a good lawyer. Your father can arrange that. He knows so many people, his own students, who are doing very well as lawyers and have set up their own practices, quite successfully. Make up your mind. No point just drifting along."

Snehlata took her mother's advice and joined a leading law firm Samartha Rai and Associates, which was headed by her father's student. While working diligently for the firm, she also decided to sit for the examination for judicial officers in the state government.

She had kept this a secret from her parents, and thought she would surprise them, if she succeeded. She did succeed, and on the day when she saw the results, she sprang a beautiful surprise on them and announced she had been selected as Judicial Magistrate First Class in the State Judicial Service.

The drug Dystanova was a miracle. She could now tell when a dysphasia attack was approaching, and would immediately start her medication. There would be a short period of slight disorientation, during which time she would just avoid any reading or writing. But within a few hours, she would be back to normal. The medication would continue for two weeks and then she would be fine until the next attack. Sometimes it happened in three to four months, sometimes even earlier.

SNEHLATA MAINI WAS now one of the special FIB magistrates in Mumbai, a most prestigious position. She had finished her course of Dystanova last month, so she expected that she would be okay for at least the next few months.

She was given a warm farewell from the judicial academy, and then she stepped into her new place, which seemed to have an air of great importance attached to it. Quite naturally, she was a bit overwhelmed by her new position.

The FIB court environment was so different from the

judicial academy. This place was always full of the FIB officers hovering around during court hours and after. They had a reputation of being very kind and considerate to the court staff. They would organise admissions for their children or their relatives' children into schools and colleges, fix appointments with the best doctors in government hospitals, provide tickets of all kinds—train tickets, cinema tickets, tickets for celebrity entertainment shows. Sometimes, they would provide for little holidays for the court staff and their families to nearby holiday locations, arrange taxis and accommodation for them. Clearly, the FIB investigating officers and their staff were flushed with secret service funds. This money was actually meant to be used for paying informants or for other secret activities connected with investigation. Perhaps, a little was spent on that too, but most of it was spent lavishly on looking after the creature comforts and luxuries of the court staff, and of the presiding officer, if he or she was so inclined, which was not really very rare.

The court staff from their side were equally civil and affectionate with the FIB officers, for whom the court really was a second home. The FIB investigation officers who wanted to switch a few papers now and then in their reports or in the court files were always allowed to do so, without anyone knowing. They would overwrite on anything, wherever and whenever they wanted. They could influence the court staff to fix hearing dates the way they wanted, could access any documents, and meddle around with the computers to change whatever they wanted. Their power in the court was supreme. And there were always their secret service amounts, if anyone in the court needed to be kept happier.

It was in this exceedingly cozy and comfortable ecosystem that the court and the FIB functioned, each working to the other's benefit, with great financial and functional synergy. Cases were relatively simple—trap cases, where extortion from the guilty followed a well-established process, after which there would be a deliberate attempt to water down the case and act dumb; or disproportionate assets cases, where again, they could play around with the evidence, depending on the accused person's capacity to pay. The FIB guys were always very fair, almost Marxian. From each according to his offence, and to each according to his payment.

The only irritant that had come to spoil this comfortable ecosystem was the GAVA Oriont case. There were too many big shots involved in this matter. The senior most scientists from GAVA and ISA, then a certain bureaucrat against whom there was no evidence, but they had instructions from the highest political centres that he had to be booked, even without evidence. All because the really guilty bureaucrats were strongly protected by politicians, god men and god ladies. Anyhow, these were small occupational hazards for the FIB. They had by now learnt the art of capturing the court to protect them, and if things tended to turn a little out of control, they could always get their bosses to send the right signals through the right channels to the presiding officers, the protectors of justice.

It was in this highly complex cauldron of justice where prosecution, politics, secret service funds and the FIB held complete sway, that Snehlata Maini took change as the special magistrate. She visited the Mahalaxmi temple before taking charge, praying that her dysphasia attacks would not disturb the smooth and efficient discharge of her duties.

She did not like her new surroundings at all. They were so stifling as compared with the green and open grounds of the judicial institute that she had just left. The court hall was small, always crowded and smelly. The bench clerk, a young man called Avinash, was always hovering around, eager to please, and wanting to provide whatever information she desired. She soon came to realize that he was the memory of the court, but would realise only much later that he was also the memory of the secret service fund management in the court.

Today, he informed her that an application for anticipatory bail had been filed by a very senior IAS officer, Manal Kumar, presently working as chief administration officer in the ISA. The matter had been listed for hearing on the next day, and the file had already been placed before her on her table.

Snehlata Maini was irritated. She had come here barely a week ago, and had not even yet settled down in her new environment. This was clearly a high-profile case and would be widely reported in the media. Well, she would just have to face it, she thought, however unsure and disinclined she felt about it.

"Yes, I know," she said, "I've seen the file. I will go through it. If I need something, I will let you know." The bench clerk was irritating her immensely, but she tried to sound in control.

She took the file home. She didn't want to open it. It took her back to the terrible IAS examination she had attempted, and tasted the first failure in her life. And then her first nervous breakdown. No, she would not see it. She decided to swallow the calmpose tablet her doctor had prescribed, whenever she felt uncontrollable stress approaching, and went to sleep. She would attend to the file tomorrow.

Next morning, she felt much better and left for the court, making sure that her emergency Dystanova tablets were in her bag.

She was confident that no dysphasia attack would occur. She had taken her prescription just last month, and didn't expect another attack for at least another two or three months.

She reached the court a good half an hour before the

appointed time. She had yet to read the anticipatory bail papers. She opened the file and tried to go through the attachments in a calm manner, but this seemed such a complicated matter, with so much of technical content, that she could make no sense of it.

She called for the bench clerk Avinash, and asked him to explain the case to her. Avinash replied that since the application had been filed just yesterday, he had not been able to read it before it was placed on her table. Snehlata was irritated. She asked whether the public prosecutor had come to the court. Avinash went inside the court hall to check and returned to her chamber. "No madam, he has not yet come. But the investigating officer is there. He's a very good and helpful man. He'll be able to explain everything to you."

Snehlata Maini pondered over this.

"Okay, ask him to come here," she said. She did not want to appear nervous or unsure in front of this damned IAS officer, whose fate she was going to decide.

The investigating officer was led to her chamber by Avinash, in full view of the open court.

Manal Kumar saw it all sitting in the court hall, and was aghast. He looked at his lawyer incredulously. "How is this magistrate calling the investigating officer privately to her chamber in full view of the open court, just before this case is to be heard? This is shocking. Completely against court procedure. Thoroughly irregular. How do we know what's going on inside? How do you people tolerate this?"

Madan Mohan replied coolly, "Don't be so agitated, my friend. Much worse things happen here. Our job is to get our work done."

Manal Kumar's application for anticipatory bail was to come up after the regular cases were over and the lawyers and litigants had left. There were just three cases today. In the first, the prosecution wanted an adjournment because the summons had not yet been served on the accused. She happily granted it. In the second, the accused wanted an adjournment because some documents they were trying to get from the Goregaon municipal office had not yet been given. She happily granted this too. In the third case, the prosecution wanted an adjournment because the witness who was to be examined today could not be produced as he was ill. Very happily she granted this too. So far, it was going well.

And then came Manal Kumar's application for anticipatory bail, which required application of her own mind on that terribly complex Oriont affair. The investigating officer, whom she had called to explain the case had spoken some gibberish, which she could make no sense of. But he had used the opportunity to make some very sincere overtures of professional friendship towards her, which she found most reassuring.

She started reading the application, quite smoothly

at first, and saw some words saying that the FIB had no grounds to seek custodial interrogation of someone who had nothing to do with the whole affair from beginning to end. The counsel started speaking and explaining.

"Your honour, my client, Shri Manal Kumar, a senior IAS officer, presently working as chief administration officer in the Indian Space Agency, apprehends that he may be arrested for some actions that the FIB is accusing him of, without any evidence whatsoever. Your honour, this case is about the GAVA Oriont agreement, which happened well before the time he joined ISA. Let me refer to page 10 of the Application, where you can see the date of the GAVA Oriont agreement, and then page 12, where you can see the date of his joining the ISA. This is well after the agreement has been signed."

Snehlata Maini felt the words coming not from the courtroom but from far away. She heard the sound of someone saying IAS. Someone was again taking her back to her bitter memory of failure… and mocking her… Let me look at him, she thought. And she saw the man standing next to the lawyer who had been speaking. Manal Kumar was looking his usual self, a little too confident and distant, perhaps even slightly condescending.

He knows that I failed, she thought. That's why he's looking at me so contemptuously.

The counsel continued, "Your honour, the entire process of investigation against my client is completely illegal."

Snehlata Maini found the words getting more and more blurred. She tried to read the application, but the words were dancing from place to place. Shc tried to write something, but the words were all wrong. A dysphasia attack was approaching, she thought in panic, but she had to remain on her seat and hear this damned thing through. Her medicine was in her bag, but her bag was in her chamber, and she couldn't leave the court at this point. The IAS man would laugh at her.

The counsel's voice kept coming from far away, "The FIB has no jurisdiction to investigate into this case against my client, who is an All India Service officer. The FIB has obtained no permission from the state government to do so. And they have no general consent from the state government to do so either."

Snehlata Maini was using all her energy to remain focused, even though she knew that the dysphasia attack was well on its way.

"What have you to say?" she managed to address the prosecutor.

The prosecutor stated unintelligently, "Your Honour, I need time to check this. Meanwhile, the anticipatory bail is opposed by us and should not be granted, as we believe the applicant might flee the country, just as the scientists from ISA have done."

Snehlata Maini's focus was beginning to dissolve, but she kept her determination going. She would refuse the petition. She would send this IAS man to jail and wipe away her past failure.

Again, she heard the voice of Manal Kumar's counsel coming from somewhere, "Your honour, clearly the FIB does not have the permission of the state government to investigate my client. Otherwise, they would have produced the state government orders before this Hon'ble Court. My client is a respected IAS officer, with the highest record of integrity. There is no evidence on record to implicate him in any offence or wrongdoing in the GAVA Oriont deal. I urge the hon'ble court to grant him the anticipatory bail that is sought."

Snehlata Maini again looked at Manal Kumar. He looked even more detached and contemptuous. The scene of the examination hall again come back to her. Her resolve kept her going. She would destroy this man.

"Who are your sureties? Have they brought their papers?"

"My client's surety is Mr Madhusudan, your honour, who is his friend from school. He now runs a publishing house in Pune called *Shaktimaan*. I am submitting his financial papers."

Snehlata Maini's resolve to stay afloat was faltering. She tried to read the papers but the words kept dancing and were not making any sense. She was trying hard to remain alert, but she didn't know how long it would last.

"Yes, that's alright. But what...what is the control... you have over Manal Kumar?" she asked the surety. "He might also abscond…run away…like the ISA scientists. What is the con…con…control…you have over him?" Her speech had also now started faltering.

Snehlata Maini was putting her life's energy into articulating her words, but the only thought that controlled her mind was that she had to destroy Manal Kumar, the man who made it to the place she couldn't.

Manal Kumar had stood silent so far. He was watching the proceedings with a sense of bemused cynicism. He could hold himself back no longer.

"Madam, your honour, with due respect I must confess to you, that if you need someone who controls me to stand as my surety, then I must in all good faith inform you that there is no such person. Control, as a word in psychology, is something that would be an extremely unnatural, if not a pathological condition, if related to a person of my age and profession. In fact, it would be a pejorative, and would definitely be considered a serious form of corruption in my profession in the IAS."

She couldn't understand a word of what he was saying…but she heard him say IAS…and the letters started echoing in Snehlata Maini's brain. They kept echoing…a sense of darkness started approaching…her vision darkened…her medicines were far away in her chamber…she had no help to revive her.

Darkness overtook her, and her face slumped over her table.

There was commotion in the courtroom. The bench clerk rushed to her. Her personal secretary, a lady, went to her and tried to raise her head, but the eyes were blank. She placed a glass of water to her month, but Snehlata Maini was unconscious and wouldn't drink.

An ambulance was called and she was taken to the Dhanraj Hospital, just about a kilometre away from the court, along with her personal secretary and someone from the court registry.

The Court was adjourned till after lunch. As per court procedure, the alternate magistrate would handle all urgent matters. Manal Kumar's counsel, Madan Mohan, did all the running around and arranged with the registry that there was an urgent matter that required the presence of the alternate magistrate, in view of the unfortunate hospitalisation of the regular magistrate.

The alternate magistrate, Mr Pramod Raikar, an elderly and kind looking gentleman came into the court after lunch. He heard Manal Kumar's counsel repeat all the arguments, and granted him anticipatory bail immediately.

NEWS FROM ISA kept coming to Maharishi from Shukra Devi and from his Delhi contacts. It appeared to be a bad scene, getting worse. The ISA was being invaded by the FIB goons, with threats of custodial interrogation.

Maharishi thought it was now time to act. Vidyasagar's health was improving, though he was still in a state of acute depression. Maharishi would speak to him every day and try and pep him up, assuring him that this whole distressing nightmare would be over very soon.

The coming Saturday, he decided to go to Washington to meet Georges and Karmaswamy, and plan out the next course of action.

They met at Georges' office and started their conversation in right earnest.

"Now Georges, what is going on is simply atrocious. I think they've all lost their minds. I simply can't understand what's come over them. But now, we really have to plan a course of action. Some strong, decisive action," Maharishi said, his facial muscles tightening.

Georges listened without a word.

Maharishi continued, "I've come to speak to you in absolute confidence. Even Vidyasagar does not know, and should not be told. He's just about recovering, but remains terribly depressed," Maharishi paused.

"Yes, go on," Georges said.

"Now, I have a lot of directly recorded evidence that the minister has approved the agreement at every stage. And that he is the one who directed that the agreement should not be mentioned in the cabinet note." He turned towards Karmaswamy, "You remember, Karma, the device that you gave me, the fountain pen? I have every intention of sending a polite message to him that if he does not stop this witch-hunt, this information will be made public. The media, no doubt, will have a field day, the opposition will lick their chops, and the government can be in a terrible mess."

Georges listened on.

"But I need the services of your agent in New Delhi to deliver this message. And before doing that, obviously I need your permission. This information should put the fear of god into him. Do I have your permission?"

It was now Georges' turn. "Of course, Maharishi. This must be done. Otherwise, we're just sitting ducks waiting for disaster to strike. By the way, you'll be happy to know that Manik Seth, our agent, is right here in Washington, working on another deal for us. Let me alert him. He'll come over immediately. This is most fortunate."

Georges buzzed for his secretary and asked her to connect him to Manik Seth. "Hello, Manik, how busy are you?...Just need you to come over for a while...It's something important...Sure, so see you in an hour." Georges hung up.

"Well, you heard. Manik Seth will be here in an hour. I must inform you, Maharishi, my information from India is that the minister is doing his best to save the deal. But he's facing strong opposition because the prime minister is being personally attacked about it by the Opposition. And that son-in-law of his, who I believe controls things to quite a large extent, is unhappy that he was not part of it."

Georges paused for a moment. "By the way, I must also tell you Maharishi, that I've not been exactly idle myself. I know a lot of the senators and their business links here—who is acting for whom in which deal, especially in India. And I have definite information of huge payoffs being made to your government, particularly one made to the son-in-law, Raja Bhaiyya, as you call him, for permissions relating to gas exploration in south India. I have been able to obtain details of the bank accounts, mostly in St Kitts and the Caymen Islands, and of all places, some in South Korea."

"Your information is absolutely definite?" Maharishi asked.

"Of course, it is. I wouldn't be talking about it otherwise, would I? And yes, I must also tell you, my people tried to get in touch with the head of TerrAkash for help, but that poor man is in deep trouble himself with some problems with his own telecom deals."

"So, what do you plan to do?"

"Simple. It will be conveyed to the gentleman. A very friendly visit from his trust fund manager, or another trusted agent, a so called *swamiji* or godman, call him whatever you will, you have so many of them out there. Whichever is quicker, or both. The *swami* is proving to be a little elusive. They say he's in seclusion and deep meditation in some grand resort that he owns in the Aegean, and cannot be disturbed. So, most likely it will be the trust fund manager. He will very simply tell the son-in-law, that there is every possibility that this information will be made public in the USA. But it could be averted, if he gives up his witch hunt against Oriont."

"Georges, this is brilliant. When are you planning for this to happen?"

"Next week, by Wednesday, that's four days from now."

"And when does Manik Seth return to India?"

"Tomorrow, you got him just in time. He'll be here any minute."

Maharishi was thinking this through. "Okay, so this is how it would appear. Raja Bhaiyya will be given the works on Wednesday by his trust fund manager or trusted *swamiji* or both. And the minister will be given a friendly message through Manik Seth, say around Tuesday. So before next weekend, we can expect some major developments. Hmm.... Long overdue."

"Yes, that's what should happen. It bloody well should happen. The whole thing is so thoroughly unwarranted. So improper."

Manik Seth arrived exactly within the hour. There was a quick introduction. Georges went straight to the point. "Now, Maharishi, just tell Manik exactly what you want him to do."

"Thank you, Georges," and turning to Manik Seth, he continued, "Please meet or get the message sent across to the minister for scientific development, Pratap Singh, as soon as you return to India, and inform him in the best manner possible that unless he stops the witch-hunt against GAVA and Oriont and makes the FIB close their case, there is every possibility that his involvement in the whole affair will be made public by Maharishi in the US. Use the best language that you can. I don't have to train you on that. You are the master. But this has to be told to him in no uncertain terms. Here is a typed note, should the minister wish to know what exactly would be made public. Anything you want to add Georges?" Maharishi handed over the typed note to Manik Seth.

"No, I think you've said it all."

"Well," Maharishi continued, addressing Manik Seth, "Any further questions?"

"No, sir. The message will be communicated in no uncertain terms. Mr Georges will have all the information by Tuesday."

"Good, and good luck. Do the job. It's very important for all of us."

Manik Seth left. Georges opened his cabinet and pulled out a bottle of Bourbon. He poured for all of them, and they drank a toast to their success and good health.

TRUE TO HIS word, Manik Seth spoke to the minister's friend and financial advisor, Param Dayal, on Tuesday morning, telling him that an urgent message from the USA had to be delivered to the minister. He conveyed the message and Dayal realised its importance. He was a loyal and trusted advisor of the minister and had been benefited greatly by him. He got on the job immediately, took the liberty of disturbing the minister during his morning hours when he met his constituents, took him aside, and gave him the news.

The minister heard him stoically. He had been expecting this and was not particularly worried. He had made his own enquiries and had been informed about the details of some huge payoffs that had come to Raja Bhaiyya from some digital communication companies in the Silicon Valley for contracts in India's growing digital market. The details and destination of payoffs had also been tracked, apart from the fact that the decisions had been taken to award contracts to them without any transparency.

This information had been conveyed to Raja Bhaiyya through their common godman, Rudrakshi Swamiji in Kaashi, who generally parked everybody's funds, and blessed them all.

The *swamiji* was a great favourite of Raja Bhaiyya.

He would lecture him on the dangers of becoming prey to *lobha* (greed) and *maya* (illusion) and if indeed he did become prey to them, then he should forgive others too, for becoming prey to them. These were human weaknesses and should be forgiven, if there was no ill will or malice.

"So, just leave Pratap Singhji alone," he advised him. "If he has done something out of *lobha* or *maya*, you must forgive him. Taking revenge on him by filing cases will not remove his *lobha*. He will only take further revenge. Anyone can say anything. People say you are getting payments from US digital companies. Of course, it's not true. But people can say anything. Already, they are trying to get information from their sources about it. People may give false information. but it becomes a scandal, and then you have to spend so much time to clear your name. So just leave Pratap Singhji alone. Tell the FIB not to pursue the case. Otherwise, they can cause great harm to you regarding the digital company contracts. All false of course, but harm, nevertheless."

Raja Bhaiyya heard everything. He got the message. It was as direct as could be. He turned a little pale, but how could he stop the FIB now? They would laugh at him if he told them to do so. He needed some time to think about it.

He thanked the *swamiji*, touched his feet and sought his blessings. He was afraid... afraid that his dealings with the digital companies would be out if he didn't stop the FIB from going further into the GAVA Oriont deal. The *swamiji* would not have come all the way from Kaashi to his house to tell him this unless it was really important. He would discuss it with his father-in-law and take his guidance. He was always so wise.

But before he could recover, the next blow knocked him down further. His trusted trust fund manager, Samir Gupta, who organised his finances all over the world, phoned and said he wanted to meet him urgently. He had a strange foreboding. Too many trusted friends wanting to meet him urgently.

The news was another jolt. "Sir, I have some information that you should know immediately. I heard a lot of talk in the US that Oriont has information regarding all the financial transactions regarding the oil exploration licences. And further, that they are planning to release it to the press by this weekend unless you stop the investigation into the Oriont affair. It can cause a lot of harm to you, sir."

"Oh, but how do you know this?" he asked.

"Sir, the investment banking world is a very close-knit world. We often share the same clients. This information has come to me from a very close and reliable source, none other than someone from the US government's financial advisory agencies. And this is very confidential information. So, as your financial advisor, it is my duty to inform you about its seriousness."

"Oh," said Raja Bhaiyya, in quiet despair, "what should I do?"

"You should ask the FIB to stall the investigation. I don't know much about these matters, but I'm sure they will know how to do it. But please remember, this is serious. It can cause great harm to you, and to the government."

"Yes, yes, I know. I'll do something."

There was no time to discuss this with anyone. This was an emergency. If he didn't act fast, the details of the oil exploration deal and his payments would be out in the open. Not to speak of the payments from the digital companies. Yes, he had to act fast.

The same evening, he summoned the FIB chief to his home office. As usual, Paul Jacob carted his deputy Sardana along with him. Now, what the hell was going on, he wondered. He hoped that the latest directive from him would not deprive him of his game of golf the next morning. Also, late this evening, his NGO staff were coming to meet him regarding a horrific case of a family of monkeys being massacred by a wild boar on the Ridge.

Raja Bhaiyya looked terribly distraught, very pale, and not at all his usual blustering self.

"Thank you for coming, Mr Jacob and Mr Sardana. This is urgent. We have important news from the US that if we persist with the FIR in the Oriont deal, it will invite retaliatory measures for a lot of business deals our Indian companies have with US companies. So, we have no alternative but to somehow stop this investigation into the Oriont affair. Otherwise, there can be serious repercussions on the economy."

"But, sir, this was done under your orders. How can we stop it now?" Paul Jacob asked.

"Nothing was done under my orders," he replied firmly, with an icy stare at Paul Jacob. "You, as FIB director, have done it under your powers. You are an independent organisation. Remember that. So, don't ever mention that again."

Paul Jacob couldn't understand a word of what the man was saying and made no attempt to do so either. No doubt, that was Sardana's forte. His mind was still extremely agitated about the massacred monkeys.

Sardana understood this language. "Yes, sir, we will try and see it is stopped. In any case, from the reports we have so far, it seems a very weak case under the present law."

"Good. So, do that. And if there's any problem and you're not able to handle it, we can always get someone else to handle it."

Both Paul Jacob and Sardana got the message, but Paul Jacob added his bit. He really didn't give a damn about this man. "Sir, we'll do our best, according to the law. You know, police procedures have to be followed meticulously. Otherwise, we get hauled up in a court of law."

Raja Bhaiyya was getting impatient. "Do whatever you have to, but do it fast. Otherwise, the government will be in a lot of trouble because of you."

Indeed, thought Paul Jacob, the government will be in a lot of trouble because of you, and we of course, are the willing scapegoats.

"How much time do you have as FIB director, Mr Jacob?" Raja Bhaiyya asked.

"Another eight months, sir."

"Don't you want to go as a Governor of some State?"

"Not really, sir. I have so much to catch up on in my work on conservation and maintaining the environment of Delhi. I've been neglecting all of this, but thank you for asking."

Raja Bhaiyya gave up. This man was weird. But then he remembered that he had been appointed only because he was weird.

"Well, please ask your fellows to go slow on the investigation immediately, and then close it up. Let the word get around."

"Yes sir, as you wish," said Sardana.

The next morning, Raja Bhaiyya called Sardana alone, and directed him that the investigation against ISA and Oriont must stop that very day.

"As for the FIR," he ordered Sardana, "close it up as soon as you can. And tell me what you want. A foreign posting?"

"Sir, it is very kind of you to ask. I assure you, this case will be closed as soon as possible, but it will still take some time. Maybe, one or two months. There are some procedures which we must follow. Otherwise, the courts will pounce on us, and it will reflect negatively on the government. Just bear with me for a month or two. Rest assured, the case will be closed. You can communicate this to the Americans."

Sardana immediately phoned Nishkam Narela, the deputy superintendant camping in Mumbai and Gyan Prakash, investigating officer at ISA, and told them that they and their team must return to Delhi immediately and report to him the next morning.

Thereafter, he went over to Raja Bhaiyya's office and informed him that he had directed the FIB team to stop all investigation, and had summoned them for a meeting at headquarters the next day.

"Sir, do not worry," he consoled him, "the investigation will be closed in just a few more weeks."

"Thank you so much, Sardana. I won't forget this. The foreign posting is yours for the asking."

"Thank you, sir."

The investigating officer was utterly confused. "What should we do, sir?" he asked Sardana over the telephone, "we're in the middle of seizing the documents and taking statements."

"Finish doing whatever you've doing. Bring whatever

statements and documents you have, and report to me by 10 am tomorrow morning." Sardana's orders were clear.

The investigating officer was bewildered. Anyway, he ordered his team to catalogue whatever material they had collected. They had to board the evening flight to Delhi and meet their chief the next morning at 10 am.

The team was overjoyed. This was the worst assignment they had ever worked on, where none of the documents made any sense to them, none of the responsible officers were present, and they were only recording statements of some minions who had no responsibility for anything. They packed up their stuff with great abandon and were at the airport at 6 pm, happily looking forward to being home again.

RAJA BHAIYYA IMMEDIATELY called his *guru*, Rudraskshi Swamiji, and informed him that the investigation had been halted in ISA, and that it would take a few more weeks to halt it in the court.

The *swamiji* uttered a few Sanskrit words blessing him, which Raja Bhaiyya couldn't quite understand, and said he'd hold a special *puja* for him. He then immediately informed Pratap Singh of the latest development.

The minister was relieved and also triumphant. Finally, the invincible Raja Bhaiyya had been put in his place. Pratap Singh then secretly spoke to Param Dayal from an unregistered phone and asked him to convey the news to his friends in the US. He had a good sleep that night.

Raja Bhaiyya then called his trust fund manager, Samir Gupta, and gave him the same information, requesting him to inform his US contacts about it immediately.

"Sir," Samir Gupta asked, "can I take it that this statement from you will actually be carried out by the FIB? Because, if I give the information that the case will be closed, and then it does not happen, it can cause even more serious problems."

"Don't worry," Raja Bhaiyya replied, "what I'm saying will happen. I guarantee that."

"My apologies for repeating. If it does not happen, it can cause even greater problems."

"I understand your concern, but don't worry. It will happen and please communicate this to your US friends. The investigation has already stopped at the ISA. You can tell your American friends to check for themselves, if they so wish."

Samir Gupta called up his Washington contact and gave him the news, which was conveyed to Georges instantly.

Param Dayal immediately gave the news to Manik Seth and asked him to inform his contacts in the US that the investigation had been halted in the ISA, and that it was a matter of a few weeks that it would be closed. The delay was only on account of some mandatory procedures that had to be followed in the court.

Manik Seth informed Georges immediately. Georges now had the news from two credible sources, but got the information double checked from his local office in Mumbai. Yes indeed, it was true that the investigation team from ISA had inexplicably left midway. He now felt confident and passed on the news to Maharishi and Vidyasagar.

The ISA staff was completely flabbergasted. What an earth was going on, they wondered? But they heaved a sigh of relief when the last of the semi-literate FIB team left. Some peace returned to ISA, but a peace wrapped in suspense and disgust. What would the next chapter be, they all wondered in silence.

THE FIB TEAM returning from ISA were to meet at the deputy chief's office the next morning, but sadly, the FIB was hit by another misfortune.

Apparently, Paul Jacob had been travelling around the ridge the evening before with his NGO staff. They were trying to locate and map out the monkey habitats and understand how it was possible for a wild boar to massacre a whole family of monkeys, and also formulate a plan of action as to how such atrocities on monkeys could be prevented in future. Perhaps, Paul Jacob had ventured a little too deep into the forest with his friend, Jack Daniels, a world-renowned environmentalist. As he raised his left arm to point out a monkey habitat, he was suddenly struck by a piercing object on the lower side of his left arm pit. He let out a shriek in pain and his right hand went out to his left side. He found himself touching some kind of a thin arrow stuck on the left side of his chest. Was someone trying to kill him, he wondered, as he slumped beside the environmentalist. Jack Daniels saw it and realised it was a porcupine quill.

Paul Jacob was immediately driven to the closest hospital, Athena Swashtha, in Hauz Khas, and was taken to the emergency ward. Several doctors worked to remove the quill, which had punctured a blood vessel leading to his heart but had fortunately missed his heart by just a few millimetres.

A minor surgery had to be performed for which Paul Jacob had to be hospitalised for at least a week to prevent any unknown infection from the quill. After all, the quill had come from the forest, and who knew what unknown micro-organisms it carried. The hospital chief also held several discussions with experts from leading hospitals in the country. He had to make sure that the FIB chief left his hospital alive and well.

Prashant Sardana felt a sense of exhilaration. He

could now handle the ISA affairs without disturbance from above and deliver on his promise to Raja Bhaiyya. He could already see himself sitting in a plush office in Paris or Brussels or Washington.

At 10 am sharp the next morning, the FIB team from ISA were asked to assemble in his office. It was a short and neat meeting. Gyan Chand, the investigating officer was asked to present a status report on what they had been able to achieve so far.

Gyan Chand started his narration, "Sir, it has been very difficult for us to function. Everyone was so hostile. All senior scientists and senior officers were absent. All important papers were missing. We did whatever we could. We seized all the papers that we could find. We took statements of all the officers and lower staff who were present there. The senior scientists have all gone abroad, and the senior bureaucrats have all got anticipatory bail. And then we returned, as per orders from your good self."

Gyan Chand produced an array of files on the table, and described each of them. Sardana's mind was far away. Gyan Chand was pointing to the file containing the statements of god knows who, and then about thirteen files containing seized documents. Sardana flipped through these, with his mind on other things. They seemed most innocuous—routine letters and notes, meeting proceedings within the department, and even some entertainment bills.

The superintendent and deputy inspector general were making notes. Sardana was examining the files, and trying hard to locate the most critical file which should disappear.

Finally, Sardana spoke. "Very good work done, Gyan Chand. It is really unfortunate that none of the senior officers were present. That is one of the reasons we had to call you back." He then turned to his deputy, Bijoy Patra, and said, "Bijoy, just go through everything, and give me a note by evening. I have to brief the PM's office about this. Unfortunately, our chief is in hospital. Most unfortunate. Which reminds me, I must visit him in hospital. What about you, Bijoy?"

"Sir, we checked with the hospital. They did not want anyone to come for some time. Some important artery has been ruptured. So, he's in a special room and no one must disturb him."

"Yes, I was told that. I think it would be proper if I called his wife, and visit the hospital nevertheless."

The meeting was over.

Prashant Sardana visited the hospital with a bouquet of flowers which he gave Mrs Jacob, spoke a few encouraging words to her, and wished a speedy recovery to Mr Paul Jacob.

BIJOY PATRA HAD a long meeting with the ISA investigation team. Gyan Chand tried his best to give a coherent account of what evidence they had been able to piece together, which was thoroughly incoherent, with the evidence completely inadequate. But Bijoy Patra had some sort of a note ready for the boss. The note and the related files were on Sardana's table by evening.

Sardana went through the note, and checked the files on the table. He removed the one relating to the GAVA Oriont contract, which contained all the original GAVA and ISA papers, placed it below one of his other files, wrapped it with that file cover, tied it securely with the file string, and put it away in his file box to be taken home. He covered the file with some more files that had routinely come during the day, and asked for the file box to be delivered to his house, as he usually did at the end of the day. The remaining files pertaining to the ISA were put in another box, to be taken along with him to Raja Bhaiyya's office for discussion, or so he told his PS.

His homebound file box reached home safely and was lodged in his home office. The ISA file box accompanied him to Raja Bhaiyya's house. He had informed Raja Bhaiyya that he would be coming over for some discussions. Raja Bhaiyya had said that he would be at a meeting with the external affairs ministry officers to run through the forthcoming visit of the Secretary General of the United Nations, but would pop in for a while to talk to him.

He walked into Raja Bhaiyya's office in the PM's residence. The doors were opened for him. The driver brought in the file box, removed the files, placed them on the desk and left.

Sardana then telephoned his deputy, Bijoy Patra, "Bijoy, I'm speaking from the PM's home office. I think you forgot to send me the file on the GAVA Oriont agreement. It doesn't seem to be here. Can you please send it across immediately."

"I'm sure all the files were sent, sir. But I'll check once again and send it across, if it got left out."

"Yes, do that. It's important."

Raja Bhaiyya walked in just then. "Anything important, Mr Sardana?"

"Actually, sir, I had wanted to brief you about the investigation so far. But I find that an important file has been left behind in the office. I'll come back tomorrow with all the papers and brief you."

Raja Bhaiyya looked a bit puzzled, but as he too was a little busy, he left the room with a hurried, "Okay."

The files were placed back into the box by the attendant and Sardana returned to his car.

There was a call from Bijoy saying that the file was not found anywhere in the office. Maybe, they could do a thorough search the next day in Sardana's office.

"Yes, I'm sure it will be somewhere. Over something or under something. I'm sure we'll find it tomorrow."

Sardana went home, had a pleasant dinner with his family, and after his wife was asleep, removed the GAVA Oriont file from the file box, and passed it through the shredder in his office along with a whole lot of other unwanted paper. The shredded paper was then assembled in a large brown paper bag and burnt the next morning in the back yard by the household help, as was the custom in the bungalow through decades.

MEANWHILE, A FRANTIC search was underway at the FIB Headquarters for the missing GAVA Orient agreement file. Every office, cupboard, desk, drawer, cabinet was searched, but there was no trace of it. The CCTV footage was studied carefully, but there was no sign of any known persons, intruders or unknown persons entering unauthorizedly and decamping with any papers.

Gyan Prakash grew nervous. He suspected that this might be an attempt to frame him by his bosses. He had already heard some rumours that a departmental enquiry would be ordered against him for the missing file. He immediately sought an appointment with the FIB deputy chief the next day, and explained to him that he had sent the file to the FIB superintendent, who had sent it to the deputy inspector general Bijoy Patra, who had discussed it with him. He told the deputy chief that this file was extremely important for the case, and that he suspected foul play from his own colleagues as a means to disgrace him, on account of the fact that he had received so much public attention because of his investigation in this case.

Sardana listened patiently. "Don't worry, Gyan Prakash. We are all here to protect you. I'm sure the file will surface soon. It must be mixed up with some other lot which is stacked somewhere else. Happens all the time. Don't worry. It'll be found."

"With respect, sir, I am worried. There is a large section of people here in Division 2, who are constantly making complaints about me. All useless, baseless complaints. Just because I do my work with integrity and fairness, and don't listen to them when they try to influence me in my investigations. This missing file will give them another issue to start making allegations against me. I want to make it clear to you sir, I submitted all the files to the superintendent, and I have the computerised entry to prove that. After that, sir, I am not responsible for what happened to the file."

"Don't worry," replied Sardana, "if we don't find the file by tomorrow, we will have to do an internal enquiry, and then if necessary, file a regular complaint in the police station. Now, don't worry. I am here to protect you, if anyone makes any allegations against you."

"Thank you, sir," Gyan Prakash left, a little relieved, but still agitated.

The file movement was tracked. It had left Gyan Prakash's office for the superintendent's office, and then to the deputy inspector general's office, when he was studying the papers to make his note for Sardana. And after that, there were no further computerised entries.

The file was not found and the matter was getting serious, though this fact had still not reached the public domain. An emergency meeting was held in Sardana's office and it was decided that a police complaint would have to be registered about the missing file. Sardana thought it necessary to inform the principal secretary to the prime minster, but the principal secretary was least interested. He then thought it was necessary to inform Raja Bhaiyya. He could not allow him to forget the foreign posting.

Sardana called him at his office. "Sir, may I come over to brief you about the latest developments regarding the Oriont case?"

"Yes, but immediately. I have to leave for an important party meeting in the next forty-five minutes."

"Thank you, sir, I'll be there."

Sardana reached the place in ten minutes. He briefed Raja Bhaiyya about the missing file, which he heard with a twinkle in his eye, smiling slyly at Sardana.

"Sir, I just thought that I should inform you that within the next few days after an internal enquiry, if we still don't find the file, we will have to file a complaint in the jurisdictional police station, that would be the Tilak Nagar police station, about this missing file. This is bound to create a lot of media sensation. So, I just thought I should tell you beforehand."

"Well, if the file is not traceable, clearly, you have to file the complaint. You know best how to handle these things." The twinkle in his eye grew brighter.

"That was all, sir. I just wanted to inform you about this. Good day, Sir."

"Good day, Sardana. You are the best. Take it to its logical conclusion. And I haven't forgotten the foreign posting."

THE FIB CHIEF, Paul Jacob, had still not returned to his office. Though the surgery had been done through laparoscopy, he had to be under observation for at least another week to ensure that no sepsis developed either inside or outside his body. Porcupine quills were an unknown entity as far as their infectious properties were concerned,

Sardana immediately ordered an internal enquiry to

trace the missing file, on which the entire case depended. He appointed the deputy inspector general in charge of administration, Amarlok Singh, an extremely upright and honest officer, to do the enquiry, assisted by a fine little team. They went through the entire computerised record, where the file was last entered in Bijoy Patra's office. They once again scoured all the cupboards and desks, but there was no sign of the missing file. There was yet another scrutiny of the CCTV footage, another interrogation of the security guards and attendants, but to no avail.

Amarlok Singh threw up his hands in despair, and submitted his report to the boss. His conclusion was an inference that it was a smart inside job, probably to disgrace Gyan Prakash, but of course there was no evidence to substantiate the inference.

Sardana now had to act. He sought an appointment to brief the prime minister's principal secretary but since he was out of the country, he briefed the special secretary, who showed no interest in the matter, and merely replied, "Do what you have to according to the law, but make sure that it is according to the law, so that the government does not have to face any embarrassment."

Sardana then called on Raja Bhaiyya and informed him that the internal enquiry had yielded no results, and now he had no option but to file a complaint in the jurisdictional police station.

The twinkle in Raja Bhaiyya's eye grew brighter. "Oh, I see, thank you for informing me. Well, let the law take its course. You know best how the law works. Who am I to say anything?"

"Yes, of course, sir. The law will take its course. Have no doubt." Sardana took leave of Raja Bhaiyya.

Promptly on the next day, a complaint was filed by Gyan Prakash in the Tilak Nagar Police station, that a file bearing the number ISA—Sect-13.1.D—GAVA Oriont Contract seized by the FIB as D—9, had been noticed to be missing since July 18. Detailed enquires and checks has been done but the file was still not traceable.

The Tilak Nagar station house officer relaxed. These were the usual tricks of the FIB fellows when they wanted to hush up a case. However, they did their routine, cursory enquiries, studied the records and statements, and took some more lengthy statements from Gyan Prakash and all the attenders and security guards, and the higher officers. Of course, they didn't dare question Sardana or the staff in Raja Bhaiyya's office. That would be for the next generation.

The newspapers and the television channels sprang to life again with their shouting sprees. There were several panel discussions and analyses. The opposition attacked the government that this was just another instance of the FIB, the captive cockatoo, doing everything at the scientific development minister's bidding. Another channel suggested that the missing file had actually been called from some invisible quarters of the PMO, and was presently secreted in some *ashram*, which was a favourite haunt for all money launderers. Of course, no names were mentioned. Yet another channel suggested that one of the previous chairmen, who had considerable clout with the US government had prevailed upon the Indian government to close the case. Of course, no names were mentioned. Fortunately, parliament was not in session, so it was just a lot of charges and counter charges flying around from all political party spokespersons, whom nobody took seriously.

Paul Jacob had still not returned to his office. So, it became the responsibility of Sardana to give interviews to the leading television channels. He categorically stated that what had happened regarding the theft of the file was completely unacceptable, and that no efforts were being spared to trace it. When asked whether the theft had happened through an agent of Oriont, he completely denied it as utter falsehood, as there was no evidence to that effect.

The scientific development minister also gave an interview to the press and stated with complete sincerity that he had no idea of what was going on in the FIB; that it was a completely autonomous organisation in which there was no interference from the government. If the FIB authorities had given an interview, he had no comments to offer, except to accept it as the truth.

For the moment the issue was quelled, and then forgotten. Suddenly, the monsoon turned violent and caused great havoc in some states in the north-east, and the entire news media was fully absorbed in that.

IN THE US, there were daily bulletins coming in for Maharishi, Georges and Vidyasagar, from their respective agents back in India. The FIB goons had disappeared from ISA; the Oriont contract file was not traceable; and a complaint had been registered about the missing file by the FIB. Vidyasagar's health improved dramatically.

These were glad tidings. All three, Maharishi, Georges and Vidyasagar, met that weekend in a quiet, exclusive restaurant hidden by the side of Central Park on Fifth Avenue. They opened a vintage champagne bottle and toasted to their success. Vidyasagar took just a sip symbolically—he was still concerned about his heart—and followed it up with some good almond and broccoli soup.

"Well," Georges said, "I'm amazed at the efficiency of your investigation system. If they want to, they can achieve anything. Anything, even the impossible." He laughed loudly.

"Yes," Maharishi added, "in India, we always say, 'let the law takes its course'. Of course, it always does. And if it doesn't, then we always say, 'we have full faith in the judiciary'. And of course, we always do."

They had a most enjoyable dinner, walked around a bit in Central Park, and had a wonderful sleep.

THE ISA WAS in limbo. The bureaucrats, all on anticipatory bail, were slowly returning to their work place. Sushil Ramu and Gurupriya had both retuned. Manal Kumar was already there. All three were deeply suspicious of each other, barely spoke, and completely avoided each other. The organisation was in a state of shock, with the FIB blokes suddenly departing without a word and without completing their work. But who knew when they would return, with even more venom. It was safer to be silent than to speculate.

Dr Nageshwar sent a note to the minister informing him that it was impossible for him to do justice to being even an in-charge chairman ISA, while also having to handle the Satellite Research Centre at Hyderabad. He requested that a full-time chairman be appointed immediately.

The minister chuckled. ISA be damned. They

had done it enough damage. Anyway, they were all a bunch of frauds, fooling the public and the press with their achievements which were outdated by at least three decades. They could all go to hell as far as he was concerned. There were assembly elections coming up in his state within the next six months, and he had to concentrate on his constituency to ensure that his men got tickets from the party. The danger from the US was over, or at least, for the moment. But he still had to be vigilant and be on his guard.

THE FIB WAITED for another month. The Delhi Police had made no headway in their attempt to recover the lost GAVA Oriont Contract file. Finally, they filed a report treating the case as undetected, and closed it.

Bijoy Patra had started examining the seized files produced by Gyan Prakash. They were laughable. All important documents were missing. There were hideous forgeries in many places and visible doctoring of documents. There were haphazard notings and even more haphazard page numeration, all pointing towards a deliberate destruction and tampering of documents.

He showed them to Sardana, who threw them away in disgust. Sardana directed the FIB team to resume their investigation in the ISA, and search for all the missing papers. And if they couldn't find them, then to file a case against the ISA for destruction of documents. That would keep everyone busy for a long, long time, he thought. Meanwhile, he directed that the FIR filed against Vidyasagar, Karmaswamy and Haridas should be closed for want of documents and evidence to file a charge sheet.

Sardana was smart. The closure of the FIR was not highlighted much in the media, but the investigation against ISA for destruction of critical documents to proceed further with the case, hit the headlines. The FIB was given kudos for their fearless investigation by several television anchors, panelists and analysts.

PAPERS REGARDING THE closure of the FIR were flown to Maharishi, Vidyasagar, and Georges in the US. Vidyasagar and his wife returned to India with great relief. Vidyasagar immediately tendered his resignation, and asked the government's permission to join the South African Space Organisation that had just started, where he had been offered a very high position as Director. The government gave him the permission almost immediately. They were keen to see him go as soon as possible, so that he would not become a rallying point against them in the scientific community.

Gurupriya put on a great show and played the perfect victim. She kept complaining about the murky affairs of ISA to the cabinet secretary, and how bureaucrats were being made scapegoats by the all-powerful and wily scientists. She returned to her parent Union Territory cadre, opted for a posting in the Andamans, and spent long hours in meditation, keeping a watchful eye, of course, on her bank accounts abroad, and on ensuring that her son's education continued smoothly.

Sushil Ramu applied for long leave and for permission to join Sri Sri Om Amma's *ashram* to take care of all her medical colleges and hospitals. It was granted.

Manal Kumar asked for premature retirement, and decided to join his family business in Chennai, which included a film production company.

He was given a warm farewell by the Tamil Nadu IAS Association, who showed him great affection and support, knowing the trauma that he had to undergo, merely for being honest. He regaled his colleagues with hilarious stories from the ISA, and had them in splits of laughter as he warned them in his thank you speech—"If any of you ever want to go on deputation to the ISA, first get yourself covered by a comprehensive insurance for life to protect you against false cases by them or the FIB. Otherwise, it is completely unsafe to go there."

Manal Kumar decided he would devote his time to writing and producing films. Uppermost on his mind was that he would make a film on this whole GAVA Oriont affair. He had already started writing the script, and it would take a little more time for him to complete it and start the film. He decided he would call it *The Asuras of Antariksh*. He felt extremely good about it, and was very excited that film distributors had already started queuing up around his family business office.

Georges and his team started preparing the papers for filing a case for arbitration for the illegal termination of the GAVA Oriont agreement. It would take time, but they would win it, he was sure. And another goldmine was in store. Raja Bhaiyya was also keeping a watchful eye on this, through his US contacts.

Just a week after the FIR had been closed and a reinvestigation started against ISA for destruction of documents, Sardana received a summons from Raja Bhaiyya to meet him. He greeted him most affectionately.

"Well, your performance has been unmatchable, outstanding. What more can I say? Get ready, you will hear from the external affairs ministry within the next few days. It's a matter of a few weeks, maximum, a month. You will be in Washington as the security attaché in our embassy. From there you can move on to the UN, if you make the right connections."

The ISA remained desolate and in shambles. They

waited for a new chairman to come and breathe back some order and life into it.

The FIB goons were back, demanding documents that had long since been cremated. There was no one to answer their questions.

THE END